Love Song of the Nightingale

ALSO BY DERYN LAKE

JOHN RAWLINGS
Book 1: Death in the Dark Walk
Book 2: Death at the Beggar's Opera
Book 3: Death at the Devil's Tavern
Book 4: Death at Romney Marsh
Book 5: Death in the Peerless Pool
Book 6: Death at Apothecaries' Hall
Book 7: Death in the West Wind
Book 8: Death in St James' Palace
Book 9: Death in the Valley of Shadows
Book 10: Death in the Setting Sun
Book 11: Death and the Cornish Fiddler
Book 12: Death in Hellfire
Book 13: Death and the Black Pyramid
Book 14: Death at the Wedding Feast
Book 15: Death on the Rocks
Book 16: Death at the Boston Tea Party
Book 17: Death on the River Thames

REVEREND NICK LAWRENCE
Book 1: The Mills of God
Book 2: Death on Cue
Book 3: The Moonlit Door

SUTTON PLACE
Book 1: Sutton Place
Book 2: The Silver Swan
Book 3: Fortune's Soldier

Love Song *of the* Nightingale

DERYN LAKE

LUME BOOKS
A JOFFE BOOKS COMPANY

Lume Books, London
A Joffe Books Company
www.lumebooks.co.uk

First published in Great Britain in 2025

Cover art by Jarmila Takač

ISBN: 978-1-83901-600-4

For Ateş Orga — if it hadn't been for a note in his wonderful book on Chopin, I would never have followed the path that led to Jenny Lind and her amazing life.

CHAPTER ONE

Delia — Present Day

This dream was different. Very much so. For a start it was in miniature, like looking through the wrong end of a telescope. Yet the picture was quite clear, showing a young woman of some twenty-odd years of age, weeping like a wretched child, her companion — a remarkably handsome man nearing fifty — sympathetic but stern-faced and quite definitely somewhat saddened.

"But what shall I do?" she was asking. "Singing is my life. I can't give it up."

"My dear young lady. It has given *you* up. Your voice is ruined beyond repair. I can speak of your teachers only with contempt."

"But they were masters at the Swedish Royal Theatre."

"They could have been masters at Heaven's Gate for all the good they did you. Your voice has gone!"

The girl stopped crying, as if by some enormous effort of will, and dropped slowly to her knees, looking up at him pleadingly. He found himself thinking that her eyes were most unusual, a vivid sparkling blue which seemed to glitter with immense inner beauty. It was almost as if crystal had been injected into them. Indeed, so lovely were they that Manuel García, the foremost singing teacher

1

in Europe, found himself having second thoughts. Should he perhaps try to get this wretched girl's voice back?

"Mademoiselle, I . . ." he started.

She nodded but did not utter a word, as if she knew instinctively what he was about to say.

"You have almost ruined the gift God gave you at birth. You have accepted parts in grand opera that should not even have been considered by an adolescent girl. It is no good denying anything to me. I have people working for me in every corner where music is played. You made your debut as Agathe in *Der Freischutz* when you were eighteen years old — may God forgive you and your wretched teachers as well. And now you are paying the price. Your voice is in tatters because of your dreams of grandeur."

He paused and the vivid eyes gave him another deep glance. He looked at her, stern-faced.

"I, foolishly and reluctantly and against my far better judgement, will *attempt* to restore it. But if you agree to my doing so you must follow my instructions completely. First of all, I must insist that you do not sing a note for six weeks. Speak very little as well. After that — we will see."

"Thank you, sir," she answered humbly.

A smile crossed Manuel García's face for the first time. "In view of what I have just said — utter no further words today, young lady."

She nodded, eyes cast down again. "Your word is my command, Señor. I will remain silent until given permission to speak." And then she curtsied deeply and sweetly, a gesture that somehow showed her total sincerity.

And now the whole vision was beginning to fade and the telescopic picture was growing smaller by the minute.

Delia gave a quiet sigh and passed into even deeper unconsciousness as the strange dream vanished entirely and left her to sleep on in peace.

* * *

There came one of those wonderful moments that could only happen when there was a full house. The audience members, who had been prattling away in a reliable hum, suddenly quietened together as if they had been given a hidden signal, and there was a second's pause before they clapped as the conductor stepped onto the podium. It was a hearty clap too, and Delia, stitching away in a small, over-lit dressing room, thought that the miracle had happened. Talk had got around that *Spring Roses* was well worth going to see, despite its old-fashioned title. That miraculous thing — word of mouth — had worked again.

It had all started as a kind of joke. Four young Irishmen, who had originally grouped together to perform traditional ditties with a hearty mixture of pop thrown in, had finally found some fame. They called themselves The Fintans and for no particular reason that anybody could understand, their song — "Oh la la, Mr Lehar" — came second in the Eurovision Song Contest. It had a tune — which was more than could be said for many of its fellow entries — and people remembered it. The story could have begun and ended there but a young music teacher, struggling through lessons with disinterested schoolchildren, having heard the song had googled Mr Franz Lehar and been rather surprised at what he had found.

Apparently, young Franz had been a prolific composer of operettas — the most famous of which had been *The Merry Widow*. Naturally, the music teacher, one Alan Pearson, had known that but what he *hadn't* realised was how closely Lehar — a Catholic — had worked with the sharp-witted Jewish community. For a start, he always used Jewish librettists to put words to his sparkling operettas. Furthermore, his wife, Sophie Paschkis, had been born a Jew and only converted to Roman Catholicism when she married Lehar. This had not generated a warm reception when Adolf Hitler came to power. Yet there, it seemed, the story grew slightly stranger. The Fuhrer eventually declared Franz one of his favourite composers, at which point the pressure eased a great deal, in contrast with earlier attempts to deport Sophie. Secretly, subversively, the composer had started a silent campaign to help his wife's people wherever he could. And so the great Franz Lehar had become a very hidden fifth columnist. This fact, together with his friendship with the great operatic tenor Richard Tauber, whose father had also been Jewish, placed him in a delicate position — which was nerve-wracking but also fascinating.

Alan Pearson had chuckled to himself and imagined the pair of great musicians smiling and joking, yet at the same time feeling the finger of fear across their backs. But did they give in? Not a bit of it. They continued to battle the horrors of the Third Reich with wit and humour, rather like characters created by the mighty and flighty film director Mel Brooks. And this had set off Mr Pearson's own innate sense of humour and, inspired, he took to writing jolly tunes — and more beautiful ones — to add to the little musical he had already started to write.

Nothing would have come of it, and *Spring Roses* would have remained in a drawer, had not one of his pupils — a skinny, frantic child called Isolde Stampe — insisted that he should come and have tea with her, a request repeated over many months. In the end, Alan gave in and was quite surprised when his battered old car arrived outside the destination he had been given: a dwelling place that was decidedly plush and expensive. Isolde came dancing out.

"Oh, I'm so glad you're here, Mr Pearson. My uncle Robert wants to meet you."

Alan went into the house and nearly fainted with shock. For, sunk in an armchair and thin, cadaverous yet brimming with vitality, sat Robert Poynes-Hamilton, the only living rival to Andrew Lloyd Webber in the world of operatic show business.

This was the reason why Delia Paget now sat in an over-bright dressing room, hastily stitching a torn costume; it was why the audience had decided that it was enjoying the show and was making rumbling sounds of approval; why Alan Pearson's name was now up in lights on a theatrical hoarding — though admittedly not very well displayed. *Spring Roses* had so far proved a hit, particularly as the part of Richard Tauber had been offered to Justyn Krasinski, an excellent and good-looking tenor and star of the Polish opera, who had allegedly entered the Eurovision Song Contest to fulfil an alcohol-fuelled bet — and won it. Yet the musical had still to be tried out on a West End stage and was currently touring in Brighton.

Delia heard the orchestra strike up the overture and began to whistle along. She was deputy wardrobe mistress and had no part in the actual show, though she was expected to cover for any female members of the chorus who happened to be missing. And tonight was just such an event — Delia was on for the great Lehar party scene, her partner none other than Mr Krasinski himself, with whom she was to have the pleasure of waltzing.

It was staged at the end of Act One and Delia made her entrance, pealing with false theatrical laughter at some off-stage witticism and then casting her eyes rapidly around the set, noticing that Miles Hepworth had a tear in his trouser leg which threatened to increase in size when he whirled in the grand waltz. Of Mr Krasinski there was no sign — he had missed his cue as usual. When he finally came on he was three minutes late and definitely had a whiff of alcohol on his breath. Delia gave him as reproving a glance as she dared — being merely a wardrobe assistant — but he just grinned and winked at her. This was a grave mistake. The real Richard Tauber had had a very slight squint in his right eye, a fact he disguised by wearing a monocle. Justyn, playing him, having had a long wait to go on, had obviously removed it, then had a swift shot of gin before putting the eye-piece back in situ. He had not replaced it properly and as a result it had now descended and wedged itself beside his nose.

Delia, smiling broadly, gave him a beautiful curtsy. She had always curtsied, from the age of three when her wonderful mother — a former corps-de-ballet dancer — had taught her how to do it. After that it had become a delightful childhood habit and even the inquisitive stare of her paternal grandmother had not quelled it.

Then the terrible day had come when the sporting little car driven by her father, the sweetest of men, had been mown down by a juggernaut, his ballerina wife sitting — and dying — beside him. Delia had been at home with Violet, a local girl who loved looking after her, and had wondered why Violet cried after taking the phone message. Then a policewoman had rung at the door and Delia, aged five, had curtsied to the splendour of her uniform. It had been too much for the professional woman, hardened as she was by life in full reality, and she had been forced to turn away her head for a moment before regaining her usual steely stance.

Delia's future, after that thundering blow, would have been impossible to bear, left to her late father's mother to handle. But her uncles, twin boys, had interceded and thrown themselves with full and wild enthusiasm into rearing a little girl. They were identical, three years younger than her father, and had of all the impossible things to do developed a magic act, which had proved tremendously successful. It had caught the attention of various managers, and the Cobblers Twins were frequently on television or touring the country. Despite the inconveniences this caused, they took Delia with them; that was, until the education inspectors decided to investigate the matter of why this child changed addresses so frequently. The result was boarding school for Delia

— an arts educational school. And it was in the making of costumes for the Christmas production that Delia became utterly fascinated. She knew then that designing the heavenly things was where her future lay. When she left school at 18 she went to art college and left there with much high praise for her work.

Unfortunately, she had not immediately landed her dream job and had to content herself with becoming wardrobe mistress for somewhat tatty touring theatrical companies. Then she had seen the post of assistant costume manager, as it had been named somewhat portentously, advertised in a trade magazine. In due course she went along for an interview. To her amazement, the wardrobe mistress turned out to be Miss T, formerly one of Delia's lecturers at art school, a woman with whom she had got on with well. The miracle had happened. Delia finally got the job she had always wanted. And now, despite her lack of performance credentials, here she was, standing on stage with Justyn Krasinski and wondering what to do about his drooping monocle.

The casting of the Polish opera singer had been a triumph for the show, in fact a major coup. Justyn Krasinski was well known throughout Europe for his powerful tenor voice and his amazing breath control and had played many leading operatic parts despite being only in his early thirties. But it was the Eurovision Song Contest that had finally launched him to household recognition.

There were several stories circulating about how he had entered the competition. The most believable was that he had been in a late bar in Krakow with a crowd of other singers — the number of people present differed according to who was telling the story — but one thing was crystal clear. They had all been performing in Opera Krakowska's production of *La Boheme* and were a fairly rowdy company by midnight. Then — so the story went — a bet was laid regarding a pop singer of the female gender who was visiting the country from England, promoting the

Eurovision Song Contest. Justyn had, of course, taken part and naturally enough had gone in pursuit of Sangeetha — a dark-eyed beauty if ever there was one. What had happened after this was anybody's guess but one result was that he had auditioned for the contest — probably as part of the wager — and, having been selected to represent his country, ultimately won it hands down.

But now he was smiling at Delia as, with a careless movement, he pulled the monocle from where it was lodged, dropped it into a pocket and gave her a charming bow. Then, to Lehar's beautiful music, they started to waltz. Just for a split second Delia experienced an enormous shiver — not from fear, fright or anything tangible, but from an icy sensation that this waltz had either happened before or perhaps was foreshadowing something yet to be experienced. Of course, she danced the waltz every night, had done so with probably every man on stage since the tour had started. Yet this distant feeling froze her to the core, reminding her as it did of something real and terrifying.

Justyn — in his role as Richard Tauber — squeezed her waist and murmured, "Don't look so anxious. I'm not an ogre."

"Oh, I'm sorry. I thought you were," she answered.

He said nothing, continuing to smile at her. The waltz ended and she drifted off stage, remaining in character until she reached the wings when her usual slightly anxious expression returned — while the show continued on its merry way, delighting all those who saw it.

CHAPTER TWO

Delia — Present Day

It seemed to be one of those nights when every member of the cast tore a hem or popped a button or ripped something on their shirt front. It was as if they had guessed that Miss T — more formally known as Thomasina Tripp — had decided to take the evening off and had disappeared into the darkness of the foggy November night. Yet nobody made any comment on her absence — good or otherwise. Miss T had made her claim to fame on a television series featuring the Victoria and Albert Museum. Her style, her wit, her voice with its slight Yorkshire accent, had all endeared her to viewers as she showed them the many treasures hidden in the museum's vaults, particularly the outfits, old and new.

After that, the costume lady so beloved of the watching public was approached to become the wardrobe mistress for a fascinating new musical. And when one of her former pupils had applied for a job on her team, she had accepted Delia Paget without reservation. Yet this night of all nights, when Delia had arranged to meet her for a drink after the show, there had been a long queue of actors and dancers leaving some garment to be mended urgently. Delia had stitched till late and Miss T had not popped in to see her as originally promised. Delia left the theatre feeling somewhat depressed and walked to her flat in Bow.

Thomasina had left three messages on the answerphone.

"Hello, luv. Sorry I couldn't make it. I've got something really intriguing to show you. Phone back."

"Delia, where are you? Have you been seduced by one of the ballet boys? Ring me tonight."

"It's me again. You can ring up till midnight."

It was just past that, so Delia left an answering call until the next morning and went to bed.

* * *

The next morning, she made the call.

"Sorry, Miss T. I got waylaid. Everybody needed something mending."

"The ballet boys as usual, I suppose."

"No, it wasn't. Why have you got such a down on them? They are perfectly respectable and are always polite — which is more than you can say for some of the principals."

"Now don't get narky!" The north country accent was slightly more pronounced when Miss T felt strong emotion. "I've got some interesting news for you."

"What?"

"You know I went to that theatrical sale yesterday? Well, I've picked something up. Something that I think could be very important indeed."

"Oh really. What is it?"

"It's a headdress. And the fact is, Delia, that I think it's really old. It obviously belonged to somebody quite important and somehow it's got bundled in with some tired theatrical tat. Anyway, I bought it for . . . Take a guess."

"I've no idea. Ten pounds?"

"No! It had got itself into a bargain box with a lot of naff old *chapeaux* from some exhausted production or other — probably introducing Mistinguett to the panting French public — and there it was, lying between all the feathers and furbelows, looking miserable."

"And how did you know it wasn't one of them?"

"Because it was *different*. I don't understand how, Delia, but sometimes a piece cries out. It says 'Help me. I'm in the wrong place.'"

"I'm yet to have that experience. But when can I see this masterpiece?"

"Now. I'll come round for coffee. It's not too early, is it?"

"No, I'm dying to see the wondrous thing."

Half an hour later, Delia's front doorbell rang loud and clear and there stood Miss T, looking as excited as a small child that had been presented with an unexpected toy. She held out her hand, which was encased, as always, in a tight kid-leather glove.

"I put it into a Harrods bag. I felt it was the least I could do."

"Let's take it into the living room."

Delia was not sure what she was expecting, but it was certainly nothing as unremarkable as the item Miss T placed before her. It was little more than a wired bed of pure — but faded and grubby — white feathers which slanted upward at the top and were surmounted by a large blue stone. Yet the more Delia gazed at it, the stronger was the stirring of her interest.

She picked the extraordinary coronet up and held it in her hand. It was like an upward-pointing tangent as would have been worn by someone playing a goddess. Or a priestess. These images ran through her mind. She looked at Miss T.

"Where did you find it?"

"As I told you, in with all the tat and detritus. Yet I have a feeling that it belonged to someone special. What do you think?"

From somewhere, a sudden and unrecognisable tune arrived and ran through Delia's brain. She looked up, startled.

"It's making me hear things. Trust you to find it."

"It's my magic eye, dear. I can always notice the wheat sticking up from the chaff — or is it the other way around?"

"I've no idea. Anyway, whichever, I think it's absolutely fascinating."

"I shall take it to the V&A and see what they make of it."

"Could I come with you?"

"Of course, my friend. Be my guest."

They fell to chattering over the coffee cups, the wardrobe mistress regaling Delia with a vivid description of how Miss T's mother had practically lived in the Covent Garden Opera House in her teens, roaring up the long and unfriendly staircase to the gods — theatre slang for the gallery — where there were no reserved seats and the front row was occupied by the youngest and fittest and those who leapt the fastest.

"I presume she had to buy a load of tickets?"

"Apparently there was a large and friendly commissionaire on the door and Mama used to slip him a half crown — this was before we went metric — which was what tickets cost in those long-forgotten days. She saw everyone, my dear. Fonteyn, Robert Helpmann, Beryl Grey, Moira Shearer. She even watched darling Freddie Ashton create the part of an Ugly Sister and Bobby triumph as Doctor Coppelius. Wonderful days."

"And what about the opera?"

"She went to everything. Even sat through a Ring Cycle at the age of 17 and fell about laughing when the Rhine Maidens' invisible wires got tangled up together as they sang bravely — but ever more closely — on."

"She sounds amazing. Who was her favourite?"

"For ballet, Fonteyn, of course. There used to be terrific rivalry in those days between Fonteyn and Moira Shearer. Moira had a great cloud of red hair and was naturally snapped up by the film people — *The Red Shoes* and all that. Anyway, in the end Margot triumphed by meeting her greatest partner, Rudolf Nureyev, and dancing better than ever. Pity she ended so sadly, though."

"She died abroad, didn't she?"

"Panama City. Her grave is out there."

"Oh, what a shame. Who were your mama's opera favourites?"

"Callas and, amongst the men, Tito Gobbi. Those great, rich voices. She told me a wonderful story concerning Maria Callas. Some years later when my mother was more respectable and had ceased her youthful flights to the gallery, she was taken by her boyfriend — a very handsome young Jewish man — to the better seats to hear the celebrated lady. It was *Norma*, and Callas — enormously fat — was singing "Casta Diva". That wonderful sound filled the theatre and detracted completely from the fact that she was shaped like a barrel. The audience shouted and cheered, threw flowers and bouquets. The great singer was much moved and bowed and curtsied to the cheering crowd.

"Now comes the good bit. Exactly a year later — to the day — Mama went to Covent Garden again, once more with the beautiful Jewish man in tow. It was to hear Callas sing *Norma* for the second time. The curtains opened and there was an audible gasp of surprise from the audience which echoed around the house. For Callas had dieted herself into someone slim and beautiful, she looked like a Dior model — which was quite the fashionable thing in those days. Everyone wondered how she had done it. The voice, needless to say, had not changed a jot."

"Good gracious. How did she manage it?"

"There were all sorts of theories circulating. Strict diet, surgery, punishing exercise, even a tapeworm."

"Ugh!" Delia pulled a face.

"To this day, nobody knows how it was done. But done it was, and the beautiful woman went on to stun audiences wherever she appeared. And then, almost imperceptibly, the voice began to go, then her love life went wrong, and Callas lay down on her bed and died."

"How old was she?"

"Fifty-three."

"Is that all? How tragic."

"That Greek rat Onassis — with whom she had been having a passionate affair — married Jackie Kennedy instead and they said it broke Callas's heart, because she really loved him."

"How ghastly. Do you think it's the fate of everyone connected with the arts to die tragically?"

"Now you're being fanciful. Some of them rollick on to a grand old age and have a thoroughly good time of it."

"Who for instance?"

"Oh, I don't know. George Formby."

"Who?"

"Oh, stop it. You're acting young to annoy me." Miss T threw a cushion and shrieked with laughter. But though Delia responded, her thoughts were elsewhere, away with the singers and dancers of the past and the concept that none of them had lived to find true and lasting happiness.

* * *

The miracle had happened. A rich Euro-Lottery winner — who wished to remain anonymous — decided to invest several million in *Spring Roses* because he had been to see it on the night his ticket had won him £159 million. His identity was shrouded in mystery, but Delia believed that he was a Welshman and lived in a small village. Apparently, he loved singing and had once been in a choir himself. Furthermore, his wife had seen and admired

Justyn Krasinski in the Eurovision Song Contest. Robert Poynes-Hamilton had invited the investor out to lunch but had received a very sweet refusal because the winner's wife was too shy to meet him. But the mysterious Welshman had backed the show and an empty West End theatre had been discovered — the St. Clements, in a side street off Shaftesbury Avenue. Work had begun on a general overhaul, prior to a grand opening.

Miss T, who was like a thing possessed as she reconstructed the costumes that had, after all, been on a national tour, decided to take her friend Delia — who had ultimately been unable to join her on her trip to the V&A, much to both women's disappointment — for drinks and a snack.

"Have you heard the rumours about our friend Krasinski?" Miss T asked as they settled at a small table for the briefest of lunches.

"No, nothing other than that he is pursuing the entire female chorus. *Are* there any other rumours?"

"Yes. Apparently he is leaving the show. He has been offered the tenor part in *La Fille du Régiment* and is very keen to take it."

"I'm not surprised. When is this?"

"Spring, next year. And it is for the Paris Opera."

"The glamour boy will be in his element there!"

"Now, now, Delia. You're only jealous."

"No, I'm not. I turned him down."

But that wasn't true, and Delia knew it. Other than by way of his generally charming manner and usual politeness, Krasinski had not so much as glanced in her direction during the production's run. Nor had there been any chit-chat. Whispered comments on stage had been about the sum total of their conversation. Delia had felt very slightly miffed. It wasn't as if she was ugly, though perhaps rather dull to look at.

Sometime later, reflecting on the situation as she worked, Delia impulsively swept her hair up and tied it back. That, she thought, was a slight improvement, giving her a certain gamine charm.

With her hair pulled back from her face, Delia vaguely resembled Jodie Comer, whose acting had enthralled her in the television series *Killing Eve*. She had once been asked for an autograph in Tesco and had felt that when she refused politely — explaining that she wasn't who they thought she was — she had been given surly glances of disbelief. Possibly she should keep her hair up for a while, see if that helped.

With a deep sigh, Delia turned back to the many layers of material that went into a Viennese ball gown and wondered what that strange tune was that kept running through her head whenever she was alone.

CHAPTER THREE

Delia — Present Day

It was the dream again — but this time very different. On this occasion, Señor García was sporting a bright magenta neckpiece, and the young woman was no longer in tears, but actually smiling — and quite genuinely at that. Her hand was on her throat and she had obviously just finished a song. She was looking at him, a silent question bobbing in the air, but Delia knew — deeply asleep as she was — that the nameless girl had succeeded and had, with the aid of this remarkable man, snatched her voice back from whatever terrible place it had disappeared to.

"So now, my dear young friend, my task is done. I have returned to you that gorgeous instrument those Swedish wretches almost took away."

The young woman tried to look sad but even though she pulled a miserable face, she couldn't conceal the smile that was gleaming in her eyes. And what eyes they were. Sparkling and brilliant as crystal, brimming with the love of life and music and laughter.

"Ah, Señor, if you had not done so I might well by now be some ordinary housewife, humming a tune at the back door as I go to peg my washing out."

17

Her teacher was quiet for a moment, suddenly becoming serious.

"It is true that you did not have the best of beginnings, young lady. But what is past, is past. They trained your voice to the very edge of ruin — but I have rescued it and will send you out into the world as a singer of great beauty and a joy for ever."

"I thank you with all my heart."

"I wish you well, my very dear Miss Lind."

It was the first time that the woman's name had been mentioned and it resounded in Delia's sleeping ears. Who was she dreaming about? Who was Miss Lind? She wished so hard to wake so that she could follow this ephemeral clue. Yet she slept on, even though the dream had faded.

When she finally recovered consciousness it was to find that the flat had grown cold and she was shivering. It was also ten minutes short of two in the morning, but Delia was nonetheless determined. Pulling on a dressing gown she made her way to the computer and, typing in the word *Lind*, sat back and awaited developments. Several things came up including an American firm based in a place called Minnetonka, a selection of luscious actresses who looked somehow frighteningly alike, and then smack in the middle of them was an old sepia print, a daguerreotype of a young woman. Instantly recognisable were those brilliant crystal eyes. Underneath was written *Jenny Lind, opera singer*.

"Oh, my God," said Delia aloud, and she felt a thrill of fear as well as triumph. She had heard the name before of course but had known nothing of the young woman's struggle to find her voice again when it had been over-strained and gone, nor of the life she had lived thereafter. Without hesitation she typed in the singer's name and waited to see what came up. There were several categories, one with a short video of an overweight American professor holding forth about how Miss Lind had sung at his hometown during her American tour. Delia hastily switched to the biography.

Johanna Maria (Jenny) Lind (6 October 1820–2 November 1887) was the illegitimate daughter of Niclas Erik Lind and Anna Maria Fellborg, who was divorced from her first husband but refused to remarry until after his death.

This was the first hint that Jenny's mother had been a difficult woman — to say the least of it — but pictures showed her to be attractive looking, that was for sure. The singer's father had been a twenty-one-year-old bookkeeper when he had first met the vivacious creature of twenty-nine. She wore vivid dresses, laughed a lot, played the guitar, flashed her eyes. He loved making music and responded to her instrument — et cetera, et cetera. The result of one of these exciting nights was born nine months later. Jenny, unwanted and kept very much in the background, had made her first entry into the world.

The flat was as freezing cold as an icicle as Delia hunched over the computer. She was enchanted, admiring the small child who had seen so little of her mother for the first few years of her life. Jenny was boarded out with foster parents shortly after her birth; Anna Maria swept in for occasional visits. There were several other children in the house; three were children of the owners, plus two nursling babies. It was clean, it was comfortable, it was in sweet-smelling countryside.

Jenny was happy and settled. Then, one day, Anna Maria — for some reason in a vile mood — called and insisted on having a blazing row with Carl Ferndal, Jenny's foster father. And this in the great outdoors where curious neighbours might catch distant conversation. They needn't have fear of missing the details with Anna M about, however — she was bellowing like a Bull of

Bashan. The result was that the wretched child was immediately dragged from her lovely, happy home and taken to Stockholm, to live with a mother who was getting more and more shrewish with each passing day. To crown it all Carl started legal proceedings against Anna Maria.

Delia forced herself away from the computer, made herself a quick cup of coffee and returned to the story. It seemed that Jenny had a half-sister called Amalia, a legitimate child, born to Anna Maria while she was still married to Captain Radberg. Due to some strange Christian ethic of her own, Jenny's mother would not hear of marrying again until the gallant Captain was well and truly dead. Meanwhile Niklas had left town, and the entire family would have to manage on Anna Maria's meagre earnings as head of a small boarding school, which took as many pupils as she could cram in.

It was Jenny's grandmother who first discovered the child's talent for music. The older lady was staying with Anna Maria while waiting for a place in the widows' home and was immediately drawn to her small granddaughter. Music filled the apartment as military bands marched past, trilling out thrilling fanfares. One day, Grandma was startled to hear the fanfare reproduced on the piano. She went to investigate and found Jenny alone, and starting to cry for fear she had inadvertently done something naughty. But the three-year-old had picked out the tune and played it, all alone, quite unaided. Her grandmother thought it was wonderful and told everyone that the child had an ear for music.

Eventually, Jenny went to live with her grandmother in the widows' home residence and used to sit on the windowsill with a delightfully characterful cat, singing to it.

A very strange sensation overcame Delia at this moment. She felt as if the computer was gone, and she was in the room with the child and the cat. She could smell them — the girl's freshly starched pinafore, the cat's feline aroma. Above all, she could hear the swell of that youthful voice, the roundness of its sound. She shivered with sheer delight. But within the next second she was back and very much alone as her eyes grew heavy and she felt immensely tired.

* * *

Delia did not return to the computer for several days, being too busy throwing herself into preparations for the grand opening night of *Spring Roses* in London's West End. Yet all the time at the back of her mind was the memory of that brief vision when she had last looked at the computer screen. The reality of the child and the cat — the feel of the cat's warmth and presence in the sturdy little arms, the muted tone of its purring — had been so true, so lifelike. In the end, Delia told the whole story to Miss T, bending down to sew a flower onto a ball gown so that her face was turned away as she spoke. The wardrobe supervisor had remained silent until eventually Delia ground to a halt.

"Do you think I am going mad?"

"Not more than usual. No, I don't. You were probably over-tired and fell slightly asleep."

"I was wide awake, I promise you."

"In the early hours of the morning? I doubt it, my dear."

At that point Delia had given up and said nothing further.

Opening night was sensational. The critics universally praised the show, albeit with terms such as "schmaltzy but scintillating"; when it came to the audience, the young looked frankly bored, but the rest of humanity who packed the place out — many of them having had to queue for hours — thundered their approval. There was a great deal of shouting, people standing up and cheering, many bouquets of flowers thrown down upon the stage. Miss T, despite being well known for her calm and slightly abrasive manner, burst into a storm of weeping and Justyn Krasinski got a standing ovation. When he finally left the stage, he shook hands with everybody backstage, kissed Robert Poynes-Hamilton and had his fingers wrung by a dinner-jacket-clad Alan Pearson, who took a bow while looking nervous. Justyn gave Delia — who was watching from the wings — a quick embrace. It was brotherly, friendly, but nothing more than that — yet against her will, her heart waltzed.

"Thank you," she said, trying to sound casual.

"You are more than welcome," he answered. "Would you like another one?"

"No. Grateful for the offer but I have had my ration for the day." And something made her move away.

Afterwards, Delia could have shouted, irritated by her own stupidity. Even though he annoyed her, being so full of himself and supremely confident, there was a definite charm about him. Maybe it was his accent, his rather dashing good looks . . . but there was an elusive *something* that she found terribly attractive despite herself.

"As if I haven't got enough on my plate," she caught herself muttering.

The first night party was given at a nearby hotel, with expenses flowing from the wallet of Robert Poynes-Hamilton and everybody talking at full voice. Miss T was surrounded by people congratulating her on how wonderfully the show had been costumed, and she beckoned to Delia to come and get her share of the praise.

"It really looked very splendid," added a quiet voice at Delia's elbow, and she turned to see Alan Pearson — to whom she had never actually spoken — giving her a pleasant smile.

"Thank you very much. But it was really all Miss T's creation."

"But you had a hand in it. In fact more than a hand, I imagine."

"She's a very clever girl," said Miss T loudly, a large brimming glass clutched to her chest. "Just as you are a very clever bloke, if I may say so, Mr Pearson."

"I just had a stroke of good luck, that's all."

"Nonsense," said somebody close by. "It was sheer raw talent, Alan. Of course you were fortunate to get Krasinski, that's for sure. But I hear he's signed a contract with France."

"No, you're wrong. He was thinking about it but has decided against."

"Well, that's a good thing. He's certainly got Richard Tauber between his teeth."

"What a nasty phrase," said Miss T, loudly. "I can't think of anything worse than nibbling his . . . though on second thought . . ." She gave a laugh.

"Really," said Alan, pretending to be annoyed. "I can't have my leading man dissected in this way."

"I wouldn't say that was quite the right word — or is it?" added some wit. "At the moment I would say he looks very close indeed to becoming just that."

And every head turned, including Delia's, to see that Justyn had been joined by Sangeetha, who was positively purring with delight as the showbiz crowd stared at her. She was extremely beautiful, black curly hair swept up tightly in a glittering chignon, huge tawny eyes overlooking the gathering worshippers, a figure that had spent hours — if not years — in the hands of a personal trainer.

"What a bitch," murmured someone close at hand, a sentiment with which Delia had to agree.

"She'll look grim when she's sixty," somebody whispered back.

Alan Pearson suddenly smiled, and Miss T — having had several further gulps of gin — joined in. Delia's own smile broadened. She knew that she ought to behave herself, but what was the point — she may as well laugh and let herself relax.

"I'm not laughing *at her*," whispered Alan quietly. "Only with happiness that my show has been so successful."

Delia turned to look at him properly for the first time. She had seen him at rehearsals, of course, but never actually studied him. He was small and neat with a pair of lustrous eyes which at the present moment were creased because he was smiling. His hair was rich, like dark wine, rather wavy, the sort of hair that you wanted to run your hands through. He was in fact a neatly formed, compact man with a rather charming look. Delia was somewhat wary of men's charms: she had in fact had only one lover in the whole of her life and he had worn horn-rimmed spectacles throughout their feeble attempts at sexual intercourse.

"Is your partner here as well?" she ventured.

"No, I'm afraid I don't have one at present."

"Oh, sorry."

"Please don't apologise. I seem to have the unfortunate habit of falling for married women and generally have one or two husbands threatening to beat the living daylights out of me. That's all I can report."

"It all sounds very unpleasant," Delia answered, and then burst into spontaneous laughter, in which Alan thankfully joined.

"And I'm not gay," he added, "just in case you were wondering."

"That never crossed my mind."

Thankfully, Miss T interrupted at that point. "Now, now, you two. This is not the occasion on which to disagree. Kiss and make up."

And then suddenly it was easy. Alan held his arms wide open, and Delia slid into them as if she had done so a million times before. He kissed her but it was as fleeting as the beat of a bird's wing. Yet for all that there was something familiar about it. It was a kiss that had happened before. Delia could have sworn it.

Soon afterwards, there was a ripple in the crowd as Sangeetha approached, waves of a heavy dark perfume making their way before her. A few paces behind — as if to demonstrate that he was not merely one of her entourage — came Justyn. There was something just a little bit amusing about the way he carried himself and Delia caught herself starting to smile. She wondered: what was there about him that always had that effect? Then suddenly, like a memory but not of anything tangible, she was listening to the immense sound of someone playing a brilliant piece of music. And she was truly happy, laughing with pleasure and with gladness that she had been chosen to hear it. Her hands went together to clap and then she realised to her shock that she was applauding Sangeetha, who was pulling a few pouting faces to please the photographers. Normally, Delia would have wanted to look away but for some reason — perhaps inspired by the music — she decided to bluff it out. Smiling broadly in the actress's direction she continued to nod and react. Sangeetha gave her a somewhat patronising grin and sauntered on her way.

"What got into you?" Miss T enquired in a voice blurred by alcohol.

Delia felt strangely defensive. "Nothing. I was just fooling about."

"I was going to join in," whispered Alan. "You see, I feel like applauding the whole occasion. Do you realise that my show was cheered in the West End?"

"Yes, I do. And I think it is marvellous, Mr Pearson," Delia exclaimed.

"I would much prefer it if you called me Alan."

"Then with your permission, I will."

But that was destined to be the sum total of their conversation, as the party began to divide up into cliques, with groups disappearing off to extend their evening's fun elsewhere. Delia watched as Alan was snatched up by Robert Poynes-Hamilton and

Justyn fell into Sangeetha's flowing train. Just a fraction sadly she turned towards home.

But the minute she got through the front door she felt a blaze of excitement and interest. She had left that poor little girl — the bastard daughter of a bad-tempered mother — sitting on a windowsill with a loving cat. What was going to happen next?

* * *

Apparently, a servant had heard Jenny singing in the street below and had mentioned the child to her mistress, who was something to do with the Swedish Opera. This woman — a dancer called Mademoiselle Lundberg —told Anna Maria that at the very least the child should have singing lessons. True to form, the mother hated the theatre and considered that actors were all nasty types. Nonetheless she agreed to Jenny's visiting a singing master at the opera house. And so began tuition of the child's voice and Jenny — much to her own relief — was finally admitted to the school itself at the age of ten and was from then on educated at government expense as a full-time pupil at the Royal Theatre.

Delia must have dozed off — or thought she did — because she opened her eyes to see a neat, compact person — a man with a tumble of reddish hair, his back straight, his fingers very long — playing the piano. But this man wasn't just playing; this music wasn't merely pleasant to listen to — this was a frenzy of emotion, of loving, of desire, of every beautiful thing imaginable. Delia sat very still, watching while the great young man poured out such a beautiful sound, the full voluptuous loveliness of every note imaginable. And then finally he stopped, slowly lowering his exquisite hands onto his knees, and looked at her, smiling.

"Hello, my dear, I didn't hear you come in. Have you been waiting long?"

The answer came from her feelings of love for this total stranger. "For you, I would wait a lifetime."

"As I would you, my beauty, my darling. My own sweet, precious girl."

Delia stood up and went towards him, arms outstretched. But as she felt the warmth of him, the well-loved scent of him, the sweet lines of his body, she lost awareness once more and fell into the greyness of deep slumber.

CHAPTER FOUR

Delia — Present Day

Waking up was even worse than usual. Delia had spent the night stretched out on her bed, fully dressed, trying to dream about the pianist with the tumble of reddish hair and failing miserably. All kinds of visions had swept through her unconscious mind: the cat on the windowsill; Sangeetha prancing through a crowd of open-mouthed fans; the cheering of the audience as the curtain came down on the last scene of Alan's West End production. But of the phantom pianist, not a sign. Delia gave a sigh and wondered why all the best things happened in dreams.

The doorbell was ringing, loud and imperiously, a ring that could only be delivered by one particular person. Miss T had arrived — hopefully having sobered up — to impart some new and exciting information. Even though she was still in her party dress, Delia made her way, bleary-eyed, to the front door.

"Good heavens," said her visitor with a wry grin. "Have you been dancing all night?"

"No," Delia answered with irritation, "I have not. I have been asleep on my bed."

"I see," answered Miss T. "Do you always slumber fully dressed?"

There was no point in further discussion. Delia merely answered "Sometimes," and opened the door to let her visitor in.

They sat down on either side of the kitchen table, Miss T obviously bursting to tell her something. Delia looked obedient and said, "Have you some news for me?" But much to her surprise it was not gossip about *Spring Roses* at all. Instead, Miss T said "I've had a reply from my friend at the V&A."

"About the headdress?"

"Yes. She's managed to give me an approximate date on it."

"Which is?"

"Mid-nineteenth century. Probably worn by somebody quite famous. The jewel on the end is semi-precious. I wonder who it belonged to."

Delia shook her head, "I've no idea, unless . . ." She paused. "There was somebody called Lind floating about at that time. But it couldn't be — could it?"

"If you are referring to Jenny Lind," said Miss T with asperity, "you are very probably right. The Swedish Nightingale herself. Why, of course! That could explain why I found the headdress in a box of tat in England. Miss Lind was a terrific favourite of Queen Victoria, you know, and sang in this country regularly."

Delia lowered her head, shaking it from side to side. "I'm afraid I don't know. But I want to. Can you tell me what information you have?"

"Well, darling, I'm not an expert but I can try my poor best. Did you know she died in England and is buried somewhere or other in the Malvern Hills? There was some funny business when she died — her husband insisting on burning all her correspondence. Letters from lovers, one asks oneself. And I believe there were a few of those."

"Really?"

"Really. Hans Christian Andersen, for one."

"I don't believe it."

"On my life. He proposed marriage to her."

"Good God!"

"Then, of course, there was the business with Mendelssohn."

Delia was aghast. "You mean the composer?"

"Of course I do. What other Mendelssohn was there?"

"Crikey!"

"An old-fashioned expletive for one so young, my dear. You must try and modernise." Miss T smiled wryly.

"Sorry. But wasn't Mendelssohn married?"

"Very much so. But he wouldn't leave his wife and Jenny wouldn't leave him. He was absolutely shattered by events and died shortly afterwards. Some people think he committed suicide. I believe there is a mysterious note in the records of some august society which that society claims as proof that he did."

"I am absolutely amazed. But wasn't she supposed to have had a fling with Barnum, the American impresario? I saw the film . . ." she added lamely.

"Hollywood, dear. Pure Hollywood make-believe. He was years older than she was and not at all attractive. Poor Jenny got herself into so much hot water. The funny thing is that she wasn't all that much to look at, that is until you saw her eyes, which — if rumour is to be believed — were absolutely stunning."

Delia stared, dumbfounded. It had never occurred to her that the woman who haunted her dreams . . . but no, that wasn't quite right. Jenny Lind did more than that. If anything, she haunted Delia's reality. She remembered the kisses given by the exceptional pianist — kisses of such brilliance that she had been hardly able to breathe. Yet he had kissed her, Delia — or had she slipped into someone else's body? Had the kisses been meant for Jenny Lind?

"You're very quiet," said Miss T, an eyebrow raised. "Does Jenny's story intrigue you?"

"That's not quite the right word."

"What is?"

"To say that her story possesses me would be more accurate."

Delia's friend looked suddenly sharp. "What are you saying?"

"I dream about her." Realising that Miss T was in some way anxious, Delia gave a light-hearted laugh. "It's probably that headdress of yours."

"What nonsense you do talk, my girl. Anyway, a stop was finally put to the poor woman's romances."

"By her husband?"

"None other. He was a reasonable musician — though hardly in the world-beating class of her previous men — and his name was Otto Goldschmidt."

"Was he good to her?"

"Apparently so. But he ordered that after her death all her correspondence should be burned — and he personally oversaw the operation."

"What a beastly thing to do!"

"Pig-like in my opinion. Though the reasons are obvious."

"Letters from other men?"

"Precisely, my dear."

"But who were they?"

"That, darling, remains a question and has been subject to a great deal of speculation."

"Ooh, how lovely. To leave all your old memories behind and people wondering."

"And you to be dead and gone, leaving everybody guessing."

"It would suit me."

"And me."

* * *

Delia slept well that night, but towards morning a dream came, bringing with it an awareness of strength, a strength which she did not possess but which was somehow seeking her out. What it could be was beyond her comprehension and then another dream drifted in. It was of a man's hands holding her and loving her, powerful mighty hands. At first she thought it must be her one and only lover, Dennis — he of the horn-rimmed spectacles — but his hands had always been rather moist whereas this man's hands were dry, and had talent and brilliance. She wanted to open her eyes to see who he was, but the dream held her in its grip and would not permit it. So, Delia instead luxuriated in the embrace of those great and magnificent fingers which spoke to her without words, telling her that he loved her.

* * *

The show continued in triumph. Ticket touts lingered by the queues and sold their goods at exorbitant prices to desperate, just-arrived Americans; old ladies hummed along delightedly to the tunes of Lehar; and Alan took over the baton. Delia was kept unbelievably busy, checking the costume changes, making sure that those of the principals were kept as fresh and sweat-free as possible, hurrying with needle and cotton when a button needed sewing on or a hidden zip fastener burst. Miss T hovered like a mystic presence and seemed to be everywhere simultaneously. Eventually, though, she cornered Delia for a chat.

"I've got it back. It's at home," she whispered, keeping her voice low because the theatre was live.

"Do you mean the headdress?"

"Yes. My friend who did the tests on it has confirmed the date as mid-nineteenth century. She thinks it was worn by the Priestess in *Norma* but she can't be certain about that. Lind first

32

took that part in 1841, when she was only twenty-one years old. Some doing. So it could have been worn by her."

"Those people had no idea about what it could do to a human voice, to sing those parts too soon in one's career."

"Poor Jenny, she learned that lesson the hard way."

"I would love to see it again, now that it's freshened up. Can you bring it round on Sunday?"

"Let's lunch at Joe Allen's."

* * *

The headdress looked fabulous, the blue gemstone glittering, the white feathers, having been relieved of their grime, preening upwards in a spiral of plume.

"Can I try it on?" Delia asked.

"Careful. Don't get it dirty again."

"Miss T, credit me with a little more sense, if you please."

Delia slipped the beautiful thing onto her head. Miss T watched as the younger woman gave a sudden broad grin and said, "I don't believe it. He can't be that tall," then giggled.

"What are you laughing at?" Miss T asked her.

"Well, this thing is giving me a picture of a young man with an ungainly body, a big nose and features that don't really fit. He's hardly what you would call handsome."

"Ah, but is he kind?"

"Oh yes, I believe he is."

"Then don't make fun of him!" Miss T leaned forward and pulled the coronet from Delia's head. "It's making you see things?"

Delia looked at her, smiling a dreamy smile. "It was rather pleasant — as was he. I wish you'd let me wear it a bit longer."

"The trouble with you, young lady, is that you tend to pursue dreams. What you need is a nice faithful boyfriend who would be good to you in bed and good-natured the rest of the time."

"If such a man existed, I reckon half the unmarried women in the world would be after him."

"And not only unmarried either."

Miss T gave her usual short laugh, that somehow resembled a dog barking, and shortly afterwards the two women parted company. But Delia could not forget the vision she had had. The tall gangly man who had looked at her with such a twinkle in his blue eyes. She wished that she had been able to identify him.

Later that evening, she wandered, somewhat disconsolately, around her flat, feeling constrained and miserable. With no idea of what was airing, she switched on the television and slumped into an armchair, bored and fed up. Then suddenly she was terribly alert, watching as some Hollywood actor whose face she did not recognise, dressed like the young man she had been watching an hour previously, ran down some old-world cobbled streets.

"Good God!" she exclaimed.

The man she had seen was none other than Hans Christian Anderson. An irresistible urge came over her — to put the head-dress on again and have another look at him, all his big, clumsy, loveable self. She got up, put on her smartest coat — though she had no idea what she was dressing up for — and went down a flight of stairs to her front door. All the flats that had a small balcony overlooking the waterway were one floor up and reached by a spiral staircase.

Fortunately, there was a taxi dropping a passenger off a few doors down and Delia shouted and raced to get it. Once inside she repeated Miss T's address loud and clear, fastened her seat belt, then began to wonder what she was playing at.

Whatever it was, she did not have long to find out. Miss T had apparently gone round to see a friend for drinks and the door was answered by Cyrus Markham, a young mixed-race actor who had recently won a Bafta for his performance in *Journey's End* at the National Theatre.

"Hello," he said cheerfully. "I'm Cyrus. And you are?"

"Delia. I'm Miss T's assistant."

"So nice to meet you. I live with her, so I suppose you could say that I am an assistant as well."

Delia didn't know whether to laugh or remain silent. She simply stared at the attractive young man, wondering what the age gap could possibly be and how Miss T had managed it.

"Come in, come in," Cyrus continued companionably. "Can I get you anything to drink? I don't expect she'll be that long."

She was dying to go in and fire questions at him, mostly about how he and Miss T had met and how they had decided to set up home together, but Delia knew that she had to take advantage of the situation.

"Thanks awfully, but I asked the taxi to wait. I've come to collect some costumes. Miss T wanted me to look over them."

"Oh, I see. Well, come in. You know where they are kept."

"No, I'm afraid I don't. You'll have to show me."

She followed Cyrus through a flamboyant home which seemed to Delia to bear all the hallmarks of Miss T and one or two souvenirs from Mr Markham's rise through the National Theatre ranks. Arriving at a back bedroom which had been turned into a glorified costumier's den, Delia turned with a smile.

"My goodness, I hadn't expected anything quite as magnificent as this. Are these souvenirs from every show she has ever done?"

"Surely are. Which one did you want?"

"It's a headdress, actually. She bought it recently from a sale and we were both very impressed by it. The V&A confirmed that it was probably used in *Norma*."

"Oh well, in that case it would be over here."

He pointed to where, gleaming and glittering, each poised on its own small stand, stood the brilliant array of headgear that Miss T had managed to gather around herself. And there it was, at the very heart of the great collection. On a stand slightly higher than the others, its white feathers clean and sparkling since its restoration, stood the high priestess's helmet.

It looked magnificent. Delia was certain that she should not take it, that Miss T would be furious with her. She knew that indeed she might get the sack over the whole affair — but despite all these things that she knew to be wrong, she still felt utterly compelled.

Cyrus must have sensed something because he said, "You're sure it's all right for you to remove it?"

"Oh perfectly. It's something she wanted me to look at in a hurry. I promise to bring it back on Monday."

"I'll hold you to that."

Afterwards in the taxi going home, her fingers clutching tightly on to the carrier bag in which the headdress nestled, she was not so sure. She didn't think Miss T would sack her but there always remained that possibility. Yet Delia could no more have ordered the taxi to turn around than throw the precious thing out of the window. She opened the bag to peep into it.

A powerful smell was arising from it, a smell of sandalwood and myrrh and other exotica that she did not recognise. She bent her head more deeply to try to catch all the scents and just for a few seconds she existed in a blur of utterly delicious perfume. Then she lifted the helmet out — for that is how it was shaped, a sparkling array of feathers pointing upwards, surmounted by a sparkling blue stone. Gazing into it, Delia wished, just like a child would.

"Let me know what it was like to be Jenny, if you can. I really would like that. Just to know something of her life. Oh, I'd like to be able to sing as well."

She felt incredibly dizzy, black circles whirling around her head. Delia tried to laugh them off. But they were growing in intensity. It was like an anaesthetic and she could not possibly resist its tempting and rich perfume.

CHAPTER FIVE

Jenny — Past

Jenny Lind woke with a start as the train gave a triumphant blast of clamorous sound and reduced its speed slightly. Pulling back a window curtain, which she had closed against the dark afternoon, she looked out and saw that now there were one or two small houses visible rather than the roaring wasteland of rural Denmark and knew that at last she was approaching Copenhagen station. With a resigned gesture she stood up, straightening her full skirt as she did so, and removed her small suitcase from the luggage rack, her larger trunk having been committed to the care of one of the guards. She presumed that she would be met at the station by Mrs August Bournonville, and on thinking that assumed her serious face, as it would never do to have a fit of grinning in front of the wife of an important man — well, as important as the ballet master at the Danish Royal Theatre could get.

She also hoped that she would recognise Mrs Bournonville, whom she hadn't seen for several years. Yet who could imitate the small, rather set, features of the former ballerina, now a mother of five? Jenny peered through the crowd, hoping to get a glimpse of a familiar face. She became vaguely aware that a long, ungainly man had come to stand beside her and was bowing. She swept her eyes up and looked at him. He was slightly familiar, and she knew that she had met him before, somewhere in the distant past.

"Miss Lind?" he said.

"Yes. I'm sorry, do I know you?"

"I called on you once when you visited Copenhagen. I don't think you enjoyed my company very much."

"I can't say I can recall the incident. But I apologise for any bad behaviour on my part. Forgive me."

He smiled. "There is nothing to forgive."

Jenny regarded him closely. The tall, oddly-shaped body; the bony face; the lovely crooked smile. Oh, my God, it had to be! Hans Christian Andersen himself had come to meet her.

Miss Lind allowed herself to peer at the famous author — that was as much as she could manage in the dim station light. He was lanky and rather thrown together; in other words, all the pieces were there but arranged somewhat haphazardly. Yet there was something utterly charming about him — an earnestly appealing long face lit by a pair of bright-blue eyes and a mop of swishing black hair.

"You will stay with August Bournonville for this visit, I believe?"

"Yes. He heard me sing and wanted me to play Alice in *Robert le Diable* . . ."

"And?"

"Originally, I said I wouldn't do it because I only knew the part in Swedish while the rest of the company would be singing in Danish. Too embarrassing."

"So what happened?"

"I refused, so he said he would cancel the whole show. Then I reconsidered."

In the darkness, Hans grinned broadly. For all her talent and beauty she was just like other women: firm until she had won the battle, then relenting sweetly. He turned his oddly-shaped face towards her and said, "I would like to call on you, if you give me permission."

"Of course you may, provided, of course, that the Bournonvilles do not object."

His beanpole body shook with amusement. "I don't think they will. Antonine, your host's father, advised me not to try for ballet dancing because of my height but to concentrate on the theatre instead. So that's why I became a writer."

Hans Andersen guffawed loudly at the image of himself as a dancer, and Jenny joined in. There was something about this great loveable giant that intrigued her, and part of it was the very fact that he seemed to have outgrown himself. But he had charm, there could be no doubting that. Taking her small portmanteau from her, he guided her to a waiting cab and helped her inside.

However, once they were at the Bournonvilles' home, which was filled with the noise of laughing children, he took Jenny's hand and said, "I will call tomorrow morning, if that is in order."

"Of course it is. I am honoured to meet you, Mr Andersen. I much admire your work."

"I am delighted to hear that. Goodnight, Miss Lind."

She looked at him earnestly. "Goodnight, Mr Andersen."

"May I say that you have the most beautiful eyes I have ever seen," he replied.

"Thank you indeed, sir. Or may I call you Hans?"

"If you do not, I shall be forced to put on mourning."

"Oh, don't do that just for me!"

In a delighted shivery dream she went to bed in the Bournonville nursery, from which his charming children had been turned out, yet stared with open-mouthed delight at the famous opera singer who was coming to spend a few days with them.

On the next day, however, following a delightful carriage ride with Helena, Bournonville's wife, Jenny returned, full of laughter and sunshine, to see the ungainly figure of Hans waiting with a large bunch of flowers clasped to his breast. Despite his vaguely comic image there was something terribly endearing about the man, with his genuine heart and blue eyes, clearly showing his admiration.

Exactly one week later Jenny Lind stepped onto the stage of the Danish Royal Theatre in Copenhagen. As always, she was terribly nervous. The opera was *Robert le Diable* and she was singing the role of Alice in Swedish. Just for a second before she launched into her opening aria, she felt terror strike at her heart and felt for a brief moment that she would not be able to sing. And then the man who had saved her voice flashed into her mind. *Thank you, Señor García*, she thought, and going into the lights, opened her mouth and let the glorious notes emerge. Out poured that marvellous, thrilling magic that the Spanish master had found when she had thought that all was lost. It was a voice like no other and the audience sat entranced by the beautiful sound she was making.

Beyond the footlights she could glimpse the shambolic figure of Hans Andersen rumpled over a chair. She only wished that she could love him in return, for his obsession was now obvious. He had fallen in love with her almost immediately and now craved her company at every hour of the day. And this night, the night of her debut, she felt that he wanted to rush onto the stage and clasp her to his kindly heart.

After the show Jenny's dressing room was packed with admirers — theatre critics, opera lovers, lusty hopeful men, plus what seemed like half the world's population. Flowers were everywhere and if it hadn't been for the stalwart figure of Hans deciding whom among the crowd was worth giving a drink to and who was fit to throw out, Jenny would have had no idea how to deal with the invasion of compliments. But eventually the crowd thinned out and she and Andersen got into an open carriage and returned to the Bournonvilles' home. In the darkness he put his arm around her waist and whispered, "You were wonderful. I would never have believed that anyone could possess a voice as superb as yours."

She smiled up at him. "Thank you. You are very kind."

"I mean it. You have stolen my heart completely."

She was flattered — who wouldn't be? The great writer declaring his passion for her — and in such a positive manner. She cuddled against him, her nose pressed, slightly uncomfortably, against a diamond brooch he wore in his shirt front.

"I love you, Jenny Lind," he whispered, and she desperately wished that she could say the same. But it wouldn't be true and she knew it, so for once the opera singer remained silent and did not reply.

* * *

"Miss Lind," whispered a small female child into her ear.

"Yes, dear?" Jenny answered, waking suddenly from oversleeping in the comfortable bed installed in the Bournonville nursery and dreaming wildly for some reason that she was called Delia.

"Mr Andersen has arrived carrying a present for you and wants to know whether you have mentioned him at all to us."

"And what did you say?"

"No," came a chorus of little voices from the posse of children who had crept upstairs behind their sister, followed by small cruel cackling.

And so it went on. The children received daily — no, hourly — calls from the lovelorn Mr Andersen enquiring whether Miss Lind had said anything about him — particularly nice things, but anything would do. The little creatures, solemn-faced, looked pious and answered no, falling around the room with laughter the moment he had left. As for Hans Christian himself, his honest soul needed love so desperately that he consequently liked men and women equally, his honest heart opening innocently to all comers. But he loved Jenny Lind greatly and each day of her visit wrote the word *foralskad* — in love — in his diary.

One night, when he was walking her home from a dinner party, he almost proposed. It was cold but there was a high, bright moon which threw their shadows onto the path behind them. Hans — as usual — had his arm around Jenny's waist and was hugging her to him as if he could never let her go. He started to speak, the words tumbling out incoherently. Yet somehow Jenny knew what was coming — and dreaded it. She loved him a little, but not enough to want to spend the rest of her life in his company. She smiled up at him, pulling a little away.

"Come on, my dear. Stretch your long shanks. We must catch up with the others. They are so far ahead, they've practically vanished." And with that she broke into a jog trot and put the poor writer in what he termed *a damned awkward position* in his diary. To compensate for the embarrassing situation, he spent the next morning working on a short poem for her, writing the finished version on a card.

> *You sang — I listened, enchanted singer,*
> *And yet my best song you will receive,*
> *One forgets the artist for the woman;*
> *I do not sing my heart beats too strong.*

He signed it *H.C. Andersen* and dated it 11 September, 1843. But by now the time had very nearly come for her to leave Copenhagen and return to Sweden. Hans felt as if his heart was breaking.

The night of Jenny's farewell performance was rapturous. The students had gathered at the stage door and followed her — and her most willing escort — back to the Bournonvilles' house, torches lit and held on high. Jenny had sung for them and they had applauded, cheered, stamped their feet and shouted. Afterwards, once they had gone, she ran into the house and burst into tears.

"My darling, what is it? What is the matter?" asked Hans, taking her into his long and loving arms.

"Nothing, my very dear friend. I am just so full of emotion. I don't think I sang all that well for the students. I promise that the next time I come I will sing some Danish folk songs."

He could not speak, realising that this talented girl meant everything to him. And realising at the same moment that she could never be his, unless he told her.

"Jenny . . ." he started.

"Don't, darling, I am too full of emotion. We will speak in the morning."

And with that she gave him a swift kiss on the cheek and ran away to her bedroom.

They had no opportunity to speak privately afterwards. Jenny was in a whirlwind of packing and Hans, realising that his time would be wasted unless they had some privacy, went home and composed a letter in which he asked her to marry him and make their relationship permanent. Then he rose in the darkness of dawn and accompanied her to the Custom House station, where the great train chuffed steam as it awaited the signal to carry the passengers back to Sweden.

He had written the words he could not say in the form of a letter, in which he asked most sincerely for her hand in marriage. He passed it to her as she set her shoe on the foot plate.

"Read this with care, my little nightingale."

"That's a sweet word to use."

"For the sweetest woman I have ever met. I intend to write a story about such a creature and how it saves the emperor from death through its beautiful song. You, my darling Miss Lind, are the nightingale of my heart."

She bent forward to give him a swift kiss on the lips, then made her way into the train, not looking back. It was a moment that would remain with them as a sweet sadness for a long time.

* * *

Jenny Lind had the strangest dream; a dream that left her breathless and frightened. She dreamt that she woke up and was hurling through a huge city in the back of a weird horseless vehicle. From where she sat — huddled and afraid — she could see the back of a solitary man, hidden behind glass. Everywhere there came the roar of sound — screams and shouts filling the night air. It was as if she had plunged suddenly into hell. Jenny — or was she somebody else, somebody other than her usual self? — closed her eyes tightly, not wanting to see any more. Then, daringly opening them again, she reached into the carrier bag and pulled out that wonderful jewel-topped headdress and slowly the noises faded and everything grew quiet as she gazed at its subtle beauty and breathed in its heady perfume. The singer drifted into sleep still clutching it and could only hear the deep thunder of the train as she sped through the night towards Stockholm and the next part of her life.

CHAPTER SIX

Jenny — Past

Very much as she had expected, the letter from Hans Christian Andersen had contained a proposal of marriage. Fond of him as she was and having encouraged his romantic dreams more than a little, she had hardly known how to reply. So, she did something even worse and ignored the letter. She could picture him sitting at home, tears running down his long nose, repeating her name over and over again. Eventually she had written, saying that though she loved him it was only in a sisterly way, and she was so sorry but his proposal had come as a great shock to her. It was a lie, of course, but it seemed the kindest way of explaining her own unforgivable behaviour.

Meanwhile, Jenny's career raced on. She was on a visit to Germany, having refused an offer from the great composer Meyerbeer to take the lead in *La Sonnambula* because she couldn't speak German, when she was suddenly obliged to return to Sweden. She was to appear at the coronation of the new King Oscar I and to give her services to the Royal Theatre once again. The Royal Theatre, delighted by her return, offered both a contract and a pension for life. But that meant no more travelling, no more challenges, just a Swedish singer restricted to her own territory. Jenny tore the contract up.

She was singing *Norma* at her farewell concert in the Royal Theatre, her voice ringing out strong and true, completely in control of herself and the sound she was making, the feathered headdress firmly on her head, when she suddenly had the strangest sensation. Just for a moment or two, she was no longer Jenny Lind but somebody else, a young female standing on a stage with no idea why she was there except to look around her and at the costumes of others — but there were no others present! She stood completely alone, desolate, washed up on some terrible strip of life that stretched from here to infinity. And then into that echoing silence she distantly recognised the thin voice of the flute and realised that she was a great singer and thousands of people were waiting to be entertained by her magic gift.

She took the smallest of breaths and sang on.

***

In Germany, Jenny had been taken to an important private party by Maestro Meyerbeer in whose opera she was playing the part of Vielka, and a strange rumour reached her ears afterwards. Though everyone loved her voice, the singer herself had been considered plain and very uninteresting until she started to sing. The words *thin* and *plain-featured* had been bandied about, to which had been added *awkward* and *nervous*. The words had been repeated laughingly by a stupid young woman who should have known better, but inwardly Jenny had frozen. So this is how she was regarded. A divine singer with no looks. A concerted effort must be made to change her appearance.

Jenny swept her brown hair off her face and into a series of curls at the back of her head. She applied rouge to her cheeks and carmine to her lips. Then she smiled at herself in the mirror and realised as she did so that her eyes were, on this occasion, crystal bright and sparkling like champagne. She decided that she was ready for the forthcoming ordeal. Putting on her sweetest — but rather false — smile, Jenny left the house and headed for the home of Amalia Wichmann.

She had been making light conversation to the best of her ability when she heard Amalia greet someone in the doorway. Even before she turned she was aware of a change in the atmosphere, of a great presence, of somebody standing there who was powerful and resplendent. Jenny Lind looked and saw to her astonishment that the newcomer was bowing — not to the company, but to her individually. Her heart flew madly as she responded with a small curtsy. He came straight towards her, his hand outstretched to clasp one of hers.

"Miss Lind," he said. "Is it really you? I had heard that you were rather a quiet little thing but, on the contrary, you are entrancing!"

And with that he bent to kiss her outstretched hand. The emotion radiating from him was tangible. For a moment she wondered who he was and then it hit her like a thunderclap. It was the great composer, Felix Mendelssohn himself.

She remained momentarily silent before whispering, "Do you mind doing that again."

"What?"

"Kissing my hand."

Felix gazed at her to see if she was making fun of him, saw that she wasn't, and allowed a mischievous grin to lighten his dark Jewish good looks.

"By all means, madam," he answered, and this time he allowed the tip of his tongue to come out for a fleeting moment in a swift and intimate greeting.

Jenny stared at him. "It is a special honour to meet you, Mr Mendelssohn."

"I should say the same, but the fact is that I feel I already know you. So many of my friends have heard you and the consensus is that you are a great and powerful performer. This is a statement so rarely given that I know it can be nothing but the truth."

Jenny just gazed, her blood racing up to her cheeks and then down again. She had never suffered this thrill of mixed emotions before. She was falling in love almost instantly and enormously with this extraordinary, powerful, dark-haired engaging man, who was smiling at her with a look which she could not interpret. She cleared her throat and managed to squeak out, "I must send you some tickets."

He grinned. Felix Mendelssohn, the great composer, master of his craft, the name on everybody's lips, was giving her such a cheeky look that all she could do was smile back, certain that she had known the man for at least a thousand years. And then . . . everything changed as a small person sidled up.

"Good evening," it said, and curtsied. Jenny looked down to see a short creature, pretty-faced, with hair in a mass of long ringlets, standing beside her and smiling politely. Mendelssohn spoke up.

"Miss Lind, may I introduce my wife, Cecile? My dear, this is the celebrated soprano, Jenny Lind."

"Oh, what an honour," Cecile gushed. "I have not had the pleasure personally of hearing you sing, but a friend of mine knows your work and thinks you are absolutely marvellous!"

Inwardly, Jenny sighed. *How typical*, she thought, *at the moment I meet a man who sweeps me off my feet, he turns out to be married.* She smiled a little sadly.

"How very kind of you, Madame Mendelssohn."

"My wife is always kind," Felix said, and gave Jenny an indescribable look that made her draw in her breath sharply. There could be no doubt about it. Married or not, Maestro Mendelssohn was attracted to her. Jenny swept a magnificent curtsy.

"Please forgive me. I see some friends over there I must speak to. It has been a pleasure indeed to make your acquaintance."

And with that she was off, her heart beating wildly, knowing — without turning around — that the great musician couldn't take his eyes off her.

A quarter of an hour later, she was proved right. He came up to her, standing alone for a second, looking around the room to find her. He approached her from behind, saying, "I have already arranged to hear you when you next sing. I am afraid you are going to find me a bit of a pest, Miss Lind."

"Oh? In what way?"

He shrugged his silk-clad shoulders. "Wherever you shall be, I will follow. If you go to London, I will hear of it. Paris, Moscow, Gothenburg — it makes no difference. I will join you there. This I promise you, my dear Miss Lind." With that, he kissed her hand and left before she could form a reply.

Going back in the carriage she shivered with delight and whispered aloud, "Oh, that Felix Mendelssohn. How he has charmed me."

* * *

On 15 December, Jenny made her debut in Berlin singing *Norma* — and conquered the city. Critics were raving about her, the audience went wild and Mendelssohn was present. When Jenny sang "Casta Diva" to a silent and sensitive house, cries of "Encore" had rung out everywhere.

But the greatest triumph was yet to come. With a sulky female star, Leopoldine Tuczek, reluctantly standing down, Meyerbeer — who all along had wanted Jenny to sing the lead in his new opera — was finally getting his wish, for Jenny had agreed.

Meanwhile, there was Christmas to contend with. Jenny had invited her friend Jacob Josephson, with his dark good looks and his vast musical talent, to accompany her to an evening party, and set off in high spirits. She had just come from a meeting with

Karl von Kustner, managing director of the Berlin Opera, who had offered her a six-month contract. This meant that her future earnings would be on a secure footing, and she could finally give Josephson — an old and dear friend — enough money to travel to Italy in order to continue his musical studies.

The carriage ride was brief and jolly, with Jacob cracking jokes, and when they arrived the holly-decorated front door was opened straight away by their hostess looking somewhat flushed in the cheeks and extremely lively.

"Come in, my dears, come in. A great many people have arrived. I had forgotten that I sent out so many invitations!" She gave an excited laugh. At that point Jenny knew there must a reason for all this merriment and, just for a second, wondered what it could be. And then she saw him, his elegant back turned, his glass raised on high, listening carefully — or so it would appear — to a woman who was speaking. Without moving an inch, Felix Mendelssohn said, "Good evening, Miss Lind. How nice of you to call."

Momentarily she didn't know whether to laugh or cry, then she regained her wits. "Good evening, Mr Mendelssohn. I didn't know that I would find you here."

He wheeled around, his whole face coming to life as he looked at her. "I told you that I would see you again soon, and thus I am keeping my word."

"And very punctually, I might add."

"I could not speak to you at the opera because you had disappeared into a swarm of German admirers. Am I forgiven?"

"Yes, of course you are. May I introduce you to my friend Mr Josephson?"

She turned around to see Jacob, scarlet in the face and eyes popping as he gazed at his hero. Felix positively laughed with amusement but gave a polite bow. Jacob, completely overcome, burst into tears.

An hour later, calm had been restored. Josephson was playing the polka, and various guests were trying valiantly to keep
up with the brisk rhythm. Jenny, nestled in Mendelssohn's arms,
was just about managing, enjoying more the warm body scent
of her partner. Felix clearly was a man who washed often and
bathed himself in fresh cologne. Jenny knew that she was utterly
entranced by him.

"So where do you go from here?" he asked.

"I rather think I might stay. I have been offered a contract
by the manager."

"Then sign it, sweetheart. I beg you."

She laughed quietly. "I rather think I will, Mr Mendelssohn.
If that would please you."

"It means, my dear girl, that I will be able to see you quite
regularly."

"But tell me, what happens if I should go to London?"

"I have already told you. I will follow. And when I am not
able to follow, I will write to you."

Jenny looked up at him, bright-eyed. "And I will reply, Mr
Mendelssohn."

"Felix, please."

She smiled. "Jenny," she said.

CHAPTER SEVEN

Jenny — Past

Her triumph in Berlin was indescribable. The previous, and mediocre, leading lady — secretly thought of as sluttish by Jenny — had been committed to memory. Miss Lind had shone like the great star she was. There had been a whisper backstage that Mendelssohn had crept into a box just as the lights were going down and Jenny's heart had soared — as did her voice and her acting ability. The Berlin audience had yelled till they were hoarse, had thrown flowers, had screamed "Lind, Lind, Lind!" until they were breathless. But Jenny's eyes had swept to the box and seen that there was one empty chair. Even in this great moment of triumph, she was filled with disappointment.

A letter arrived just as she had got into bed that night. Even as she was climbing into its comfortable warmth, she heard a knock on the door and a minute later her companion had put her head around the door and said, "Post, Miss Jenny."

The warmth and affection that poured out of the letter was unbelievable. Mendelssohn apologised for not having seen her afterwards, said that he had to hurry away but also that she was a great star, a triumph, and that she had raised the art of singing to a new level. Jenny leapt out of bed and poured herself a small glass of wine, which she raised to her lips with the words: "To you, Felix Mendelssohn. With the hope that I shall see you again soon," she murmured, then hastily got back into bed as she heard her female companion moving about in the next room.

* * *

She had not realised how much her physical state depended on contact with the man with whom she had fallen so in love. She did not see him for several weeks and to add to her problems she was desperately trying to get out of a contract she had foolishly signed to sing in England for Alfred Bunn, who owned the Drury Lane Theatre. The stress of everything came to a head during a performance of *Euryanthe* when she felt faint and nearly lost consciousness. She was rushed home and put to bed, then examined by a doctor and told to rest for at least a week. So she was glad to get a letter from Meyerbeer — at least she *thought* it was from him, as it was signed *M* and nothing further. It said that he would send a carriage around to her house one evening, which would convey her to a well-known dining place, and there they could relax and discuss her future. Jenny tried to brighten her appearance for the occasion and put on a lace dress that swished enticingly as she walked about. Then, when she heard a carriage pull up outside, she put on her new red cloak and went to get in.

The conveyance was dark and fashionable, but sturdy-looking, the driver sitting aloft. He tipped his hat on seeing her and Jenny climbed inside. Then her flesh crept as what she had thought was an abandoned garment let out a muffled laugh.

"Where are you going to, pretty young lady?" it asked in a piping falsetto.

"I'm sorry. I thought that I was being collected. I apologise. My mistake."

She stood up but at that moment the coach trundled forward, and she sat down again rather hastily. An arm reached out from the bundle of blackness and grabbed her hand.

"Tell your fortune, little sweeting."

"No. Be off. I am sorry, I have got into the wrong vehicle. Kindly release me."

"So soon?" asked a masculine voice and the bundle threw off its disguise and revealed Mendelssohn roaring with laughter.

Jenny stared for a moment, then: "You cheeky young man. You frightened me almost into a faint!"

He chortled. "I've obviously got the wrong woman, then. The girl I sought was not afraid to face an audience of hundreds. Furthermore, she had a magnificent voice and was wanted by warring impresarios. She was afraid of nothing and nobody. But *you* are squeaking like a little mouse."

"Oh, Mr Mendelssohn, what trick are you playing now?"

"I'm sorry. My name is Felix, so why don't you call me that? I assure you that as far as I'm concerned, we have moved on from ceremonial greeting."

Jenny did not know whether to laugh or weep, she was so wildly attracted.

"I'm sorry, Felix. I was rather frightened." She couldn't tell him that she had in fact been absolutely terrified.

"Then I apologise. It was just that I wanted to see you on your own and couldn't quite work out how."

"Please don't say any more. I shall simply ask the coachman to stop and I shall go home as if nothing has happened."

Felix's face was suddenly lit by a passing streetlamp and in its brightness, Jenny saw that his eyes were shining, alight with emotion. It struck her very forcibly then that, despite his childish prank, he really meant what he said and actually had some feelings for her.

"Very well," he said. "I am sorry to have disturbed you. Goodbye."

She did one of her spectacular turnabouts. "I would not like that," she answered quietly.

"What are you saying?"

"I said that I would prefer not to do that. I would rather spend some time talking to you, Mr . . . Felix."

"I could fall very much in love with you, you know."

"But what of your wife?"

"Cecile? I love her too — but not the way I feel about you. She was sixteen when I met her, and she hasn't grown up much since."

Jenny turned away and looked out of the small window. "I think we are going around in circles."

"As you are — in the circle of my mind. Never to leave it. That is what you have done to me, Miss Lind. I am for ever your captive."

* * *

Meeting up with one another was a difficulty they managed to overcome with a certain amount of good fortune. Jenny continued with her season at the Opera House in Berlin, to thunderous applause. Mendelssohn attended as many of her performances as he could manage, sometimes slipping away without seeing her, leaving just an empty chair in a box which he had shared with other theatre goers. But at her very last performance in *Norma*, he sat amongst the crowd in the stalls and shouted his enthusiasm with the rest. He stood up — as did all but the most senile — and cheered as Jenny took curtain call after curtain call. Then he vanished.

Afterwards, as she was making her way out of the stage door — crowded with eager young men and wrinkled old roues, plus those who just wanted to glimpse the great Miss Lind in the flesh

— she saw him, muffled in a huge scarf, cap pulled well down. He thrust a piece of paper into her hand, growled, "Brilliant, little lady," and vanished. On the note were written the words: *Well done, my sweet. Au revoir for the present.*

A reception had been arranged by Meyerbeer, which was being given in a local hotel. Attending, devoid of both scarf and hat, was Felix, beside him the small woman whom Jenny had met before. The singer's heart sank. So little Cecile had been brought along. Jenny smiled at them distantly and continued her conversation with the wife of the orchestra leader. After a while, she saw the Mendelssohns determinedly making their way towards her. At that moment she hated the entire situation, but nonetheless managed a smile.

"Mademoiselle Lind, do I recall that you have met my wife, Cecile?"

"Of course, Maestro", Jenny answered, all sweetness. "How do you do, Mrs Mendelssohn?" She gave a small bow.

Cecile responded with almost a complete court curtsy. "Oh, Miss Lind, I have been hoping to meet you again. My husband speaks of little else all day."

"How boring," were the words on Jenny's lips before she could stop but which she rapidly accounted for with, "I expect he was talking about opera in general."

Felix spoke up rather angrily. "Nothing of the sort. I was talking about you and how talented you were."

"Yes, he was, truly, Miss Lind. He is very struck indeed with your singing."

Jenny simply did not know how to answer. Cecile was not only sincere but quite definitely unsophisticated. But there was nothing at all to dislike about her. It was fairly obvious that Felix had outgrown her and remained by her side for the sake of their children. And, Jenny thought wryly, because she was comfortable and unchallenging. Yet she found herself warming to the little creature and thought that she — the great opera star — was in a truly horrible situation. With an intuition that Jenny had not realised he possessed, Mendelssohn spoke.

"Mademoiselle, tonight everyone sitting in the audience loved you with all their heart. When you sang "Casta Diva" one could hear nothing but your golden and great voice ringing out into the darkest recesses of the opera house. That accompanied by the quiet fall of their tears as the magic sound consumed them. Miss Lind, I salute you." And he knelt down on one knee and kissed her hand.

She couldn't help it. She was so very much in love with him. As he rose to his feet he stared her straight in the eye and she could see that he was in the same state. Yet he owed allegiance to his little wife — and always would — even while she, Jenny, absolutely fascinated him.

CHAPTER EIGHT

Jenny — Past

The steamer slipped into the dock at midnight. Stockholm was a city that usually put its lights out at 12 a.m. but to Jenny Lind's amazement it was glowing with illuminations, and she could see hordes of people thronging the streets. As the ship finally moored a mighty cheer rang out and the crowd, as one, called out, "Jenny, Jenny, Jenny, Jenny Lind! Welcome, welcome, welcome, welcome home!" This was followed by an almighty shout of triumph, and a mass of fireworks lit the dockside and Jenny — standing so small and so vulnerable — could hardly believe that all this rejoicing was entirely about her return to Sweden. But it was true. People had stayed up late just to glimpse her and cheer. Her triumph in Germany had given rise to a Swedish national celebration. Finally, she timidly stepped ashore and was immediately picked up by a group of hearty young male students and carried to her hotel. She did not know whether to laugh or cry and ended up doing both.

Of course, it was lovely to be back in her native land but she found her thoughts wandering to Germany and to Felix and how much she missed him. Jenny was in some ways still a slip of a child with a wayward mother, and the great composer — the wonder boy — had been the first person to show her any true emotion.

Of course, dear old Hans had amused her and had flattered her to no end, but now she knew what it was to feel the drama of great emotion. And then, one day, a letter turned up, sent directly to the Royal Theatre, and she had known even by the very feel of it who the writer was. It simply said, *I miss you terribly, little lady. Come back to me soon.* It was signed *F.M.* Jenny held it to her heart and whispered, "As soon as I can, sweet man."

Eventually, the season in Sweden came to an end and Jenny set forth on her tour, starting in Germany where she had been asked to sing by the King of Prussia himself. Crowned heads of Europe abounded in the audience and included Britain's Queen Victoria and her husband, the young, musically minded Prince Albert. Lord Liverpool, an old cynic, was also amongst the throng. He regarded himself as a great critic and raised a cynical eyebrow when Jenny took to the stage at a private concert given that night in the chateau of Bruhl. He ended up weeping, bowled over by Jenny's style, skill and quality of voice. He was completely charmed and a little bit in love.

Very much thrilled by the cordiality of Victoria and Albert — who invited her to sing in England — Jenny moved on to Frankfurt and met someone who would become a great friend. Tall, good-looking, somewhat masculine of character, politically powerful — as powerful as it was possible for a woman to be — Harriet Grote took to the singer immediately, offering to deal with Alfred Bunn — who still thought Jenny was under contract to appear at Drury Lane Theatre — on the singer's behalf.

They heard Jenny in *La Sonnambula* that evening, Harriet declaring that the orchestra was coarse and noisy, the rest of the singers worse than mediocre, the opera house crammed to suffocation, but Jenny herself could both act and sing.

Before leaving Sweden, Miss Lind had thoughtfully left her forwarding address with the stage door keeper, a jolly man with a great understanding of actors and singers, all their little foibles and all their secretive little affairs being known to him. Aware of this, Jenny had tried to look exceedingly demure as she handed the man a good tip and a card.

"My first address in Germany, Mr Lundgren. I will write to you with a new one the minute I move on."

The stage door keeper had smiled a secretive smile. "Expecting a lot of mail, are we, Miss Lind?"

Jenny had looked at the floor. "Not a great deal. But I would like to get what there is."

And now it was here. At last she had received a postcard, well-thumbed and somewhat ancient in appearance — and from England, of all places. The singer read: *Touring Europe. Very beautiful. Back next year.* Then came the signature *Felix Mendelssohn X.* What the X was for, Jenny wasn't quite certain, but she liked it anyway.

Her next stop was Denmark — Copenhagen, to be precise. And there mouldered a glowering Hans Christian Andersen, angry but still very much in love. She decided to smother him with affection, which raised his hopes once more. So much so that he wrote in his diary, *Jenny is kind and loving towards me; I'm happy and hopeful — although I know—!* But it was the only way that she could think of to sweeten the atmosphere. Anyway, she had received another postcard via the Royal Theatre — not as soggy or as well-travelled as the last one — that announced *Returning home* with a date confirming her belief that he had already done so. So despite the fact she was treated like a goddess and that Andersen followed her around like a lovesick puppy, Jenny was pleased to get on the train to Berlin, where Hans wept openly as he flapped a large hand in farewell.

She arrived in the city, at the small house she had rented for a few days, to find that an anonymous admirer had filled it with flowers. She knew at once who they were from. The next morning a note arrived:

I shall be at the Wichmanns' house tonight. Make my happiness complete and be there. F.M.

And so Jenny put on her very best day dress and swept her hair up, decorating it with one of the flowers he had sent. And even before Amalia Wichmann had met her in the hall, she could hear his voice. She practically threw her cloak off, then paused, suddenly terribly nervous. He knew, even as she stood in the doorway, that she had arrived. He turned immediately and gave her a smile that left her in no doubt whatsoever. He was as deeply in love as she was. She almost felt herself pulled to where he was standing.

"Good evening, Herr Mendelssohn." All this said with head bending, not looking him in the eye.

"Good evening, Fraulein Lind. God, how I have missed you." The first part spoken loudly and clearly, the second in just above a whisper.

She looked up, as if she was gazing at him for the first time. Saw his beautiful large dark eyes — and the expression in them — as he surveyed her. She smiled a delicious smile that transformed the whole of her face.

"And I have missed you too."

"Are you in Germany long, my dear?"

"Five months. I have been booked for the winter season."

"And you could not spare a second of that time to come and sing with me in Leipzig?"

"I will think about it."

"You wretched girl. I shall abduct you unless you come willingly."

"Now that sounds as if it could be enjoyable."

He laughed, his wonderful eyes lighting up. "Consider yourself under contract, Miss Lind."

"Yes, *Herr Orchesterdirigent*."

And it was true enough. Felix was now conductor of the Gewandhaus Orchestra and a towering figure in the world of music. To ask Jenny to sing for him at one of his concerts — the finest in Europe — was the greatest compliment a singer could get. She blushed with sheer pleasure and said, "Oh, it is so lovely to see you again, Felix. Now, tell me all about your adventures last year."

"Dear little girl, it would take all night — which is quite a pleasurable idea! — to describe it all. I never got to bed until half past one in the morning. I got through more in two months than I did in the rest of the year. But just to be practical for a moment, are you staying with the Wichmanns?"

"I move in in a few days' time."

"Then I shall visit frequently. There is no chance of seeing you alone, I suppose?" This he added in a whisper.

"Perhaps," she answered quietly — and smiled inwardly with excitement.

"Shall we dance?" he asked and held out his hand to lead her as someone had started to play a waltz on the piano.

"Thank you, Herr Mendelssohn. I would enjoy that."

He made no answer but gave her the shadow of a wink as they went together to join the others.

* * *

Her body was telling her one thing, her conscience another. She had been brought up very strictly by her mother; that was, until she escaped to the Royal Theatre school. Once there, of course, although the teachers tried hard to protect their charges, weird rumours which she had not fully understood were whispered by the older children with much giggling and cries of 'shush' as they noticed a younger pupil listening in. Jenny had managed to steer a faultless course — though operatically, her voice had been pushed to the limits by singing in *Der Freischutz* at the ridiculously early age of eighteen — but romantically, all was well until she was introduced to Julius Gunther, who was so good-looking that he regularly had a team of young female singers — and one or two males — following him wherever he went. He was the son of the musical director of a nearby church and he auditioned for the part of leading tenor, a role that the company was most anxious to fill. He had a fine voice, though not large, and the slightest of lisps, which was most becoming. He also had impeccable manners. Young Jenny Lind fell in love for the first time in her life. As for him, he noticed that her magnificent eyes widened at the first sight of him and he, in turn, was immediately smitten.

During their operatic scenes together, Jenny's gaze would stare deep into his and one night, possibly when he had mistakenly swigged from a glass of beer during the interval, he winked at her — upstage, of course. This broke his code of good manners and after the show he apologised, even having the courtesy to flush deeply as he did so. Jenny had laughed good-naturedly and had been rewarded by him flinging his arms around her and stealing a kiss. After this they became a regular couple and had even stretched out on a bed together, though doing nothing more than kissing and cuddling. It had all become too much for young Julius, who had begged her to marry him. Jenny — a little tease — had answered, "Please keep the dream alive, my dearest friend. Maybe in the future. But we are both so young and at the very start of our careers." And with that, the poor man had to be content.

At nineteen she had had a similar experience with Adolf Frederik Lindblad, the distinguished musician, poet and piano teacher to the nobility, in whose family home she was lodging. He had a plain and kindly wife, and three children. His passion for the youthful singer was growing daily and even though she called him *Uncle* he could hardly conceal what he was feeling. His friend Erik Geijer was suspicious and wrote to his wife, *However I fear that she (Jenny L.) is a comet, whose path may come to upset the domestic peace.*

And Jenny knew, deep within herself, that it was true. She was born to flirt with men, and by holding them off — apparently — led them on. She charmed everyone, continued to call Lindblad *Uncle* — a fact which drove him mad — was sweetly teasing to all, though not without those who saw through the act and accused her of being a downright little madam. In the end, however, things had come to a most painful conclusion and she had left the Lindblad home with Adolf's nerves shot to pieces and his wife Sophie offering to stand down, taking their three children with her. It had almost been a tragedy of the first order, while all along Julius Gunther remained quietly in the background, adoring her madly despite it all.

There followed a period of flirtatious glances, of quiet glasses of wine, of surreptitious hand holding, until that fateful night when she had gone to a party at Amalia Wichmann's house and met the great Felix Mendelssohn, at which point her desire to tease had vanished as that wonderful, handsome man had captured her heart completely. That had led to a whole year apart while he had gone on one of his great European tours and she had worked on completely changing her vocal tone, following the García method. And now, the miracle had happened. They had met after a year apart and she was still totally in love.

He stayed long and late that evening, sitting on a chaise longue, his head close to hers. They laughed a great deal. Indeed, there were quite a few present who raised an eyebrow as they observed the young couple so absorbed in their own world.

"I wonder where dear Mrs Mendelssohn is tonight."

"At home, minding the children no doubt."

"Those words slide off your tongue like silk."

"Now what on Earth made you say that?"

"Because that is what you are, my dear. A snake rustling silkily in the grass."

It was true that the couple's happiness in each other's company was obvious to all — but this was a fairly sophisticated crowd of music lovers and after the initial surprise, the majority of people moved on to other less indelicate subjects. So it was that they were quite alone when Felix whispered, "Where can we be more private? I am longing to kiss you properly."

Jenny looked at him. "I thought that was what you *had* been doing for the last half hour or so."

Felix swelled his chest. "Good heavens, no. This has been merely playing."

Jenny sat up straight. "Playing? What are you? A hunting gorilla?"

For no particular reason, this struck the great conductor, the musical genius of his age, as hilariously funny and he laughed uproariously. So much so that one or two wandered in from the other room to see what all the laughter was about. Jenny swiftly took the decision to smile as well and let out one or two operatic laughs, moving a small lace handkerchief to her mouth and grinning over the top. Tobias Feilner — who had recently imbibed a great deal of wine and who was also a great one for giggling — walked in and, spying Mendelssohn doubled up in a fit of enjoyment, slapped his thigh and roared his approval. Amalia, his daughter, never quite sure how to behave amidst such splendid intelligentsia, let out a nervous guffaw. Then her husband walked in and looked around him.

"I see that you are all enjoying yourselves. Can I be told the joke as well?"

Mendelssohn looked at him through streaming eyes. "Sorry, Wilhelm, you're too much of a gentleman to understand."

"Piffle," answered the other — and emptied the remnants of his wine glass over Felix's head.

* * *

Two days later, Jenny moved into the Wichmanns' voluminous apartment, a fact which delighted Mendelssohn — whose visits became extremely regular — but which also presented him with a problem. The trouble was that he had fallen in love with Jenny completely and would not rest until they had become lovers. He had had sincere but brotherly feelings for Cecile and shrank away from doing anything that would hurt her. But for Jenny his love was overpowering, and he needed desperately to express it in physical form. The opportunity came in December when they were both going to Leipzig. There, Felix wielded the baton for the Gewandhaus Orchestra, which made him a towering figure to work with. Jenny had been asked to sing at the Gewandhaus Concert under his direction. It was a great honour as the concerts were considered the finest in Europe. Tickets sold out immediately and the customary sale of cheap seats for students was withdrawn.

Jenny was as nervous as a small animal before her entrance but when she heard Felix speak to the audience she listened carefully.

"And now, ladies and gentlemen, it gives me enormous pleasure to introduce to you Fraulein Jenny Lind. I never quite recovered from hearing her sing for the first time and I am sure that she will have the same effect on you. Please welcome — Miss Jenny Lind."

He then dropped his baton and started to clap, turning to look over his shoulder to where Jenny was making her entrance. As their glances met there was no further pretence. He winked at her, silently wishing her all the good luck in the world. She gave him one of the most loving looks of which she was capable, held her head high and walked onto the stage.

There followed one of the most memorable performances of her career. Her gorgeous high voice, unique in its unblemished purity, yet filled in its lower register with the whisperings and rustlings of midnight, soared above them all. When she had finished and stood for a moment in silence, head bowed, there was suddenly a great clamouring from the audience as programmes were thrown high in the air and people rose to their feet, shouting for an encore. Felix stepped down from the podium and taking her hand, kissed it, then raised it high above her head. Looking at him, Jenny asked a silent question, and he whispered, "Till my death." She nodded quietly, then sang a gentle love song, both as an answer and an encore.

The audience sat in rapture until the last sweet note had died softly away — then they went berserk and the great walls shook with their appreciation.

CHAPTER NINE

Jenny — Past

Felix had rented an apartment, consisting of various spacious rooms, one of which had a balcony fluting out to meet the leaves of the glorious trees in the park below. His reason for doing so was manyfold: he needed somewhere absolutely quiet where he could compose in peace, he longed for a place where he could just stretch out on a sofa and close his eyes when his work was done, he wanted total solitude, away from the noises of ordinary family life. Above all he longed for . . . He stopped thinking for a moment, feeling a demanding stiffness grow in his stylish trousers. This was neither the time nor the situation. Yet the truth was that constant visions of Jenny Lind had sent him out looking for just such a suitable property, where he could make love to her all the rapturous night long, if they so wished.

He sat very still, waiting for that delicious twitching to go away, trying to think of anything other than the exciting Miss Lind. He was madly in love with her, of course, completely and utterly obsessed. But truth be told, they had so far never been near a bed together. And yet he knew by the sparkle in those eyes which seemed to have been made of pure crystal — and glimmered and shone and drove him to the point of insanity — that she was considering the idea. Whether she had ever been tempted, he did not know. Though he took a shrewd guess that her young operatic partner — Gunther — might have suggested it. But Felix did not care. Though his family had long ago converted to Christianity he had Jewish lineage and enjoyed the singing in his blood that this had always given him.

The couple had met, of course, at the home of Amalia and Ludwig Wichmann, who took more than a little pride in the fact that their house was regarded as *the* place for artistic intellectuals to gather. Though the composer and the singer's initial time together had been short, now things were different. Jenny was under contract to the Berlin Opera for the winter season and was actually staying with the Wichmanns. Felix Mendelssohn's visits became more and more frequent, so Jenny sat up later and later. One night she had actually fallen asleep and woken up in his comforting presence. He had pulled his chair right up to hers and transferred her into his arms, where he hummed an old Jewish lullaby and stroked her hair. She had opened her eyes and felt enormously comforted.

"Oh Felix," she said. "I am sorry, I dozed off."

"No apologies to me, young lady. I've been dying to hold you like this for weeks. May I steal a kiss please?"

"I shall cry if you don't."

"That has to be one of the nicest things you have ever said to me."

It was the best kiss that either of them had ever had. It was true that young Gunther and she had exchanged a few youthful embraces, and that Mendelssohn was a married and experienced man, but neither of them had ever felt anything like the blazing fire that was lit when they first embraced. They had been made for each other, that was certain.

"Come with me to my apartment," Mendelssohn whispered urgently.

"But what about Cecile?"

He clicked his teeth with annoyance. "She lives at home with my children. I have another apartment where I can compose and think quietly. And entertain a few private guests."

"Such as?"

"Listen to you! You sound as if we have been married for years. Darling girl, please believe me when I assure you that there are gentlemen who can get a bit rowdy when they have had a drink or two and might wake up my peacefully slumbering offspring. That suite of rooms is where I can usually be found when I am not working or paying court to you. I am telling you the truth."

She laughed quietly. "Oh, my dear man, you have the sweetest frown when you are serious. Despite many offers from well-meaning old gentlemen — you are not included in that number — I have not yet accepted anyone. You will have a great deal to teach me."

"I can think of nothing that will please me more. Come, my lovely, let us steal out while we can."

* * *

It was a night that continued until the first pink rays of sunshine blinked over the edge of the world and lit the two sleeping forms of Jenny and Felix. They were entwined, holding on as if each feared the other one would escape back into the ordinary world of music and orchestras and fine and beautiful operas and wonderful compositions. If you had looked closely you would have seen that Jenny Lind had told the truth, because drying on the tops of her legs was blood, lost in that exquisite night-long tournament with Felix Mendelssohn. Meanwhile, he slept as contentedly as only a warrior who had won a battle could. Yet it had not been a battle at all, for she had given so willingly and so lovingly that it had been a triumph which they had both wished for desperately and wanted with all their hearts. Even though he was still asleep Mendelssohn gave her a fairy kiss on the nose and she, sweet soul, raised her hand to stroke his cheek. This couple loved each other deeply.

The sun continued its majestic rise and Felix woke fully. "I must go, my angel. I must get home before Cecile wakes."

Jenny sat up and the golden light nestled on her beautiful breasts. "Will she be furious if she suspects something? That you were with someone else if you did not come home?"

"No, of course not. She is still a child in many ways. She was very young when we married and she has grown sweeter and kinder with the passing years. It would be the last thing she would think of — that I have fallen in love with another woman."

"And have you?" asked Jenny earnestly.

"Oh yes," Felix answered, drawing her close to him, "I have indeed."

It was beautiful but painful, too. For though both lovers felt they had gained the world, they had also lost something. However, at this point in their relationship they lived for the moment, seeing each other frequently, spending nights together as often as they could. When Felix was away from his proper home, working for other people, she would write to him at his married address — and friends of Jenny's who had been told the magical secret would quietly roll their eyes and think that La Lind skated on the edge of disaster.

Christmas came, 1845, and Jenny was positively bubbling with happiness. Felix had sent her an album of songs which he had composed especially for her, written with an inscription so loving: *. . . only do not change. I think I should have invented that remark if she (The Queen of Prussia) had not said it first, and as often as I have read your letters, and as often as I think of you, I always come back to those words.*

However, everything has its downside and the arrival in early December of Hans Christian Andersen — glowering at the very mention of Jenny's name — put a black cloud over events. His arrival at the Wichmanns' pulled the feeling of festivity down and he only started smiling again when the singer had appeared in *La Sonnambula*, much to his great enjoyment. By Christmas Day he was angry once more. "There is a veil over my thoughts, but they fly towards Jenny! What have I done to her! Is it out of caution for her reputation that she is taking so little notice of me?"

The rest of the festivity was spent in constant mood swings and the uneasy Hans got the worst of it as Jenny teased him, until one evening Felix shouted at her angrily, "Leave the poor devil alone, can't you."

She turned to look at the butt of her jests. "I was only joking. I'm sorry, Hans, my dear."

The great writer gazed at her wretchedly. "Don't worry, it was just meant in fun — I think."

However, Mendelssohn whirled around, obviously in a terrible mood, probably after an argument with Celine for leaving his family alone at a time of togetherness.

"How can you be so forgiving to her? If I were in your shoes I would never speak to the wretch again! Joking is one thing, downright rudeness is another," he screamed at poor Andersen.

Jenny — who was badly in the wrong and knew it — burst into tears, and to crown it all, Mendelssohn swept out, then came back for a second to regain his hat, which he had forgotten. Cramming it onto his head, he gave the singer a malevolent stare, then flounced from the building. There was a terrible silence, broken only by Andersen's cracked voice which whispered, "Please don't upset yourselves on my behalf."

After that dreadful behaviour, Jenny pulled herself up short. In a few days' time she was due to make her debut as Julia in *Die*

Vestalin. The opera had been translated into German from the original French and the translation was — in parts — a little rough, to say the least of it. The audience did not receive it well. Jenny got a curtain call, but the public booed the opera. The next day Hans Christian Andersen and Jenny, together with her friend Louise, set off for Weimar, where she had been invited to sing at the court of the Hereditary Grand Duke. Finally, Hans came into his own as he knew everybody of importance there and was well loved by the ducal family and their courtesans.

Jenny had been asked to sing two nights after her arrival and on this occasion was taken to the concert hall by the Dane, who was dressed mightily in full court gear, including a three-cornered hat and a noisy rapier which clanked at his side. In other circumstances Jenny would have smiled with puckish delight, but this night she was terrified out of her wits. Her reception at the Berlin opera house had not gone well and she had heard boos ring out when she took her curtain call. She was being repaid for all her silliness — and she knew it. When they arrived, Hans kissed her hand very formally, his tricorne slipping down over one eye as he did so, then he solemnly left her. Normally she would have smiled, maybe even have laughed gently, but not tonight.

She sat in a window seat, like a child waiting for physical punishment, staring at her lap, dreading the moment when she was called to her fate. And then, suddenly, it was upon her. The pianist arrived and her name was announced, loud and clear. She looked up and saw that the place was packed with the high and mighty of Weimar and that as she stepped forward they were applauding her. Hans was sitting in the front row and gave her a mighty wink, one blue eye completely disappearing as he did so. Jenny smiled back and just wished that she had had the good sense to fall in love with him rather than that human tempest, Mendelssohn. But she hadn't. She was a complete fool, and she had to live with it.

Yet even thinking about Felix gave her courage and, happily, she sang her first note. She heard it, clear as a bell and beautiful, and she gathered herself together and sang on.

Some two hours later, as her last crystal tone died away, she heard a sound like the approach of a mighty army. It was the audience rising to its feet in one great echoing movement. Jenny bowed deeply and as she stood straight again, a veritable flurry of flowers dropped delightfully at her feet. She waited, motionless, and watched the courtly gathering as they clapped and cheered and shouted, then suddenly she gave the deepest curtsy, dropping almost to the stage. At this, the cheering was renewed.

How she and Hans ever escaped she couldn't quite recall. He had suddenly become masterly and somewhat commanding and was giving members of the audience instructions not to keep the singer in conversation for too long. Jenny guessed that his consumption of local beer (specially brewed for the Hereditary Grand Duke) had been somewhat excessive. But once outside the beautiful hall he became silent, his face deeply lined in thought, in fact he did not say a word until they had reached her lodging.

She turned. "Oh, thank you so much . . ." But she got no further.

"Jenny, I have something of importance to say to you."

Her heart plummeted. The last thing she wanted was a lecture of any kind and the expression on Hans's face told her that was what she was about to get.

He gazed at her intently. It was obvious that he was still madly in love. "Can we go indoors, please. I want you to concentrate, my dear."

She didn't answer but strode inside, mentally groaning.

"Well?" she said, settling herself in a chair and pouring out a small sherry. Hans remained standing, tearing his tricorne hat from his tangled mass of rumpled hair.

"It's about us," he said.

"I thought we were friends," Jenny answered, just a fraction coldly.

"I know we are, yet I keep asking myself why you still treat me so coolly. Is it an act to hide the fact that you *do* love me but want to hide it from the world? Is that what this is all about? Because, if so, I beg you to tell me the truth."

He was like a child, crying. Tears ran down his marvellous cock-eyed cheeks and into the tricorne hat, which he clutched to his heart.

Then she was suddenly on her feet, holding him close. "Oh, my dearest friend. Oh, sweetheart. You have come near the truth but not quite close enough. I am in love but not, I'm afraid, with you."

"Then who? Unless he agrees to marry you, I'll run him through."

"No, you must not say that! You would rob the world of an overwhelming talent."

"Do you mean he is married already? The beastly hound. How dare he toy with your affections?"

"Because he loves me — and I love him too. And always will. Oh please, dearest Hans, try to understand."

"No, I can't. I love you far more than he does."

"How can you possibly say that? You don't even know who he is!"

"He is a braggart and a bastard whoever he is. Who is he?"

"Mendelssohn," Jenny answered, and fell into an armchair, laughing and weeping simultaneously.

Hans gaped, his jaw practically hitting his knees. "You don't mean . . . ?" he gasped once more.

"Yes, yes, I do. Felix Mendelssohn."

"Good God, not him," he said, and dropped into another ancient chair which groaned with the unexpected weight.

They sat in terrible silence, both continuing to sob quietly, until Jenny finally said, "Dearest Hans, have you nothing further to say to me?"

He looked at her, his crumpled face strained. "But he is a married man, Jenny."

"I know," she answered, her voice little above a whisper. "I know, and I hate it. The entire situation sickens me. I wish with all my heart that it could be different — but I just can't help myself."

"And he," Hans answered, regaining something of his composure, "feels no prick of conscience, I take it?"

"He will not desert his children, and Cecile is such a sweet creature that he could not possibly leave her."

"How convenient for him." This was said with a sharpness that Jenny had never heard before. "Poor fellow. My heart bleeds for his unhappiness. But then — I nearly forgot — he holds all the trump cards. An adorable and loving wife *and* a brilliant mistress. I would say, summing up, that he is one of the world's most fortunate men." Hans Andersen rose from his chair, looking drawn but determined. He peeped out of the window. "It is still raining. Will it never stop? I ask myself. Goodnight, Miss Lind. I wish you good fortune."

And he swept out. Jenny collapsed, weeping; meanwhile, out in the street Hans Christian was in floods of tears. Would they see one another again? Of course. They were true friends despite the awkwardness at the start of their relationship. Would their association become what it had been before? No, that was not possible. But for the present two badly fractured people wept in the darkness and mourned the horrible situation. Indeed, Jenny felt so faint that she poured herself a glass of something — she had no idea what and didn't really care — and drank it.

And then, unbelievably, it happened again. She was lying sprawled in the back of some vehicle, which was hurtling along so fast that Jenny had to clutch some rough-sided material to stop herself tumbling forward. Out of the darkness a voice spoke, rough as blades and hard on the ear.

"Where did you say you lived? Is it them flats near the river?"

But she could not answer. All she knew before total darkness came was that she was clutching a headdress worn at some time or other by a famous singer, but who that singer had been she was not at all certain. Nor did she want to know. It was all in the past — wasn't it?

Wasn't it?

CHAPTER TEN

Jenny — Past

On her final night at the Hereditary Grand Duke's theatre, Jenny gave a concert. Up till then she had sung in opera, given recitals, done her absolute best. But no one could have been more grateful than she was when the curtains finally swished shut and she stood off stage listening to the uproar from the audience. Then she walked slowly forward as the curtains opened once more, and she saw the people in all their splendour and elegance, all their glitter and gleaming, all their arrogance and affectation. She bowed very low and the usual hurling of flowers began, including a small bunch of forget-me-nots which she knew instinctively had come from Hans. However, she did not see him again as she was leaving for Berlin, stopping on the way at Leipzig to dine with the Mendelssohns. Oh, how marvellous to be in his absorbing company once more — even after his angry departure from the Wichmanns' on Christmas, and even if it did mean having to stare at Cecile jealously, wishing she were out of the way, yet at the same time pitying the poor little wretch.

Mendelssohn's wife seemed to sit in a golden beam, always smiling, always serene, the perfect mother. The more she thought about it the sicker Jenny felt. Why could she not sit beside him, the superstars of the music world together? Dinner guests whispering to one another, men muttering that the two must have the most incredible sex life, and winking. Instead, she was seated several people away from him and had to make the best of it.

She felt grumpy about the whole situation, drawn to the man quite hopelessly yet unable to overcome the immovable obstacles between them. Thankfully, her singing voice had not been affected by her recent hard work and emotional stress, and she sang superbly through six different operas in Berlin.

Then she ended the season by spraining her ankle during a concert for the poor, which she had considered a happy duty until the beastly accident.

There followed an intimate evening with Mendelssohn, during which Jenny, crying within at the terrible pain in her ankle, defiantly stood up regardless. The doctor came the next day and prescribed leeches and complete rest. Mendelssohn came on the sprint and, most irritatingly, was accompanied by Cecile. Writing in her secret diary, Jenny's friend Louise commented that, *I think it is the most unfortunate thing to fall in love with someone else's husband, and at that so obviously.*

* * *

At last — at long, long last — they were alone together. Her ankle back to normal, the season in Berlin ending, him bounding with enthusiasm to have her alone in his company. The first thing he did as soon as the door was closed and the key turned in the lock, was give her a kiss that seemed to last a lifetime.

"I have missed you to despair. Oh my darling sweet little girl."

"It has been horrible for me too. Thank God I have had so much to do, otherwise I think I would have gone crazy. Oh Felix, why do I love you so much?"

"I would ask Cecile for a divorce, but it is the children who make me realise how evil that would be. Oh, dear heart, I must wait until they are older."

"And *then* will you?"

"You have my word on it."

And after that they spoke no more and concentrated on making love, made all the sweeter by the delay the pair of them had recently endured. Felix started gently but ended with shouts of joy, thrusting like a healthy young animal. Jenny was just as bad, forgetting that on stage she was the beautiful diva and yelling out her enormous pleasure at top voice. Afterwards they lay, spent, in each other's arms, talking in whispers.

Jenny said, "That was absolutely heavenly. Just for a few moments I went there."

"What was it like?" Felix murmured.

"I was completely taken over by a gorgeous feeling."

"In which I shared. Oh, my dearest girl, I do love you with all my heart."

They lay quietly in each other's arms for a while and then Mendelssohn gave a gurgling shout and leapt off the bed, dancing a strange little dance. Watching him, Jenny suddenly had the oddest feeling that she had seen him somewhere before — not hiding in a carriage pretending to be an elderly occupant or putting on a funny hat at the stage door or doing the thousand and one glorious and silly things of which she knew he was capable — but in a different place altogether. Showing off, but nonetheless gently, smiling confidently to the world.

She exclaimed in surprise and Felix stopped his ridiculous routine and said, "Do I look strange?"

The illusion vanished and Jenny gazed at him with laughter. "Come back to bed," she said, and shivered delightfully as with a wild whoop he did so. But later, when all the kissing and loving were over and he was dressing in his ordinary clothes, she looked at him with sadness.

"Felix."

"Yes, my darling."

"Did you really mean what you said?"

"To which part of my conversation do you refer?"

"When you spoke of our future together. Did you really mean that when your children are older you will leave Cecile and we could be together?"

Felix let his neckpiece go, turning towards Jenny with quite the most startling look. "Does it bother you that much?"

"A little," she answered, turning her head away so that he could not see the expression on her face.

He stopped dressing and went towards her.

"Don't grimace like that, little sweet. I truly love you with all my heart. It is just that . . ."

"It would not be fair on the children. But you knew that when we started."

Mendelssohn stared out of the window and said in a quiet voice, "I did not realise, when I started, how very serious I was going to get."

Jenny stood stock still, a sudden quiver of fear chilling her spine, and he, sensing something, gave her a deep look.

"I mean it, Miss Lind. I would rather be dead than live without you."

"Well, that's not going to happen, is it?"

"Do you swear to that? Do you give me your word?"

"As long as you want me, you only have to beckon."

And Jenny laughed and wondered, later, why her words had sounded so hollow.

CHAPTER ELEVEN

Delia — Present Day

The opera house in Vienna was grand beyond anyone's wildest imaginings, for the director, Franz Pokorny, had spent every bit of money he had in the world getting it ready for the arrival of the greatest singer of them all — for in such glowing terms Jenny Lind had been described to him. Bristling with importance, sporting formal dress of plum-coloured velvet, he stood on the steps and positively tingled with excitement as the carriage, which had been sent to the station to fetch her, drew to a halt at the bottom of the steps. He rushed down them and opened the door with a flourish.

A very small, rather dull woman, with hair revealing a reddish touch and a very pained expression on her face, got out.

This can't be her, please don't let it be her, Franz thought wildly, stooping to kiss her hand.

"Miss Lind, I bid you welcome," he intoned grandly.

"No," uttered the other, "I am her personal attendant. How do you do?"

Flustered, Franz stood back and watched as another even smaller mouse got out of the carriage, much the same in build and physique, although this one had a wonderful pair of crystal eyes which looked at him very nervously.

"Miss Lind?" he asked tentatively.

"Yes, I am. I do hope we are not late. We slept on the train and were rather flustered when it pulled into the station while we were still dressing."

"Oh dear. How awful for you."

Her crystal eyes looked solemn. "It was somewhat unnerving."

Franz felt the hand of doom reach out and tap him on the shoulder. From that moment on, things would only go from bad to worse. After a quick tour of the resplendent opera house, Jenny was reluctantly ushered onto the stage. A wretched young pianist sat eagerly awaiting her arrival but made matters worse by rising to bow and sending the score to the floor, to which he rapidly dived to rescue it, fumbling as he did so.

Jenny, meanwhile, had apparently gone into a trance, standing motionless on the vast arena, her small hands clutched together as though they were the last living things she would ever see. There was a profound silence. The pianist, blushing violently, finally stood up, the rescued score in his hands. He looked near to tears. Still nobody spoke. Into the echoing stillness Franz harrumphed his throat.

"Miss Lind? Is everything to your liking?"

"The auditorium. It's so huge. I don't think I can sing here."

There was a stunned gasp from those present and the pianist went white as a sail, while Franz Pokorny briefly contemplated suicide. He had spent his entire fortune on this venture, including — and especially — on Jenny Lind's fee. To say nothing of refurbishing the entire theatre and losing his leading lady who had walked out, hissing at him as she did so.

"You are probably tired from the journey, Madame. I suggest we repair to the green room and have a cup of something refreshing."

Meanwhile, Pokorny was hissing frantically at his assistant: "Go now. Run. Franz Hauser the singer lives not far away. Beg him to come back here with you. Maybe she will listen to him."

When Hauser arrived, red in the cheeks and panting, it was to find Jenny Lind, frozen-faced and the colour of ash, staring blindly into the depths of the auditorium.

"My dear Miss Lind, how lovely to see you again. Will you step into the green room with me? I've developed a raging thirst suddenly and I'm sure we could find you a nice cup of something so that you can join me."

A pair of wild eyes gazed into his. "But my dear Mr Hauser, have you *seen* the size of the auditorium?"

"It is absolutely splendid for the voice, you know. The rebound effect. As you were taught by the great García himself, you will already know this. It somehow seems to hold and magnify song. I personally adore the place. Now do let me escort you to a more comfortable spot for a chat. I really would be so delighted if you would allow that."

How he did it nobody afterwards knew. Slowly, slowly, Jenny — who had been seized and frozen by a violent attack of stark fear — began to thaw. She sat, a strong cup of well-brewed coffee clutched in her hands and listened to every word he said. He told her, gently but firmly, that she would be a laughing stock if she withdrew. He also pointed out that Franz — who sat dismally in a corner trying not to listen — would be ruined. That the man had poured every last drop of his funds into the renovation and restoration of the theatre and stood to lose the lot if she withdrew.

"But I am so nervous," Jenny whispered.

"I do understand. We all are when we see the grandeur of the place but those of us who know how to project the voice — as you were taught by the great García himself — feel nothing but final satisfaction."

The pianist, who had now lost all the vivacity with which he had entered the theatre, was sent for and reappeared rather diffidently, still clutching the score.

"Miss Lind will sing for us," Franz announced in a grand voice and gave the poor boy a broad wink that startled him more than ever.

And sing she did, the lovely lyrical sound rolling out and around the great arches and columns of the Theater an der Wien. On the opening night she was recalled by the audience several times, their applause reaching its peak only when she had taken sixteen curtain calls. She was ecstatic. The next day she wrote to Felix, a letter full of love and energy, enough to make him smile broadly, almost as if she had manifested in his house.

The bond between them was incredible. They were both in love as never before though still he continued to address her as Miss Lind and act — that is, in public — with an air of respectability, which caused hoots of mirth and a great deal of amusement behind their backs.

The season in Vienna ended with *Der Freischütz*, Jenny Lind sang incomparably, and was attended by the entire elite of the city crammed into the opera house. Johann Strauss the elder came with his full orchestra to play at her party, but was forced to perform in the street outside, so great was the number of guests gathering within. Naturally, this drew the attention of every drunk and layabout the town had to offer. They grew unruly when Jenny Lind finally appeared and in a drunken effort to pull her coach themselves, they tipped her unfortunate manservant onto the ground and proceeded to walk all over him.

His injuries were sufficient to make Jenny postpone her next journey by a day. And this was a journey she longed to make, for it was to Frankfurt for the Lower Rhine Music Festival conducted by Felix Mendelssohn himself. In the end she travelled through the hours of darkness and arrived at midnight, yet the very next day she went to meet Felix on board a Rhine cruiser, where he stood waiting, surrounded by a party of old friends — and the fire of love alight in his eyes. Jenny was radiant, joyful beyond words. They had to clasp hands behind their backs to stop themselves embracing one another.

It was with a great and golden grin that Felix bowed before her and seriously introduced her to the River Rhine. With equal sincerity Jenny begged the Rhine Maidens to be kind to her, dropping her bouquet into the sparkling water as a token of esteem. Felix gave her a swift kiss on the cheek and a discreet wink for reward. Then, with the engine chugging and the sun blessing the landscape, the river boat took off.

Friends said later that they had never seen Mendelssohn in such high spirits or Jenny so radiant with joy. To amuse her he sat on a chair pressed close to hers and told her how all the various wines growing on the slopes or in the valleys represented musicians, comparing them with classic composers and others less reputable.

"And there's a sweet Mozart," he said, pointing towards a gently growing Johannisberger, "peaceful at last. And that vine fighting its way up the cliff is quite definitely Beethoven."

She laughed a great deal, enjoying herself thoroughly, and when her companion, poor Louise Johansson, approached her and asked if she would like to repair to her cabin and rest, Jenny positively shouted at her that she most certainly would not. But Mendelssohn picked up on it and whispered, "Is it because of me that you're staying up?"

Jenny was even more annoyed that he had thought so. "No, indeed. I am enjoying the fresh air after spending so much time in stuffy opera houses. Besides, I like your company."

"And I like yours. Jenny, I have been thinking about you day and night and I have finally come to a decision."

Deryn Lake

She turned to him, her sparkling eyes vivid in the river light. "Have you? May I know what it is?"

"Yes, my darling, my own sweet girl. I have decided . . ."

But a blare of music from an approaching landing stage blasted out his next few words. A male voice choir had already gathered on it and were giving his *Antigone* full throat. Felix rolled his eyes. "No peace for the wicked," were his final words.

The festival that followed was a triumph. As always when she sang and Felix conducted, Jenny felt transported. On the first night she gave tremendous voice to Haydn's *Creation*, on the second she soared her way through Handel's *Alexander's Feast* and on the final night succeeded as never before in Mendelssohn's *Fruhlingslied*. Then she left, with Mendelssohn, for an idyllic little retreat on the Rhine.

On a small upper deck — which they had to themselves — they lay somewhat less well dressed than usual. Felix was wearing a shirt, open with no vest beneath, so that his tanned body was clearly visible, leaving space for Jenny's loving fingers to tickle and tease. She had defied fashion and wore a pair of silken trousers, copied by one of the theatrical dressmakers.

Felix said, without opening his eyes, "I have come to an important decision, Jenny."

"Oh, and what is that?" she answered, sipping a cordial, which was highly relaxing for her throat.

"That when the children are older, I am going to leave Cecile and ask you to come and live with me. I cannot go on with this life much longer."

There was complete silence during which Mendelssohn opened his eyes and looked deeply into hers. "You *do* love me?" he asked anxiously.

Just for a moment, the whole of Jenny's life collapsed. It was like the air escaping from a child's balloon. She knew that without

Mendelssohn her existence would become much emptier, because it was the side of herself that was not totally preoccupied with singing. Very briefly a picture of Manuel García flashed into her head; she knew that he had brought about such a change in her vocal powers that she had conquered worlds. But he had not reckoned with Felix Mendelssohn, for that momentous meeting had changed Jenny completely. She did not wish to give up her career, but she longed for a child — not in the foreseeable future but one day, when she and Felix could live together. But now that he had talked of it, she had taken a nervous step back.

"What's the matter?" he said, suddenly sharp.

"Nothing. Oh, don't look like that. It's just that you startled me."

"Is that your usual response to a lovesick musician telling you that he wants to marry you?"

Jenny fought down her answer, which had been on the lines of *it would have flattered more had the lovesick man been free to make me his bride instead of being heavily married with a brood of yelling children*. She did her best with a smile that broke into a million sunbeams — just like the smile she had given the cheering stalls on an opening night. Felix, however, was not impressed and feigned sleep once more. Feeling helpless, Jenny closed her eyes and immediately plunged into a deep and vivid dream.

She was in the back of that strange, swaying vehicle, travelling along the road at a great and frightening speed. But this time it was more clear, more sharply realistic than before, she could even see the outline of a figure sitting in the front, protected by a sheet of glass. She must speak to him, somehow attract his attention. Tell him to stop driving and return her immediately to the lazy deck of a Rhine steamer as she did not want to be in this strange place a moment longer.

With a great effort, Jenny struggled to sit up straight. She could see him more clearly now, stubble-headed and needing a shave. But her movement had attracted his attention, and his voice spoke over some strange and magical device.

"Are you all right, young lady?"

She did not know a lot of English, having had to work so hard to polish up her German, her French, and any other language that an opera had been written in, but she managed to gasp out, "Please. Where am I?"

He laughed. She never forgot that.

"You're back home, love."

The sound of his voice grew louder and louder until it rang around the taxicab sharp as a clarion. The echo of it filled Jenny's head like a military band — a military band that had come marching up the street playing the high, bright notes which had made a small child toddle to the piano and pick it out. Then suddenly came darkness and no sound whatsoever.

Jenny Lind was completely unconscious.

When she came to, she thought she had died and gone to hell. She was surrounded by dark shadows out of which arose a black spiral staircase. She appeared to be in some subterranean pit which was completely strange to her. Behind her was a front door, firmly shut, above those winding stairs. With all her strength Jenny pulled herself upright and grasped the curling banister. And then came the biggest shock of them all. Because her hand had changed, it belonged to someone else. Jenny Lind had gone away.

"Oh God," she said, crying aloud. "What is happening?"

There was no answer but behind her there suddenly came a thunderous knocking on the door.

"Let me in, you little idiot!" shouted a voice that somehow was vaguely familiar.

But Jenny was once more wavering on the brink of consciousness and could no longer answer as this time she lost her grasp on what was real and what indeed was a phantom of her mind. When she finally awoke it was to find that she was tucked up in Delia's own bed — she recognised it because of a harp-shaped stain made by spilled black coffee on the pillowcase — and that Mendelssohn was sitting on the bed, looking at her anxiously. Only it wasn't Mendelssohn, but another man who she knew quite well — if only she could remember his name.

"Miss T, Miss T," he called excitedly. "She's waking up. Delia's waking up."

She shook, she physically shook, while memory after memory came rushing back like an avalanche of the mind. She recalled everything from her lovely curtsying ballerina mother right up to the moment when she had walked into Miss T's bedroom and stolen Jenny's headdress. For that had to be the link, surely? It was nothing that she would have done in normal circumstances. Jenny Lind had entered her reality and had quietly taken control of her. And because of that unbelievable control she had adored every one of the thrills of the soaring notes of grand opera, the physical reaction when the notes were not so pure and the audience uneasy, her inner fury with herself. Her overwhelming and frightening reaction to the enormous size of that theatre in Vienna. Her passionate love for Felix Mendelssohn. And, after all that passion, she had woken to find not the great composer — it wasn't him sitting on the bed — but Justyn Krasinski, winking at her.

When she next regained consciousness it was night time and her curtains had been drawn. Out in the kitchen she could hear somebody busying around and knew that though she may have no family, at least she had friends.

"Miss T," she called quietly.

Delia's old acquaintance appeared in the doorway. "My dear girl, how are you feeling?"

"I'm not sure. Miss T, I am so sorry for what happened. I think I must have had a brainstorm."

"Yes, my dear. You probably did. Anyway, you weren't yourself. My lodger said you were acting very strangely."

"Your lodger? The young man from the National Theatre?"

"Cyrus Markham? Yes, he lives with me. Only because London is so damned expensive. We are not lovers — more's the pity! — but we get on well and that's what really counts. Anyway, he said that you looked very strange and icy — yes, that was the word he used."

"Icy?"

"Yes, emotionally frozen. Like someone that the Ice Queen had cast a spell on."

"Crumbs!"

"That's a very old-fashioned expletive," Miss T commented.

"My mother used to mutter it when her curtsy went wrong."

"How sweet."

"Oh Miss T, you are an angel. I am so sorry to have done all this to you. But I can tell you one thing, it wasn't really me. I think I must have been possessed."

"Do you do drugs?"

Delia shook her head. "No; I know most people do but I just don't want to join that club."

"Then Cyrus was wrong on that point. Ah well, let's not talk about it anymore. *Something* happened. We don't know what. So let's now put it behind us. Agreed?"

"Relieved, more likely. Thank you, Miss T. You're a truly marvellous person."

After that, she slept deeply once more and woke the next morning, wondering whether the Jenny Lind occurrences could have been merely the stuff of dreams. Yet the memories of Mendelssohn and dear Hans were so vivid. Delia felt completely mentally exhausted. Nonetheless, she got up, looked for Miss T who had apparently gone home taking the headdress with her, and eventually made herself a cup of coffee. The radio was on and she could hear Mendelssohn's *Midsummer Night's Dream* bursting forth. It moved her to tears. He had been seventeen years old when he had written this lovely, haunting piece. Jenny had not even met him yet. It had been long before the start of their great and passionate love affair.

Slowly, very slowly, Delia carefully considered her plight as she sipped her coffee. It seemed to her that now she had three options. Go to her doctor and beg to join a course for people who had terrifying dreams. Naturally, because of the crisis in the NHS, she would be well down on a list of other dream-laden cranks and might have to wait a year for her first appointment. Secondly, she could ring all her friends and keep them talking for hours about her experiences, with a horrendous bill and nobody believing a word of it at the end. Thirdly, she should just shut up and say nothing at all and if people should ask questions just look vague and smile. *Least said, soonest mended* had been one of her beautiful mother's favourite sayings — and this was the least, though in some ways the most, appealing of the routes that lay before her.

CHAPTER TWELVE

Delia — Present Day

Delia went back to working in the costume department, aware that the situation had changed — subtly, but for all, still that changed. Justyn Krasinski was paying her much more attention, presumably having been dumped by the gorgeous Sangeetha. Indeed, he had invited Delia out to dinner but so far had not named a date, his diary being somewhat full. And dear Alan — the unassuming genius behind the whole *Spring Roses* phenomenon — had taken leave from his role as conductor, saying that he was suffering from a wretched cough and would be spluttering throughout the entire show.

Discreet enquiries and looking through reference books had revealed to Delia that while she had experienced Jenny Lind's life over many months, as she was feted and loved by crowds and in particular by the great maestro Mendelssohn, in this life only a few days had passed. It was all too difficult to understand and she found herself thinking more and more seriously about seeking professional help. Then one day, when she was feeling particularly glum, Miss T had approached her with a wide smile.

"Come along, little friend, I haven't seen you fall about with laughter in an age. What do you say about our having a day out?"

Delia didn't know how to answer politely. She couldn't think of anything worse. Her current mood was black. She was considering handing in her notice. She feared that she was suffering with delusions. If there had been a cliff edge handy, she would have jumped off it. Instead, she looked at Miss T and her eyes filled with tears. Miss T read all the signs correctly and took her into the most enormous hug while Delia sobbed unashamedly.

"It's all been too much for you, hasn't it, my dear? Whatever it was really frightened you, didn't it?"

Delia shook her weary head. "No, it's not that. In fact I loved it. I would go back tonight if I had the chance. It's just that I don't know if it was only a dream. I mean . . . is it possible to dream that you are a truly great person?"

Miss T's eyes were very close to her friend's face. "Now come on. What does it matter if it *was* just a glorious figment? It was a splendid one and you enjoyed it. Wipe your eyes, sweet maid. I thought of going to Hastings and having a look around the antique market stalls. Finding things for the shows. I would like it very much if you came with me."

When Miss T was like this, sweet and unbelievably kind, she was impossible to resist. Delia nodded.

"Yes, I'd be interested in that. I've never been to Hastings."

"My dear, you haven't lived!"

* * *

They boarded a train to the south coast at Charing Cross and Delia's heart leaped with sudden unexpected joy as, looking out of the window, she realised that the landscape had changed from the eternal suburbia that had overcome the once fine city of London and saw rolling green fields. At last, here was countryside as she remembered it from her childhood. If she closed her eyes she could picture London as it had been when she had first seen it too, with clean streets and sweeping views — all gone as thanks to some rich politician, lining his pockets, assuring his constituents that it was all for their own good, the town was being thoroughly modernised. She remembered her father sadly saying "The City of London was once known as the Square Mile. Think of it now, bulging with skyscrapers."

It began to rain a little as they made their way to Hastings' centre, passing the remnants of what had once been the beloved escape of the Victorians, who would pop down to get a breath of briny on the slightest excuse. In her imagination Delia could almost see them, strolling forth in lightweight suits with feather-weight caps upon their heads. Or with long skirts swishing the pavements, which were kept spotless by an army of boy sweepers who looked fit to die of exhaustion as they did battle against the local dirty dogs who squatted all over the place.

Hastings' old town was fascinating, full of antiquities, shops that had remained unchanged apparently for centuries and stalls that had hidden gems from the past hiding beneath murky coverings. Miss T fished out one or two interesting items, exclaiming as she did so, while Delia wished she could work up a little more enthusiasm for the things that were being handed to her for approval. By now, it was pouring with rain. What had started as a gentle shower when they left the station had turned into a drenching downpour and Miss T looked about her with a frantic roll of the eyes.

"I can't stand this. Shall we go and get a drink?"

"Yes, please. Is this weather a speciality of Hastings?"

"I have no idea but have no intention of finding out. Look, there's a pub across the road. Shall we go?"

Delia nodded and started to sprint towards the building, pausing slightly in her flight as the sound of men's voices raised in song grew suddenly louder. There were several of them, a decent choir, and they were bursting into full voice with an old sea shanty that she recognised. *Hoorah for the Arethusa* was being given the works by a group of enthusiastic vocalists.

She rushed through the door, out of the pouring rain, to find herself in a long room with a stage at one end and tables and chairs scattered through the length. It was packed to the doors, full of jolly people all looking at a fully constructed stage, small but sturdy. This was covered by a choir of merry men, all grinning, plus their accompanying accordions and a drum. They were singing their hearts out and Delia felt that she could never remember in this life — before she became Jenny Lind — seeing so much massed enjoyment. And then she looked up and thought for a moment that time had gone crazy again and she was once more in the throes of a dream. For there, high on the wall behind the singers, was painted in large bold capitals one name — and that name was Jenny Lind.

"Good heavens," said a voice in her ear and Delia turned to see that Miss T was standing right behind her, also looking up at the painted name. "It can't be," she continued.

"But it is," Delia answered. "It's her. She was here — in Hastings."

"But why? For what purpose?"

"I don't know, but somehow I must make it my business to find out."

The choir came to a rousing finale and the whole room went into a shout of loud applause. Delia turned to a stranger and said, "Excuse me, but is this a regular occurrence?"

"You bet it is, girl. There's music most nights. But you can get solo singers and choirs as well. This lot call themselves The Shanty Boys. I like 'em."

Miss T spoke. "And what about Jenny Lind? Did she used to sing here?"

"Not that I know of. Who is she, anyway?"

"She was a famous singer in her day."

"Good for 'er," answered the man and giving them a cheery wave, walked away.

"I need a drink — badly," said Delia.

"And so do I."

"My round, I believe."

But though they continued to stare at the name painted clearly across the back of the auditorium neither of them had anything of importance to add. Yet there was a firm belief in Delia's heart that she must pursue the trail of the opera singer, however flimsy it was, and discover the story behind the name appearing in such strange circumstances in a little seaside town called Hastings.

Eventually, greatly replenished by alcohol, they tore themselves away from the merry Jenny Lind — for this was indeed the name of the pub, though nobody seemed to know why — and picked their way slowly through the rain towards the station. As they rounded a bend they noticed somebody plodding towards them, head down, shoulders hunched, but for all that a familiar figure. Delia clutched Miss T's sleeve.

"I say. Isn't that Alan Pearson? It is him, isn't it?"

"Yes. I wonder what he is doing in Hastings."

"What are *we* doing in Hastings, come to that?" Delia answered and called out, "Alan, Alan, is that you?"

The composer looked up from within a bundle of coats and scarves and gave a huge cough.

"Good heavens! Surprise, surprise! What are you two girls up to in a seaside town on a rough night like this?"

"Heading for a train bound for London," Miss T answered, just a trifle sharply.

"We've been in the pub, the Jenny Lind. It's amazing. Full of noise and lovely sounds. How does it come to have an opera singer's name? Do you know, Alan?"

"I do, a bit. Listen, why don't we all go back there? If I get any wetter I shall die of something grim, I know it. Come on, ladies. Allow me to tempt you."

Miss T was clearly in a funny mood, because she politely refused, though with just the amount of irritation in her voice that told the world she really meant it. Delia hesitated, not wishing to upset her friend but simply longing to go back into the confines of that warm and friendly hostelry and discuss the mysterious opera singer who had apparently come to Hastings and given the building its name. She wavered and Miss T suddenly at that moment felt something resembling a pang of pity.

"Go on, girl. Alan will take care of you. And he looks as if he could do with a bit of cheering up himself."

"I'm fine, really. Just nursing a cold," he protested.

"Then nurse each other better for heaven's sake."

With that, Miss T departed, and delightedly they went in and found a table. Alan made a progress towards the bar and came back with two delicious gins.

"There, this should put a smile on your face, dear girl."

"Why? Is it frowning?"

"No, it isn't. In fact you look rather wan and beautiful."

"I don't know how to do that."

"What?"

"Look both wan and beautiful at the same time."

Alan changed to mock severity. "Now you're being irritating. Stop it at once!"

She giggled with enjoyment. It was suddenly just such fun to sit in this extraordinary pub, bearing the name of her dream-state alter ego, and make silly jokes with the creator of the whole marvellous show. Alan, seeing her happiness, laughed till he coughed.

"I'm really interested in this," he said, indicating their surroundings with a sweep of a rather shapely hand which Delia had not truly noticed before. "I intend to go to the library and find out all I can."

"Can I come with you?"

"Of course."

"Do you think she stayed here?"

"In Hastings — yes, I do. In this hostelry, no. I reckon this was built after Miss Lind's time."

"I find it all very exciting."

Alan had looked at her sideways, amusement showing in the glint of his eye.

"Yes, I suppose it is."

About an hour later they left the wonderful pub and stepped out into the dampness of evening. The shower had ended but the night was brisk, the streetlights showing all that was left of the town's Victorian grandeur. Alan slipped his arm through Delia's in a companionable way. She felt truly relaxed for the first time since she had undergone what she could only think of as her out-of-body experience. He smiled at her, and she found herself looking closely at a slimly built young man, probably three inches taller than she was and handsome in his own particular way.

"Where do you live, Delia?"

"In London."

"Whereabouts?"

"In Stratford. What about you? Is it true that you've moved somewhere rather posh?"

"How I love that word! *Posh*. It sums up everything that one has always wanted to be while the little squirts who are born with it are actually rather ghastly people."

"You are speaking of several reprehensible famous names".

"True — but still seriously grim."

He coughed and laughed simultaneously, looking at Delia with a warmth that made her head spin a little. Momentarily, she wondered why she had reacted like that.

"Have you ever been married?" she found herself asking.

"Yes. I know that not many people are aware of it — but yes, I was once. Susan was killed in a cycling accident, which was a tragedy because she was such a sweet and good person. She truly held no ill-will for anybody, which would have been easy because there were many, many flautists better than herself. But her single-minded parents considered her the *champion*. They were a pair of terribly earnest people called Mavis and Maurice, who lived in a house called *Mon Repos*. She was the only child, and they worshipped her. Talk about obsessed. They used to give tea parties as opportunities for spying out possible friends and future husbands. They couldn't bear me — a humble music teacher in a state school — so I did not pass the sandwich test. But, to add to the tragedy, Susan believed the nonsense her mother spewed forth and couldn't understand it when she wasn't picked to enter young musician competitions, when she did not pass the entrance exam for any of the music colleges and was not accepted by any of the big orchestras. She was truly puzzled."

"Poor girl. She must have been very upset."

"She was — completely. Something I blame Mavis for. Maurice did not say much but he always referred to Susan as *my son*."

"Really? That's slightly sinister."

"You're telling me." There was a moment's silence, then Alan added in a low voice. "She was very, very pretty, you know. Or perhaps that is an understatement — she was absolutely beautiful. Her parents wanted a full-blown wedding for her. Cathedral, choir boys, famous organist, elegant guests, husband top-flight merchant banker with titled parents. Royalty as guests of honour."

"So how did she end up getting married to . . ."

"Poor, broke, little me? Very easily. We went to a register office and officially booked our wedding. I know everyone says registry office, including Mavis, but they are all wrong. It's register office. Anyway, some weeks later we went with a crowd of good mates, and we got married, then went for a honeymoon in Gloucestershire, near Berkeley Castle."

"Hasn't that got a nasty reputation?"

"Yes. It was there that poor old Edward II had a red-hot poker thrust up his anus by way of execution."

"Sounds horrible."

"That's what he thought, I imagine." Alan paused, then said hurriedly, "Let me give you a lift back to London. I've got a taxi here and more rain is forecast tonight."

"Did you come from town?"

"No. I live near Battle, famous for being the scene of the original and ghastly fight. But I've got a tiny little pied-à-terre in Covent Garden which I stay at when I'm in town."

"It all sounds very beautiful. Except I don't know where Battle is."

"I live outside the town. In rather a remote mansion. But not that far away from Hastings."

"So that is how you came to be near the pub."

"Right, Sherlock. Now, no arguing. I am giving you a lift home and then going to my pied-à-terre. Right?"

"Right."

* * *

She slept very soundly for the first few hours, but at around three a.m. Delia began to have quite the most vivid dream. She was standing close to the sea somewhere — surely Hastings? — and could hear its low rumbling murmur as a background to all the other sounds. But that was the trouble. There were no other sounds, only the constant murmuring mutter of the sea as it pursued its relentless course. Without knowing why, Delia turned to the beach and began to pick her way slowly toward the lulling, moaning expanse that lay beyond. But a light touch on her arm made her stop in her tracks. It was her beautiful mother — as slim and youthful and charming as she had always been. She did not speak but dropped a spectacular curtsy and — though she said nothing — gestured with her head that there was someone with her. Delia peered and gradually she could see the figure that her mother was indicating. It was a man with deep, deep red hair. Not the scallywags' ginger colour but the autumnal fire that blazed in the trees before the death of winter claimed them. He was superbly dressed, she noticed: swishing topcoat, elegant trousers, beautiful gloves.

"Who are you?" she whispered.

He shook his head from side to side, like a child that has been forbidden to speak.

"Tell me, please, so that I will know you when we meet."

He smiled, again such a sad deep smile and then, slowly turning, he made his way out into the icy ocean and there disappeared from her sight. Delia went back to her mother but she too was walking away.

"Mummy," she called out — but there was no reply, only the constant rhythmic beat of the unforgiving waves.

She made to get out of that terrible sea but instead — in her dream state — she wandered out of her front door and fell on that black ironwork of her ultra-modern staircase and cut her head.

"Damnation," she said aloud and slowly crawled indoors and headed for the medicine chest in the bathroom.

CHAPTER THIRTEEN

Jenny — Past

Jenny could overhear — quite distinctly — the voice of Harriet Grote, to whom she had been presented some while ago. A larger-than-life character — a free thinker and advocate for the rights of womanhood — she always dressed unconventionally, with high red stockings on full show, as Harriet despised crinolines. The voice answering her comprised the loud and self-assured tones of Josephine Ahmansson, a tough being whom Jenny Lind had appointed to take the place of her former companion, Louise. It was a change well needed.

For a terrible blow had occurred and proven to be almost more than she could bear. In November 1847, suddenly and without warning, Felix Mendelssohn, aged thirty-eight, collapsed and died. In spiritual terms, Jenny had died as well. She had loved him so much and for so long that the thought of a future without his great and charming self was more than she could possibly comprehend.

Harriet Grote's voice was ringing out. "Jenny, my dear, it is time you left that bathroom. Your presence is required."

"What is the date?" asked Jenny.

"You know perfectly well," Harriet's voice shouted back. "It is your opening night and the crowds at Her Majesty's Theatre are already desperate to buy any tickets left. There's an absolute mob out there. So come on, Jenny, best foot forward. I know you are going to delight them."

"I hope you are right, old friend."

Jenny smiled, but inside she was quaking. Could she still sing, she wondered. This was going to be an interesting way to find out.

Miss Lind had chosen to open the operatic season with *La Sonnambula*, a role that she had played to perfection before. But tonight, of all nights, her confidence was low. She was nervous of London, of the huge, restless audience. Because she was so afraid of them, she decided on an action that she personally considered cheap and vulgar. It was to peep at the crowd and see for herself how many people were packing the theatre. It was an action that was way beneath her — as star and focal point of the whole affair — and yet she felt irresistibly drawn to do it. Very much to the amusement of the stage crew she looked through the tiny spying hole in the curtains.

At first all she could see was a head, bearing a cloud of dark-red hair framing a member of the audience's face. The hair was beautiful, wavy and full, though the features beneath were some-what intense. He was looking assiduously at his programme, read-ing the notes with some difficulty, which meant that he was not an Englishman, but came from somewhere else. And then he sud-denly looked up and straight at her. For a moment Jenny thought he could see her but then realised it was impossible, besides which she was being asked to return to her dressing room as there was only a quarter of an hour left before curtain up. She stepped down from her vantage point, wondering who the man was.

It was a miracle but somehow, something special happened — to her ears, anyway. Her voice had slightly improved in tone.

If there had been any change in her acting all she could do was be grateful for it. As the great opera came to its spectacular finale, she found herself shaking with the emotion that such a feat evoked. The crowd, which had behaved as if enchanted and sat extremely quietly throughout the performance, now let rip. They bellowed in their thousands, cheering and stamping, throwing cascades of flowers onto the stage, handing bouquets up via the conductor who was frankly in tears. Jenny took her last curtain call like a true artist. Walking to the front of the stage then sweeping a deep curtsy with lowered head, she slowly rose up as the audience went finally mad, taking in the front rows of the stalls with her eyes.

He was there, his hair gleaming under the lights, standing up with the rest of the crowd and applauding madly. Jenny graciously inclined her head several times, and once looked directly in his direction. He smiled at her — or appeared to do so; the house lights were coming up and it was difficult to tell. Jenny smiled graciously in return and swept off to her dressing room.

When she finally got home, members of the public blocking her way for hours, Jenny fell exhausted onto a sofa.

"Would you like a cup of tea?" Mrs Ahmansson enquired, her voice somehow grating. "I sat up for you. I hear it was a triumph."

"No, I am going straight to bed. If you would be kind enough to leave me."

"Very good. Goodnight, Miss Lind."

Once she was by herself, the singer closed her eyes and the next minute — or so it seemed to her — she was dreaming of Mendelssohn and all the passion they had shared. She remained like that, sleeping on the sofa, until the lights of dawn swept London, and she was awoken by a knock on her front door. It was answered by a maid and there was a brief conversation and then came a gentle tap on the living room door.

"A letter for you, ma'am," said the serving girl, holding out a folded paper.

"Thank you. Please don't look shocked. I slept here all night. I was somewhat exhausted."

"I'm not surprised, ma'am. It's the talk of all the servants that you were a triumph. Albert's brother had a ticket in the gallery, you see. And he was beside himself, he was."

Jenny could not help letting out a small yelp of sheer delight. "I'm so glad. Thank you for telling me."

* * *

Later that week, on 12 May to be precise, Jenny finally had a wonderful night off. She put on a rather daring dress and wrapped herself in a fur-lined coat. Then she called a taxi and made her way to her friend's house, for Harriet Grote was giving a small party, naming Jenny as guest of honour. Upon arrival, Jenny paused in the doorway, to show off her splendid dress as much as anything. And then she stopped dead — for standing there, his clothes elegant and his hair quite amazing, was the man whom she had seen at the opera, the man who had clapped her so enthusiastically. He looked up, smiled at her, and gave a bow.

"Miss Lind," he said, in French.

"I am afraid I don't have the pleasure," she answered in the same language. "You are . . . ?"

"Fryderyk Chopin. I am staying in London presently. I thought you were superb the other night."

"Thank you so much. I am afraid that I couldn't see the audience distinctly," she lied, having picked him out instantly, attracted by his looks as much as anything.

Chopin thought of the letter he had written to his friend Grzymala and the words he had used to describe her: *This Swede is indeed an original from top to toe! She does not show herself in the ordinary light, but in the magic rays of an aurora borealis. Her singing is incredibly pure and sure.* Et cetera, ad nauseam.

"It is truly my pleasure to meet you. I had heard rumours that you were a good singer — but they were not true. You are not *good*, you are *astounding*."

Harriet Grote came over, wearing something extremely short. Her legs were clothed in vermillion tights.

"Ah, my dears, so you have met at last. This is going to be a very small party, I'm afraid. I so wanted you to see one another that I have not invited anyone else at all."

"Good," said Chopin firmly. "With your permission, my dear Harriet, I will take Miss Lind to the piano after we have dined. I want to hear her sing again."

What followed the meal was one of the most blissful experiences that Jenny could remember since the death of her beloved Mendelssohn. Fryderyk threw back the piano cover and started to play, looking up at Jenny and smiling. It was exquisite. The notes poured out from beneath his elegant fingers till she felt tears start in her eyes.

"Oh bravo, Mr Chopin. You play excellently well."

"Fryderyk, please, Miss Lind."

"By the same token, my name is Jenny. All right?"

He smiled, his dark eyes gleaming a million thoughts. "Would you like me to sing to you? Polish songs that show the spirit of our nation? Mind you, I can't really sing. But I can make a noise."

"Please do."

Chopin gave voice robustly, his dark-red hair flying as he gathered speed and emotion. Jenny listened, entranced, realising that she had not felt so joyful since the death of her former lover.

"Oh bravo again, Mr Chopin, I mean Fryderyk. Now I shall sing some Swedish national songs to you so you can compare the two cultures."

"It will be my pleasure."

They laughed and sang and played for one another until Chopin eventually looked at his watch.

"My God, it's one o'clock in the morning. We've been singing all night."

"Poor Harriet. We've probably kept her awake."

Chopin chuckled, a deep, sweet sound. "I think she has taken her purple legs to bed, don't you? We shall creep out of the house without disturbing her further."

"Yes. Of course."

Chopin stood up from the piano. It had been his turn to play again. He bowed suddenly, his tight-fitting clothes not wrinkling at all as he caught her hand.

"Good night, Miss Lind. Jenny. I would be very honoured to see you again."

"But you must. I have rented a cottage in Old Brompton — it's awfully rural, but I think you would love it — all my friends call on me there. Please come in whenever you like."

"I will, most certainly. Thank you for a wonderful evening."

He kissed her hand and held it a second longer than he should — and elsewhere in London a Scottish woman screamed, high and shrill, and sat bolt upright, weeping loudly.

She was tall and terribly thin, her breasts small and loose, her face quite sparse, lacking a firm chin and shapely mouth. At the moment she was crying at top voice and one of her arms thrashed.

"Oh, sister," she was sobbing. "Something is wrong with dear Mr Chopin, I know it."

The older woman, sleeping on a couch nearby, sat up crossly. "Whatever is it, Jane? Why are you weeping like that?"

"Because I know he is in danger. I dreamt it. He has so many admirers and one of them is overstepping the mark, I believe. Lord above, have mercy on me! Do not torture me like this!"

"Oh, calm down. You'll wake the neighbours."

"But Mr Chopin is in danger? I feel it deeply."

"It's your over-stuffed imagination, Jane, caused by eating too well. Now be quiet, do."

Jane sniffed loudly, but reluctantly lay down again, her face — which could have been reasonably attractive in normal circumstances — sagging as she breathed heavily and sighed.

* * *

Waking later than usual and feeling better than he had done for months, Fryderyck Franciszek Chopin called out to his manservant Daniel, an Irishman who thankfully could speak French. "I'm awake and could do with some breakfast. I shall join you when I have had a bath."

Daniel's eyes popped. His master had not been so cheerful since he had arrived in London, complaining bitterly about the air being unfit to breathe and to the constant presence of the two Scotch ladies — but his late night yesterday seemed to have blown all that away.

"Very good, Mr Chopin. Shall I bring it in in half an hour?"

Fryderyck's head appeared in the doorway. "Most certainly not. I am getting up."

"Well," Daniel muttered to himself, "*somebody's* done him some good. I wonder who? It can't be that blathering Scotch creature rolling her eyes at him. Personally I can never understand a word she says. So who is it?"

When Fryderyck finally entered the breakfast room, a whiff of a strong scent accompanied him and his hair was literally bouncing from the amount of washing it had received. Daniel's eyes practically hit his brows as he gazed at the transformation in his master.

"Did you enjoy the dinner party last night?" he ventured to ask, determined to know more.

"Very much indeed," Chopin began — and then stopped short as he drew a theatre ticket from the covering letter, which had just been delivered to the door. He whistled softly. "Well, well," he said.

"You sound surprised, Mr Chopin."

"It is from Mademoiselle Lind. A ticket for tomorrow's performance."

"Will you go, sir? I mean, you went only two nights ago."

"If you think I'm about to ignore it then you've judged my character incorrectly. Of course I shall go! Now where's my breakfast? I'm famished."

At that next performance Jenny Lind stole Chopin's poor heart away and so he wrote to his great friend Count Wojciech Grzymala, to whom he poured out most of his emotions: *She is enormously effective in Sonnambula. She sings with extreme purity and certainty, and her piano notes are steady and as even as a hair.*

The fate of these two vulnerable people was sealed. They were about to embark on a passionate relationship which could only end in the most bitter way of all.

CHAPTER FOURTEEN

Jenny — Past

Life had become interesting again. Jenny Lind had been so deeply and passionately in love with Felix Mendelssohn that she felt dead herself when he had died so suddenly and swiftly. She had often wondered about his death — so strange in someone so young. Yet his family had not queried the cause, nor had his friends, and so Jenny had accepted it along with the rest of humanity.

But now, here in this wonderful opera house, with all the world singing her praises and the wild applause still ringing in her ears for an hour after curtain down, she had come to life once more. And the cause? A skinny young man who was one of the world's greatest musicians, who had no money to speak of and was racked by a terrible cough, had stolen her generous heart — and all she wanted to do was sing her joy from the rooftops.

As for him, he was a creature transformed. He, who had spent so many miserable nights listening to the two Scots ladies talk interminably about nothing except their family connections, dining with them, watching their jaws eat methodically, feeling Jane's pale blue eyes drinking him in as if he was a glass of Highland water, had driven him crazy. Yet, what could he do?

His composing brought in precious little, recitals were few and far between. He was caught in a web of poverty and was only able to afford his apartment, his manservant and his little luxuries, by the skin of his teeth.

And now, as if some all-powerful being had interceded in his life, a love had come to him. A love like he had never experienced before. God — or Fate, whichever one wished to call it — had sent him Jenny Lind and he would love her till the moment of his death.

After they had met, he had left it one night and then called at Clairville Cottage, walking in through the iron gateway, then relishing the scent of the newly mown lawn, the flowers and the general sweetness of the atmosphere. His mind went back to the time when he had moved into Nohant during the period — far too long a period, in his opinion — when he had lived with that ghastly creature George Sand, a transvestite woman who dressed in trousers and smoked cigars, which had done nothing for her breath, he remembered. How he could ever have been attracted in the first place puzzled him now. But attracted he had been, so much so that they went on holiday together to Majorca and stayed in a creepy convent with cavernous corridors, and it was there his wretched cough had come to wrack him.

Baudelaire had called George Sand a *stupid, heavy and garrulous slut. A man-eating nymphomaniac* was another delightful soubriquet. But she intrigued Chopin, her choice of clothes being fantastic, her lips rarely without a cigar. She invited him to stay with her in the spring; she had legally separated from her husband and was more than ready for new meat. And in the following year she scored. With her strange cigars from the east — probably hashish or opium (or both) — she managed to get Chopin into bed, in a 'maiden room' she rented immediately. She was relentless, he was sexually aware — very much so — but she was voracious. She devoured him in her huge and exploding kisses. She cooed sweet words into his eager ears, her very experienced hands caressed every part of his body, she turned her power — gained through many years of practice — onto him with full beam. He gave in — who could resist such a phenomenon?

Thinking about it now, as he approached the front door, Chopin felt an unseemly flush at the memory. It had been wonderful at the start; he had to admit that. He had been consumed — body and soul — by that marvellous, voracious creature. But she was a mother — though the two children were immediately handed over to servants while she and Chopin made love. It had ended bitterly, of course, the problem being that he was not content with kissing the days away and wanted to compose. But, at first, he had fallen under the spell of living in France, teaching and writing music and spending his summers in Nohant, at a place rented by George Sand and a delight to both the eyes and the senses.

They lived as the pinnacle of the arty set. Musicians, actors, writers; all plunged through their door at a great rate, everybody drinking too much, eating like wolves, smoking those strange cigars of hers. Sand dressed like a dandy man, talking non-stop to her appreciative audience in a gravelly voice. Chopin had adored it all, a prowling cat in a den of lions. But eventually, it had begun to wear thin.

The front door opened at this juncture of his thoughts and a young maid servant stood there. "Good morning, sir."

"Good morning to you. Is your mistress in?"

"I think she might be, sir. If you will wait in the library I shall go and make enquiries."

"Thank you. I'm sorry to trouble her if my call is inconvenient."

But at that moment there was a whirl of frock as Jenny Lind herself rushed through the library door and said, "Why, it's Mr Chopin. How lovely to see you."

He kissed her outstretched hand in a restrained and formal manner. She looked up at him, thinking he was thin but so attractive, wearing clothes that could have been cut on him.

"Will you step inside for a cup of coffee? I am just about to have one myself."

"Nothing stronger?" Chopin asked with a laugh, remembering how George Sand had welcomed many a day with a shot of wine.

Jenny shook her head. "No. There is a full rehearsal of *Lucia di Lammermoor* this afternoon. In the theatre itself."

Chopin's face lit up. "How marvellous. I love that opera. You will be singing Lucia?"

"You know the work? But then of course you do. After all, you are Chopin."

He laughed aloud at this, his face cracking into a grin that had been notably absent during the last few months.

"Thank you for telling me. Sometimes I forget that is who I am."

"Why?" And then a knowing look passed over Miss Lind's face. "I think I can guess."

"What has anybody said to you?"

"Oh, Harriet Grote of course. She is the best of company, a very knowledgeable and well-connected woman. But occasionally she lets little bits of gossip escape her. She said that you and George Sand were deeply entwined."

Chopin looked glum. "*Were* being the operative word, I think."

The coffee arrived and Jenny Lind poured him a cup, noticing as she leaned forward that his ruby hair was streaked more darkly, here and there. She took a sip and smiled brightly, hoping that he would tell her more.

"I have a knack for attracting all the wrong sort of women," he said with some reluctance, then, after a pause, "Not including your good self, Miss Lind."

She smiled into her cup but made no reply.

"First of all — no, not my first but the one that harmed me most — was the novelist George Sand. She came after me with such power that I just crumpled into a corner and let her play with me unmercifully."

"Sounds frightening," said Miss Lind with a smile.

Chopin warmed to his theme. "I was driven crazy by her constant attentions. You must know how awful that is."

Jenny replaced her coffee cup on the tray. "No, actually, I don't."

"But hundreds of people adore you. You are a goddess with a vast following. You are worshipped by the crowd."

"But by no one in particular." She looked at her watch. "I'm afraid I will have to go in fifteen minutes."

Chopin collected himself. "I am most terribly sorry. I shouldn't have burdened you with my shoddy recollections. I realise that I have overstayed my welcome."

He stood up, looking thin and smart in his fitted black velvet waistcoat. Jenny Lind rose as well.

"Oh, Mr Chopin — or would you prefer that I call you Fryderyk? — you do allow yourself to be plunged into gloom. What is past is done, dead, buried. You will only make yourself miserable the more you dwell on it. Look forward with pleasure — otherwise your looks will be ruined."

A small smile twitched Chopin's mouth. "I apologise, madam, for my ill behaviour. And I wish you great success in your latest role. Don't worry, I will be there to see you."

"Will you? Why don't you come now? I know that you are aware of the rules. Strict silence and be very discreet."

"Do you mean accompany you to the rehearsal?"

"Of course I do. Cheer up, Fryderyk. You can tell me your opinion later."

"Nothing — I repeat, *nothing* — would give me greater pleasure."

"Then that's arranged," said Jenny Lind.

* * *

Chopin sat perfectly still, as did the rest of the company gathered in the shadowy haunts of the great London theatre. Nobody spoke except the conductor, and he with a voice at low pitch as he conversed with the leading violinist. Fryderych had slithered into an empty row and quietly taken a seat. For absolutely no reason that he could think of, he felt nervous as the members of the chorus suddenly trooped in, not conversing but all totally silent. When they were in their places there were no whispered comments that Chopin could detect and it was with a sense of relief that he saw the conductor finally stand up straight and look at the chorus master, who nodded. And that was it. Without further ado they started off, setting the scene for what was about to happen.

Then, from the wings, a hidden Jenny let out a wonderful musical trill of greeting and Chopin felt the tears sting on his cheekbones.

What the hell is the matter with me? he thought, as he silently continued to weep, suddenly terribly aware of immense gladness that his long-standing affair with the weirdest woman in the world was well and truly over. He reached for a handkerchief and applied it liberally to his face as Jenny let rip vocally. How pathetic seemed Madame Dudevant — now an ageing hag — by contrast. *I must have been mad*, he thought.

It was quite honest to say that nobody stirred throughout the opera, which ran through from start to finish without a single pause. Then Fryderyk stepped outside and, going to a flower-seller, bought a bunch of roses for Jenny. He made his way back within via the stage door — and there she was, still in costume and in private conversation with the leading tenor. He just gaped, silently and like a schoolboy, and his heart did some strange things, starting on an irregular beat that caused him to pause for breath. He must have gasped, because Jenny turned around.

"Oh, it's you! I thought it was the theatre ghost."

"No, it's only me. I'm sorry I startled you." He bowed in the direction of the tenor. "A very fine performance, sir. Those high notes were most impressive."

The singer bowed back, said "Thank you" in a tuneful voice and departed. Jenny turned to investigate Chopin's face.

"And what about you? Did you enjoy it?"

He shook his head. "*Enjoy* is not quite the right word. I was so near to heaven that I heard an archangel sigh."

Jenny twinkled. "With pain — or with pleasure?"

Chopin, straight faced, answered, "Both, simultaneously."

He would have escorted her home and left her to rest but Jenny — suddenly overflowing with well-deserved pleasure — did not want to hear about it. Instead, they went out for an early supper and then returned to Clairville Cottage, where Jenny insisted that he play for her. Chopin did so, his fingers shaking terribly as every possible mixed emotion flowed through his body. If he had been younger and stronger he would have kissed her. He remembered the power with which he had swept the hateful George Sand off her feet. Or had he, really? Rather, hadn't he been overwhelmed by her, snatched into her grasp, treated with such torrid enthusiasm that he had mistaken lust for love?

A small sigh from the sofa had him turning around to look at Jenny. She had fallen asleep where she sat, a compact bundle of kindness. Very quietly, Fryderyk got up and with the aid of his stick, walked home through that fresh spring evening, his body ailing, his heart on fire.

At breakfast the next morning Chopin was unbelievably quiet. Usually at this hour of the day he would try to make conversation with his manservant, Daniel, but this morning hardly a word came out of him. Looking at him closely, Daniel thought that he had an exhausted face but the expression upon it argued the contrary. The unbelievable fact was that inwardly, Chopin was smiling.

"Had a good night, sir? I didn't hear you come in."

"No, I was very late. Too late to disturb you."

"And how about your health, sir? Are you feeling any better?"

"Yes, very much so. In fact, yesterday I went to the opera."

"Good gracious, what would that have been — a matinée?"

"No, my good Daniel. I was invited to a dress rehearsal by Miss Jenny Lind."

"Gracious me alive! I thought you had to be royalty to get asked to one of those. By the way, sir, the ladies called while you were out."

"Oh God. What did you tell them?"

"The truth, sir. That you were out and I knew not where."

Fryderyk smiled. "That sounds very poetic. How did they take that?"

"Not well, sir. Mrs Erskine looked haughty and grand. Miss Jane went bright red, then blanched to white. It was extremely dramatic."

Chopin then did something so unlikely that Daniel looked quite alarmed as a result. He exploded into a loud fit of the giggles, his lean body rocking with laughter, his morning coffee spilling wildly, his plate of porridge flying into the air and landing on the floor.

"Oh, I wish I could have seen that," he gasped. "I would like to have witnessed that very much."

"It was not a pretty sight, sir."

Chopin quietened down. "I can imagine. The trouble is, Daniel, that she and her sister are so good to me. I would not be here in London if it had not been for their kindness to me."

Daniel gave his master a long look. "Do you mind if I tell the truth, sir?"

"No, of course not. What is it?"

"Miss Jane Stirling is madly in love with you, sir. She is dying for you to make her Madame Chopin. She has the expression on her face of a lady at the bottom of a lake when she looks at you."

Fryderyk shuddered. "I realise. But she is the last woman on Earth that I could love in return. Frankly, my dear Daniel, she is boring, past it and has had her day."

"If she heard you say that, she would die of grief."

"I speak only the truth," Chopin replied with dignity and picking up his bowl of porridge, he started to eat.

* * *

The season at Her Majesty's Theatre continued to flourish, to everybody's satisfaction. Chopin would slip silently into a seat, unrecognised by the masses, apart from Prince Albert who leaned towards Victoria and murmured, "Isn't that Mr Chopin over there?"

She raised her opera glasses. "Indeed, it is. I think he must love the theatre very much."

"Or somebody in it," came the whispered reply — and a raised eyebrow.

Jenny was inundated with visitors, particularly Hans Christian Anderson for whom she rushed out into the road outside Clairville Cottage to help him locate her. He was older and plainer than she remembered but as attentive as ever, and still in love with her in his funny, sad-faced way. One or two people who had gathered to stare at her home raised a faint cheer when they saw her, but Jenny scuttled into her house with Andersen whirling beside her.

It was during this time, when the singer was busy with other visitors, that Chopin yet again invited the two women of Scotland to his house to dine. The elder one — Mrs Katherine Erskine, watchful and non-smiling — was the guardian of the younger, who was a tallish, light-haired woman, who had never married and was madly in love with Chopin, over whom she hovered endlessly. When she was persuaded to talk, she declared that she loved him with all her heart and had always done so. She bored people endlessly with this tale.

Miss Stirling had first met Chopin in France, where she had gone for piano lessons several years before. She had immediately fallen tremendously in love with him but unfortunately, the sentiment was not reciprocated. Jane was tall, pale, thin and boring, but Chopin was a god in her eyes and thus she lived out a life of fantasy in which he eventually fell in love with her. There was no hope of that whatsoever. In fact, the reverse happened.

Political revolution in France had seriously undermined Chopin's work as a piano teacher and he became terribly short of cash. Jane Stirling came from a wealthy background. The Clan Stirling had been around for centuries and there was no special regard as to how Miss Jane spent her money. With disease and poverty wracking Paris, Fryderyk decided to give England a try — paid for by Jane, of course. So he had set out, unaware that he was at last going once more to meet his great and only true love. Behind him, unsmiling and unrelenting, came Jane and her legal guardian, Mrs Erskine, growing just slightly tetchy with it all. And to make it worse, Jane had heard rumours about a certain singer: one Jenny Lind to be precise.

But now, this evening, the Scottish ladies were coming to dinner and Chopin was very slightly on edge, wondering who his sweet young lady was entertaining in her home.

"Ah, Daniel," he said as his servant walked into the dining room, "have the guests arrived yet?"

"Not yet, sir. You have another few moments of peace."

But from the hallway they heard the front door open and Miss Jane announcing — in French, which she spoke with an appalling Scottish accent — "Please do tell Mr Chopin that his lady dinner guests have arrived."

"Your moment of calm is over, sir," Daniel informed Chopin.

"Not for too long. I am going to feign ill health. And there is no need to look like that. It will be better all around if the evening is brief."

"Very true, sir."

And there they were, Miss Stirling displaying a good-humoured smile and Mrs Erskine looking around her for dust or any other detritus that a man living on his own might accumulate. Chopin bowed.

"Good evening, ladies. Pray, sit down."

"It is nice to see you looking so well, Mr Chopin," said Jane.

Mrs Erskine said nothing but accepted a drink of cold spring water from a tray that Daniel was carrying, which also held various other beverages. Miss Stirling took a small glass of sherry. Chopin, on the other hand, swallowed a large brandy and demanded another one. Mrs Erskine said nothing, her gaze focused determinedly over his head.

Miss Stirling spoke. "It has been quite a fine day today, has it not? Did you go out, Fryderyk?"

They were on first-name terms, even though it had taken her a couple of years to get used to it.

"Yes, briefly. I walked in the park for a breath of fresh air."

Mrs Erskine cleared her throat audibly. "I believe in my parents saying that casting a clout before May was out could be highly dangerous."

Jane pretended a shower of loud, pealing laughter. "Honestly, Katherine. You do come out with some ancient sayings!"

"And what is wrong with that, pray? I believe that the previous generation had more sense than all of us who follow."

122

Her expression was serious; it was an expression which Chopin detested.

"Really. I truly believed that you had more intelligence, dear. And don't interrupt me . . ." Mrs Erskine raised a large white hand. "No, I can honestly say that we of a younger generation . . ." — she darted a look at Chopin, who was toying with the idea of having another drink — ". . . are more sensible than that, would you not agree, Fryderyk?"

He nodded, his thoughts a million miles away, wondering what Miss Lind was doing and saying at this very second. Then he guiltily remembered that he was in company and moreover, that he was the host. With a deep but silent sigh he gathered himself together.

"You are probably right, madam. As always."

Miss Stirling shot Chopin an anxious look to see whether he was jesting but he remained as usual, staring into his glass, he did not even look up as he addressed her.

Thus the evening plodded on until — eventually — there was nothing further to say or do. Jane decided that her boykin — as she thought of Chopin with a secretive smile that disguised nothing — was not well and that she and Mrs Erskine must make for home.

"Goodnight, my dear. Thank you so much for entertaining us. I really think we must depart as Katherine is beginning to wilt."

"I am doing no such thing."

Jane sighed affectedly. "Oh hush, dear. Goodbye, Fryderyk — for the present, that is."

Chopin, who had been miles away wondering what Jenny Lind wore under her beautiful costumes, snapped back to attention. He had never been more delighted to see guests leave and now he saw them off with a handkissing that sent Miss Jane into silent raptures. As soon as their conveyance was out of sight he whispered urgently to Daniel.

"Fetch me a taxicab, will you? I'm off."

"Very good, sir. May I ask where you are going?"

"No, you may not. Let me have some privacy."

A few minutes later a cab was at the door and Chopin, with a spring that surprised both himself and his servant, leaped aboard, pulling on his cloak and jamming down his hat. As it turned out of sight Daniel could have sworn that his master winked at him — but then the servant had always had a rich imagination.

CHAPTER FIFTEEN

Jenny — Past

He had definitely drunk more than he normally did, Chopin was well aware of that. First of all it had been to get away from Miss Stirling's fixed gaze, secondly it had been a strong arousal of his passion for Jenny Lind, as yet not affecting him physically. Given half a chance, however, it most certainly would. He allowed his mind to wander down that slippery path and decided that he was strong enough to make the effort providing, of course, that she agreed. He wondered just how much experience she had had before — and then recalled a rumour he had heard about herself and Mendelssohn. Had it been true, he considered. He rather thought so because she was warm and kind and affectionate, unlike Miss Stirling who was firmly *intacta*. He turned the thought of the Scottish woman over in his mind and shuddered visibly.

There had been several people leaving Clairville Cottage as his cab pulled up outside. The two men raised their hats to Chopin and the ladies nodded graciously, but no words other than "Good evening" were exchanged. But once out of sight one of the men nudged the other and said, "Did you see who that was?"

"Yes, Chopin. He doesn't mind calling late, obviously."

The first speaker winked at him, "It all depends on your purpose, of course."

The two ladies, all ears, stared at one another. "You don't think . . . ?" said the older one.

"Yes, I do," replied the other. "After all, they're not children, are they?"

The two men, overhearing, started to laugh aloud and they walked down the street chuckling heartily.

Inside, Chopin was busy divesting himself of his cloak and hat and making his way purposefully to the living room. Jenny was yawning, sitting alone on the sofa, having sat there previously with a group of opera lovers who had all been to see her in *Sonnambula*. She turned at the sound of the opening door.

"Why Fryderyk, it's you. I thought you were entertaining at home this evening."

"I was, the two Scottish dames. But they were tired, and I had something else on my mind."

"Really? What was that?"

"You," he answered and, sitting down beside her, pressed her against him as hard as he could.

"What's all this about?" she asked, though she did not try to move away.

"Can't you guess?" he answered, then bending his head, he kissed her — having been shown the art by the wretched woman he had once lived with. Jenny did not object, nor did she try to leave. If anything, she pressed herself a little more closely to him.

"That was nice," she breathed. "Please do it again."

"Oh, my God," Chopin said quietly, more as a thanks to the Almighty than anything else. "Don't you realise that I have fallen in love with you?"

"No, my dear, I did not have any idea," Jenny answered truthfully, though a sudden feeling of wonder seized her.

"Well, I have, and that is all I have to say on the matter except to wish that my love may last for ever."

"Is it true?" she said and gave him a kiss, then led him up the stairs to her bedroom where — without a word of protest — she let him unbutton her clothes until she was out of them and stood looking at him.

There was something awfully sweet about her, something young and appealing and extraordinarily vulnerable. Chopin stood, staring at her, thinking that she was the most precious thing on God's Earth and thankful that he was being granted all his manly sensations. Illness or no illness, he was determined to give her pleasure.

"Jenny, my dear, you are so lovely. May I touch you?"

"You already have."

"Oh, damn it! Invite me to your bed. I can only make a fool of myself once."

But that fear was not to be realised. Instead, Jenny cried aloud with joy as she flew above the blazing stars and Chopin — for once not coughing — heaved a great sigh of contentment as he felt the comfort and tenderness that he had almost forgotten. He sighed with fulfilment and Miss Lind — who had loved another so dearly and who had sought nobody since his death — knew that her days of loneliness had ended, and at that she laughed with sheer enjoyment.

They spent the night together and finally parted at dawn. Jenny, seeing first light, said, "I think, my dear friend, that you should leave. We'll have the servants in an uproar if you should be seen."

"I shall slip out like a wraith — on one condition."

"Which is?"

"That I may come to see you soon. That I can hope for something of your company in the future. I promise you that I don't ask for more. Oh, my darling, you have brought back such happy memories for me."

"Of your lady friend?"

Chopin, struggling into his underwear, decided to ignore that question, for no two women could be more unalike than George Sand and Jenny Lind.

"I don't know what helped me. Perhaps I do believe there is some kind hand guiding me."

"Oh, I so hope you are right," Jenny answered. "As long as it is mine," she added cheekily.

* * *

It was the beginning of a wonderful relationship, light-hearted and loving, but Jenny was beginning to have thoughts. Vocally she was at her peak, something that she hoped would remain the case for the next few years, and she was in terrific demand. The audiences everywhere were more than appreciative, and yet she wanted one thing more.

A child.

She smiled whenever she thought of it. If Chopin was the father, she could picture her son. Long tawny hair, her eyes, Chopin's wonderful mouth. Jenny would hug herself and smile. She was now twenty-eight years old, and the idea haunted her. But she said nothing to her lover, who came and often stayed the night, enjoying nothing more than being held in her arms while he slept. It was the nearest to heaven he ever got, and he wept over her hand when they had to part.

However, Jenny's career was soaring like a rocket. Having sung to vast applause in *La Sonnambula*, *Le Nozze de Figaro*, *La Fille du Régiment*, *Lucia di Lammermoor* and *I Puritani* and given a concert to raise money for the Brompton Hospital for Diseases of the Chest — the thought of Chopin wheezing and coughing was never far from her mind while she sang for them — one day she told her lover that she would meet him north of the border.

Chopin was confused. "But darling, where shall I go? I can't just travel north and hope for the best. I have no bookings — and nobody to stay with. God help me, I can't bear this. I am not good enough for you. I love you deeply, more than I have ever loved anyone else, especially that revolting woman from Nohant."

Jenny smiled. "Why was she so hideous?"

"Her breath smelled of her foul cigars."

"I see. Well, I don't smoke so I can't be blamed for that."

Chopin did not reply. They were sitting outside Jenny's cottage for the last time.

"Jenny, would you consider living with me when all this awful touring has ended?"

She turned to him, her face wearing that far-away look people get when they are thinking of something else.

"Darling, I can't imagine anything I would like more. But first I would have to retire. And — quite importantly to me — we would also have to be married. You see, I have no wish to live like the Cigar and play with men for the rest of my days."

Despite the misery of the occasion, Chopin let out a bellow of laughter.

"I love it — and I love *you*, Jenny. You make me happier than I have ever been, despite my declining health."

"And we shall have a son, Fryderyk. A sweet child that will look like you."

"I should hope so indeed. And a pretty daughter, very like a famous singer I know."

"Now who could that be?" Jenny answered, before they kissed and parted company.

* * *

Chopin looked as depressed as someone at a funeral and, so far, had added nothing to the conversation but a few unseemly grunts. Miss Jane Stirling, however, strode on bravely, keeping up a loud conversation about nothing at all.

". . . and then you will never guess, the donkey chaise took off and poor wee Mrs Miller fell right off and crashed into the earth below. Fortunately she suffered mild bruising alone and was able to attend Mrs Cameron's ball a few nights later. Now what do you make of that?"

There was total silence. Chopin stared silently at his plate, his head well down; Mrs Erskine was chewing on a piece of tough meat and did not wish to talk. Miss Jane looked around brightly.

"Tongue-tied? My, my, what bad company. Now, if we were entertaining in the Big House, guests would feel it incumbent upon themselves to keep up a lively chatter."

Chopin let out the mildest of moans, as Mrs Erskine continued to chew malevolently.

Miss Jane felt a momentary panic. Had she said something to upset *him*, her man, chosen for her by kind Fate, and she would let nothing and no one stand in the way of that.

"Fryderyk, dear. Are you not feeling well? I thought you let out the tiniest groan."

At last, he looked up. "I don't feel too good. You'll have to excuse me."

"What is it, my dear? A headache or a stomach pain?"

He looked up suddenly, his dark eyes glistening. "More of a heart ache."

"Oh!" Jane clutched her hands to her heaving bosom and a scarlet patch appeared in either cheek. "And may one guess at who is the subject?"

Chopin was sorely tempted to shout *No, you may not*, but at the last minute stopped himself, saying instead, "I would rather you didn't."

Jane gave a wide smile of triumph and said, "Oh, you naughty man. Leaving us all to guess." She looked at her sister triumphantly and saw that she had at last chewed the meat. Mrs Erskine appeared thunderstruck. Her sister could have screamed with rage. At last she had something like a commitment from her beloved and Mrs Erskine sat there mumchance.

Chopin rose to his feet. "If you will excuse me, ladies. I am thinking of retiring early."

"Of course you must. Take the greatest care."

He did not answer but walked quietly through the door which Daniel had held open for him. A few seconds later he followed his master into the hall.

"Are you all right, sir?"

"Of course I am. I just had to get out. That younger woman is driving me insane."

"I think," Daniel answered solemnly, "that I would probably have murdered her by now."

"But she has *me* by the throat, as you know. She is keeping me. My music is not earning me a thing. I could weep with frustration. And then, to crown it all, I must go and fall in love with a great and wonderful star. What am I to do, Daniel? Where am I going?"

"My advice would be to marry Miss Lind."

Fryderyk burst into tears, not making a sound but nonetheless weeping like a child.

"There, there," Daniel said quietly. "It will work itself out, I promise you."

"But how can I marry her when I am a pauper?"

"Does she worry about that?"

"No, I don't think she does."

"Then do so, my dear sir. Do so."

* * *

They parted company a few nights later. Jenny, brimming with excitement about the great and wonderful tour that lay before her; he as miserable as sin because he could not join her.

"But Fryderyck, why don't you just get on a train so we can meet in Edinburgh? Perhaps your Scottish ladies will invite you."

"*Don't* — I mean this with all the sincerity of which I am capable — don't mention those creatures to me again. Those two women bore me so much that I don't know which way to turn. They absolutely insist on my going to stay with their family in Scotland."

"That could be quite pleasant."

Chopin groaned. "I will have to listen all day long to their interminable stories about what this ancestor did or didn't do. I shall end up in a lunatic asylum."

Jenny burst out laughing and Chopin adopted a hurt and miserable expression. "They have me over a beastly barrel. Jane Stirling is mad for love of me."

"As am I. But I am not breaking my heart because I am going on tour. Instead, I suggest that you join me wherever and whenever you can."

"It will mean great personal sacrifice."

"Oh, rubbish." And Jenny gave him a theatrical punch. "You are probably glad to be rid of me."

Fryderyk looked aggrieved. "You are suggesting something that wounds me deeply."

"Don't let it. Darling man, I love you very much. And part of that love is because you understand, better than most, that I have a wonderful career, and I aim to fulfil all my commitments."

After this they kissed one another and spent the night together and the next morning Jenny was off in a whirl of waving and shouting from various followers, who knew that she was going on a tour that would open every door for her. Chopin cried, silently and alone, but came to a decision. He would go to Scotland with the two wretched women, who were horribly kind to him in every degree. He did not know how to shake them off but in his present dire financial position had very little choice in the matter. Put up with them he must.

CHAPTER SIXTEEN

Jenny — Past

He couldn't help it; he was excited and full of a sudden hope that everything was going to turn out well for him after all. On 5 August he and Daniel and a manager appointed by Broadwood, the great and highly favoured piano makers, boarded the express train to Edinburgh. It was nine o'clock in the morning and the flyer promised to arrive at Edinburgh Lothian Road in twelve hours' time. Grinning like a happy cat, Fryderyk turned to John Muir Wood, the man from Broadwood's.

"It was so kind of your company to ask you to accompany me."

"No, maestro, it is entirely my pleasure," John Muir answered in terrible French.

Chopin felt the weight of years lift from his shoulders. To be called maestro (though officially that was an honour given to conductors) always pleased him. Besides, he had a letter from Jenny tucked into his breast pocket and was full of eager anticipation. This buoyancy had partially left him by the time they arrived in Edinburgh, but was restored when they made their way into the Douglas Hotel. He then proceeded to get just the slightest bit inebriated with several bottles of excellent red wine and fell asleep in his armchair. His first impressions of Scotland were excellent indeed.

They stayed in these luxurious surroundings for two days and then the adventure really began. They were to make their way by carriage to the estate of Lord Torphichen, who was Jane Stirling's elderly brother-in-law. Something told Chopin to be on his guard, but whatever fear there was, was removed by the glories of the Scottish countryside. A carriage duly arrived harnessed in the English style, the driver being mounted on the horse. Chopin's spirits were raised even higher by the sight of it. And the views were glorious. Whichever way he looked they were frankly gorgeous. His thoughts went out to Jenny, *his girl* he thought comfortably, and a smile broke out on his clever face.

Lord Torphichen spoke French but with an irritating lack of care, so that his conversation consisted largely of a high whining sound which fell with gross heaviness on Chopin's ears. However, it was not as bad as the female versions which burst upon him as soon as he and Daniel alighted at the great front door.

"Oh, Mr Chopin. So you've made it all the way to Bonny Scotland" — the translation used was *Jolie Ecosse* — "to see us."

Chopin bowed low. "Indeed I have, Mademoiselle Stirling. And what a grand estate it is. You know my servant, Daniel, of course."

"Oh yes. We're old acquaintances."

Daniel bent to the ground, his hair almost touching the driveway. His face, thus hidden, was a study.

"Well, we'll do our poor best to make you comfortable, Fryderyck. Is there anything in particular that you would like to order?"

"Miss Lind," muttered the servant, still bowing low.

"What was that?" asked Jane swiftly.

"Nothing, ma'am. I merely coughed."

"I thought you said something in English. We speak French here." She trilled a girlish laugh. "Don't we, Mr Chopin?"

It was all so arch, so coy, in a terribly old-fashioned way. Daniel felt a momentary nausea.

From that time on, Jane Stirling went out of her way to be subtle — as she thought of it — succeeding with all the power of a man-o-war. Chopin, despite the beauty of his surroundings, felt himself dragged from pillar to post, meeting peers and peeresses who desperately tried a few words in half-hearted French — but he found that he was mostly listening to them drone on in their Scottish burr while drinking heartily and eating vast quantities. He became an expert on knowing when false teeth were about to slip on the rim of a wine glass or vanish momentarily when eating a nut. Oh, what fun it all was.

Things came to a climax when one day both coaches skidded off the road and Miss Stirling, who had been riding in the first with a grim-faced Mrs Erskine, was catapulted out to the ground below, followed by her sister who was screaming wildly because her underclothes were temporarily on show. Chopin and Daniel were tilted heavily towards the road but managed to keep their seats.

"This is it!" exclaimed Chopin. "Never again will I allow myself to be hoodwinked into crossing the Scottish border. You have my permission to heartily punch whoever suggests it."

"Very good, sir," Daniel replied in French. "Including Miss Lind?"

Chopin ignored him. "I shall leave these two ladies very shortly. We both will. All I do here is wander about aimlessly or read the Parisian newspapers — which Miss Stirling provides daily — and I still haven't seen the bloody ghost that's supposed to haunt the corridors."

It was too much for Daniel, who burst out laughing and was thus quite unprepared when the coach was shaken straight again by a pair of sweating farmers. But Fryderyck was completely sincere and departed for Edinburgh a few days later, leaving a bewildered Jane to indulge in a bout of weeping.

"My poor Fryderyck," she wailed aloud. "How will he manage without me?"

"Perfectly well," said Mrs Erskine sharply. "He always manages to fall on his feet, that one."

"How can you be so horrid, Katherine? You know how heavily he relies on me."

"Only because you encourage him, Jane. If you had any sense left, you would let him live his own life."

"He does. He's gone of his own free will. All the way to Salford, I hear."

"Staying with friends on the way like the good boy he is."

"Your accusations are vile," Jane answered, and burst into a fresh phase of tears.

* * *

Fryderyck stood — for once unaccompanied — watching the London train pull in at Edinburgh station. He looked the height of elegance, dressed as only a handsome man could; slick and eye-catching, with a certain innate style about him. Harriet Grote, her legs clad in bright-blue tights, spotted him and waved as she got off. Chopin waved back, then stood motionless, realising how very much he had missed Jenny Lind.

His first glimpse told him that she was as attractive as he remembered, and he wanted nothing more than to hold her in his arms. As she got off the train she made a polite curtsy but all the time grinning like a Cheshire cat and looking quite delicious. However, they were in a public place and it would not be wise to embrace in full view. Mrs Grote, however, had no such inhibitions and flung her arms round Chopin's waist.

"My dear boy," she said, "I haven't seen you in an age."

"And neither have I," Jenny whispered quietly and gave Chopin a most welcoming smile.

He, never conventional, bowed very low, stood up when he felt his hat begin to wobble, and kissed her outstretched hand.

"My dear Miss Lind," he said, "life has been so much quieter since we parted company."

"I wish I could say the same. It must be lovely to have a peaceful existence."

Chopin grinned, rather sadly. "But boring in the extreme."

"I suppose you are right."

"I know I am," he answered — and threw a coin to the waiting porters to pay for their service.

A few minutes later, they were off. It was not often that Harriet Grote was silenced, but on this occasion she was happy to relax and feel the warmth that was filling the cab as the two people, whom it had been her pleasure to introduce, chattered excitedly to one another. She remembered the night they had sat up at the piano and played and sung into the small hours. She wondered now if it had been a *coup de foudre*. Love at first sight. Slyly, she watched while Chopin peeled off his gloves and noticed that Jenny did the same thing a second or so after. And then, as the singer's hands flew through the air, telling some tale or other, and came down to rest on Chopin's immaculate, talented fingers, Harriet knew. Two people whom she admired above all, who had been born and destined to meet one another, had finally done so.

A contented smile appeared on Harriet's face, and she turned to look out of the window, pretending not to be aware of her fellow travellers at all.

CHAPTER SEVENTEEN

Delia — Present Day

In a funny sort of way, Alan Pearson, now busy composing another musical and eating only when he remembered to, was more than somewhat depressed. He knew — or thought he did — that music was his entire life and was more than grateful that Fate had moved him — rather like a chess piece on a mighty board — to meet Robert Poynes-Hamilton, all through the machinations of Robert's young niece. That had been his lucky moment and he had had the sense to grab it with both hands. Now he had everything he had ever wanted; a place on the Musically Important list, a wonderfully tidy income, people — well, a few — waving at him in the street, and — above all — the house.

It had been built in the mid-eighteenth century and was Grade ll listed. It had originally been the creation of Lord Basil Fountain, who had lived life to the full there, giving wonderful parties and dances and fancy-dress balls and other goings-on. And yet — if rumour was to be believed — Fountain also had a love of investigating the world of ghosts and the unseen, including fairy folk.

Alan could well believe it. When he had first seen the place — built on a small hillock two miles outside Battle — it had borne that tired and frustrated look of an exquisite gem left to suffer the ravages of time alone. And also, latterly, the presence of a dated rock band, who had behaved within its shuddering walls like uncaring yobbos. It had been going for a relative song because the sad house needed so much spent on it — but something about its innate beauty had clutched at Alan's heart. He had bought it and started to offload his comfortable bank account upon it.

But today, walking in his reviving garden, sniffing the spring flowers thrusting through the earth, Alan felt an urge to speak to someone; anyone, any living being would do. But no, that wasn't strictly true. He was actually thinking of female company. At that moment, into his mind came an image of the good-natured Delia Paget and he wondered how she was. He raced into the house and picked up his phone as if it were a reflex action — and was just about to dial her number when there was a tiny disturbance. There was the sound of distant laughter, as if a man and a woman were sharing a joke.

Alan jumped with sudden fright. He knew perfectly well the house was empty and unless someone had entered it while he had been in the garden, it still was empty as far as he knew. Thinking himself brave — which in fact he was, quite — he made his way swiftly into the gracious entrance hall and looked around.

The beautiful creation, which he had had repointed and repainted, was empty. Not a single soul occupied the space, except for an elegant cat which had obviously come in while the place stood unguarded. The cat looked at him and gave him a lazy wink, but other than that there was no movement anywhere. Hurrying, Alan went into his music room. It was completely empty — but a score he had been playing had fallen onto the floor. It was a *Prelude* by Chopin, a wonderful, glistening piece which Alan adored. He picked it up and could have sworn that there was the faintest rustle of clothing behind him. But the house was empty, and a full search revealed nothing. Alan gave up and switched on the television.

Later that evening, the cat got up and walked out of the room and Alan was reminded of his funny, soaking little friend Delia. Not that Delia and the cat were alike, except that both had a similar way of moving, a fact which amused him. Looking on his list of numbers, Alan dialled Delia's.

There was no reply but eventually an answerphone kicked in and asked him — in rather husky tones — to leave a message. He replaced the receiver, undecided, wondering why he felt so alarmed. Where could she be, and why would she be out on a Sunday evening? But after all, she was single and attractive and that wretched Krasinski was after her. Maybe that was it. Perhaps it was just plain jealousy kicking in.

Alan grabbed the phone and dialled her number again.

* * *

With a pain in her head as if it had been used as a football by some street urchin, Delia woke to hear the phone. Two nights ago she had fallen on those wretched stairs and cut herself, and had staggered into bed. Presumably she had been there ever since. And now the phone was going, and she could hear Alan's voice on the answerphone. He who had brought her home so gallantly when she had had *more than a drop in* — a lovely saying that, she thought. Pulling herself together and with a certain determination which she had always rather lacked, Delia rang his number.

"My dear girl, there you are. Have you recovered from your recent outing?"

"Yes, I have indeed. It was very kind of you to give me a lift back."

"Think nothing of it. It was my pleasure. Actually . . ." He trailed off.

"Yes?"

"Actually I was going to say, would you like to do it again? Explore the mystery that you seem to be uncovering about Miss Lind."

She gasped with pleasure, although she really didn't know quite why. "Yes, yes, I'd love to. When did you have in mind?"

"How about tomorrow? Does that fit in with your social calendar?"

"Oh yes, yes it does. But where can we meet? I mean . . . we live so far apart."

"Nonsense," Alan lied gallantly. "I'm staying in my little cubby hole at the moment. I'll come by taxi and collect you."

It was a bit of a bore, having to leave his lovely house, but as he was locking up the cat came strolling down the grand staircase in a leisurely manner.

"I hope you've got something to eat," he said to it, "because I'm off to town and I'll be away a couple of nights."

It winked its eye again and Alan bent down to stroke its head. "Have you got a name?" he asked.

The cat did not respond but made its way to the kitchen, where it stood expectantly.

"Dammit. This is emotional blackmail. Go back to your real owners," he said sternly. Then he opened a small tin of salmon and put it on a saucer as a gesture of good faith.

* * *

No sooner had she put the receiver down than the phone rang again.

"Hello," said a voice that was instantly recognisable. "Are you in, or just going out?"

"I'm in but going out shortly. Where are you?"

"At the bottom of your horrible staircase. May I come up please?"

For a Pole he had mastered the nuances of the English language to perfection. Delia laughed, despite the fact that she had a large sticking plaster on her head. "Of course you can."

A minute later, he knocked. "What's this bloody mess here?" He pointed to where she had fallen the other night and left a smear of blood on the stair rail.

"Sorry, I overlooked it. I promise to clean up tomorrow."

From behind his back Justyn produced a bunch of flowers. "Something nice to look at. Smells good, too."

"Justyn, are you being kind to me?"

"I am always kind to beautiful young women."

"And don't we all know it," called a voice from the bottom of the stairs and Delia looked down to see Miss T in full flight upwards. Fortunately, the Polish singer saw the funny side and gave the woman a huge hug when she reached the top.

"Sadly, my darling, you are not included on my list."

"Just as well I imagine," Miss T answered brightly, chucking him under the chin, just a fraction painfully. Justyn continued to smile, his lips growing slightly more tense. Delia, meanwhile, was mentally rapidly going through her drinks supply and wondering if there was enough to go around. But she need not have worried. No sooner had she poured Miss T a meagre draft of port — found lurking at the bottom of a bottle left over from Christmas — than there was another pealing of the bell.

"I think it's Alan," she said to the others.

Miss T made a dramatic mouth but Justyn merely chuckled and said, "I might have guessed."

Trying really hard to remain calm, Delia made her way to the front door to be greeted by an enormous bunch of flowers with Alan's hand holding on to it.

"I hear you've got company," he said. "Shall I go away?"

She shook her head. "No, please don't do that. I've really been looking forward to your coming."

From the living room came the sounds of Justyn laughing and Miss T joining in, though not as heartily. Alan pulled a semi-serious face.

"I'm not sure that they like each other," Delia whispered.

Alan grinned. "I'm sure that they don't."

"Oh, well." And Delia walked into the living room saying, "Alan's here", very brightly.

There were two reactions. Miss T looked momentarily bug-eyed and then gave the newcomer a beaming smile. Justyn, on the other hand, smiled his very own special grin and winked a dark-blue eye, then slowly rose to his feet and put his arms around Alan's shoulders.

"It's good to see you, my friend," he said.

Alan's small and modest beer drained the party dry, but they moved with great determination to a bar situated pleasingly near Delia's home, where they proceeded to down several glasses of wine each. However, eventually the impromptu gathering broke up and Miss T and Justyn drifted off in separate taxis. Alan resolutely climbed Delia's sinister staircase and stood in the doorway, obviously wanting to be invited in.

"I can't stay long," he said. "There's just something I want to tell you."

"Oh? What's that?"

"It's about my house. I know you don't know the area but it is within hailing distance of Hastings — no, that's not quite true, actually it would take a very loud shout — but I thought you might like to visit it."

"I'd love to — I love old houses. Tell me, when was yours built?"

"In 1754, by an old roué called Lord Basil Fountain. There's no record of his marriage so my guess is that he lived a life devoted to pleasure."

"How wonderful!"

"I suppose so — though one could become bored with it in the end, I imagine."

"I imagine one could apply that to anything," Delia answered slowly, opening a bottle of wine she had bought in the bar and carried upstairs in case Alan had wanted any more.

"You're not driving?" she asked, laughing but serious, before she handed him the glass.

"No, ma'am. I shall taxi it back to my cubby hole and fall asleep immediately."

"So what is it you wanted to tell me about the house?"

"It has a presence. I'm not joking. I heard them the other afternoon."

Delia felt herself grow tense. "What do you mean exactly?"

"It was so brief I thought I might have imagined it — but I know I didn't."

"What happened?"

"It was terribly quick. A couple — man and woman — were talking. And then they laughed."

"Is that all?"

"Yes. I know you will think I dreamt it, but I didn't. To make it more intriguing, they were speaking together in French."

"What did they say?"

"Goodness, you sound like a quiz organiser. I'm not a master of languages but I know it was French and that's all I can tell you."

"I'm sorry. But I thought you seemed rather anxious when you spoke about it."

"Well, I wasn't. Not much, that is. I personally am only slightly uneasy at the thought of my occupying the house in the company of talkative Frenchmen."

He said it with such a straight face that Delia wondered if she had upset him. Then she saw that his lovely grin was appearing and felt infinitely relieved. So relieved, in fact, that she drank a great mouthful of wine and felt much better. Alan smiled.

"So — now you are aware that you might bump into somebody gesticulating wildly — when are you coming to see me?"

"It will have to be a Sunday."

"Or a Saturday night. If you can get the 20.05 train from Charing Cross I can pick you up at the station."

"I could leave early, before the curtain call. Provided no one has fallen over and I have to go on."

Alan's face was a study. "When I wrote the show I never gave the people who slaved away in the background much thought."

Delia grinned. "It was ever thus. Do you think Wagner considered his singers' comfort."

"You're hardly comparing me with the Great Man, are you?"

"Yes. Why not?"

"The reasons why not are too profound to discuss further. Now, are you coming or is the thought too nerve-wracking?"

"I shall do my very best to be there."

"I look forward immensely to entertaining you."

And he nodded his head as he kissed her hand.

CHAPTER EIGHTEEN

Delia — Present Day

It seemed that Fate was on her side. Nobody had a costume that needed taking in, out, up, or was unwearable. As for the men, luck was really on the seamstress's side: not one zip was refusing to go up or down, in or out, or sideways — or even malfunction, a favourite trick of the ballet boys after a series of grand jetes in one of the ballroom scenes. They would laugh and put their hand over their privates, saying ,"Oh lovey, I've done it again." And Delia would laugh back at the woebegone faces as the boys stood in their underpants and talked shop. Occasionally, she would pick up pieces of gossip.

"That Alan, do you think . . . ?"

"Could be. He lives alone apparently."

"He's been married, so I'm told. His wife was killed in a motoring accident."

"Then there's hope for us all."

The closing remark always left the question of Alan's sexual preference open and tonight Delia had decided to leap to his defence should his name come up.

It did.

"I'm going to visit him shortly, by the way."

"Sorry, lovey, we were only messing about. When is this?"

"Tonight, if I can get my train."

"Ooh, I say. Well, good luck then."

"We shall be ghost hunting," said Delia, trying desperately to look severe.

"Oh, is that what they call it nowadays? Well, good luck, sweetie."

And the ballet boys trooped out, leaving Delia alone with her thoughts.

Fortunately, there were no further calls on her expertise and she was able to pack her things up and have a brief word with the stage manager, who gave his permission rather sourly — or so she thought — when she asked whether she could leave early. But he grunted "yes" in a sullen voice and Delia whirled out of the theatre before he could change his mind. She got a taxi to Charing Cross and dodged her way through the crowd who, unhelpfully, always seemed to be standing in her path. And then she was chugging through a brilliantly lit London and wishing that she had brought an elegant suitcase with her rather than the tatty old rucksack she had strapped on her back.

After a good many miles the train passed through Tunbridge Wells, where a great mass of people got out, and then gained speed on its way to Wadhurst. Clutching her unattractive ruck-sack, which had decided to slip half off her back and halfway down her arm, Delia got out and looked anxiously up the dimly lit platform. He was there, standing under a lamp, peering at the passengers passing.

"I'm here," she called, and he turned on her a look she had never seen from him before. It was so welcoming, so lovely, that tears sprang into her eyes and in that moment she knew that she must do her very best for him and never let him down if she could possibly help it. Alan hurried forward and at that moment, the rucksack broke free and hit him in the chest.

"I see that you travel in style," he said, and laughed before giving her a brotherly kiss on the cheek. Deep inside, Delia felt disappointed and decided that something would have to be done about the situation. That thought crept in again as they approached his car. It was a Porsche, a neat affair, sturdily built and ready to take on the challenge of Sussex roads. Delia was so overcome by its compact design that she automatically did one of her beautiful curtsies.

"I'm sorry," she said, straightening up. "It is something I do when I pay my full respects. My mother taught me, it's a sort of instinct now."

"Think nothing of it," Alan answered. "People do it to me all the time."

"Really?"

"Oh yes. As I walk along I can hear them mutter, ''Ere, ain't that the bloke wot writes them funny musicals? No, that's the other one, the rich one.'"

"What's the name of your house?" she asked, changing the subject.

"Rosehurst Place. It's been very grand in its day, but some recent owners have let it slip a bit."

"Which you are hastily putting to rights, I believe."

"As quickly as my bank manager will allow."

The car turned into a drive which had once been spectacular. Trees, preparing for spring, lurched together in a great weaving tapestry, with here and there a leaf unfurling to advertise the colour which was to follow. Delia, clutching her rucksack once more, leaned her head back so that she could see the stark loveliness that the glare of the car's lights revealed.

"I like your place already," she said.

Alan did not answer, glancing at her as she sat entranced by the miracle that nature had in store, noticing the glow of her hair in the flickering light, the lift of her small but determined chin, and deciding that he liked it very much indeed. In fact, as he drove along he had felt a warmth for her that he could not explain. Then he suddenly turned left — almost forgetting where they were going — and the house came into view.

"Oh my goodness," she whispered, and — lit as it was by a flickering moon that had finally decided to make an appearance — Alan could only agree.

The house stood mysterious and white and quite magnificent in its ageing glory; so much so that Alan felt his heartbeat quicken. The house definitely needed another coat of paint, particularly where the group of would-be rock wonders had attacked a wall and painted it the colour of sick. But Delia was looking beyond all that, her face enraptured, as she breathed the words, "It's so beautiful."

Alan quite literally felt a melody fly into his head and out again and knew that it was the start of a great and marvellous musical, and that all he had to do was concentrate and it would come back to him. He turned to look at Delia, but she had already got out of the car and was running towards the house with an expression of wonderment. Alan gave a quiet chuckle at her patent enthusiasm as he turned the key in the lock.

They stood in the magnificent entrance hall — on which Alan had spent a fair amount of money — and she gasped at its breathtaking lines.

"It's gorgeous," she said. "I had no idea you lived in a palace."

"Dear girl, it's eating up my money. Previous tenants left it in a hell of a mess and I'm afraid I can't live with that. I had and shall have to put it right, even if it costs me."

"I'm so glad," she answered.

"Come into the living room. I've laid a fire which should roar into flames in a second or two. Or would you rather see your bedroom? You must excuse me. I really am the most terrible kind of host."

They were standing, speaking, and not a bottle had been opened, drunk or touched, when they both heard a distinct sound coming from the first floor. A man and a woman laughed, briefly and joyously, and then were silent. Alan stared, as did Delia.

"Have you got someone staying?" she whispered.

He shook his head. "No, I haven't. Other than a very talented and clever wardrobe mistress. Look, I could pretend that I heard nothing — but that wouldn't be true. I do hear them occasionally, laughing and chattering. I've tried looking them up, but they weren't residents here and I think they must have popped in and visited whoever was. That's the only explanation I can offer for it."

"Were they English?"

Alan shook his head. "I don't think so. When they talk I could swear it is in French."

Delia grinned. "It sounds like yo-ho-ho and a bottle of rum. They were probably smugglers."

"You're more than likely right. Anyway, that is all they get up to. Converse — and giggle. I have never seen either of them and I don't particularly want to. Now, will you be all right with this or do you want me to go and book you into a pub nearby?"

"And not talk to this elegant gentleman?" Delia asked, and bending down began to stroke the cat.

"Ah yes. It arrived when I moved in and has been around ever since. I rather like him."

"What's his name?"

"I haven't quite decided. What do you think?"

"Sylvester — after that great big brute in the cartoon."

Alan looked puzzled. "I don't remember that."

"Yes, you do. My mother used to watch it, pretending that I was a fan."

"Surely that was Tom and Jerry?"

Delia paused, looking thoughtful. "Perhaps it was. Then who was Sylvester? 'I am that great big puddy tat, Sylvester is my name.'"

Alan laughed. "You do that awfully well. Missing teeth and all."

"Thank you. It's my party special."

"Well, special guest, what can I get you to drink? Do you like champagne?"

"My mother always told me it was the first drink I had. The midwife put her finger in the glass and then into my mouth."

"What a wise move. Here, Little Princess, a full glass for you."

As Alan handed it to her his hand briefly touched hers, and Delia felt herself loving the sensation; that clever hand that could produce wonderful music and set audiences alight. She let out a slightly Sylvesterish sigh and Alan smiled.

After supper he played what he called *background music*, and they talked quietly. Sounding plaintive — though not meaning to — Delia told him of the bad dream she had had about the cold sea at Hastings and how her mother had featured in it.

"What worried me, Alan, was that she was so cold and miserable."

He stopped playing. "But how can you know that, sweet girl? Was she shaking or crying?"

"No, but she looked unhappy. She really did."

"Well, so would I, standing in the sea up to my oxters. It was only a dream, dear girl. I promise you."

"Really?"

"Really and truly upon mine honour."

"You're so nice," Delia murmured somewhat drunkenly. At that moment the cat let out a particularly loud purr — perhaps to disguise an escape of wind — and its new owners both laughed.

"And so are you," said Alan, then severely to the cat, "And there's no need to accentuate everything we say."

Sylvester lay motionless, but one of his ears flicked forward. Delia, watching him, said, "Perhaps he can hear things that we cannot."

"And no doubt you will hear things in the night. All old houses have their sounds. But there is nothing malignant or to be scared of. Old wood creaks as it settles down, chimney places sigh, the wind can produce some ghastly moans if you listen to it on a stormy night. And don't forget the couple in the guest room."

"You remind me of my mother. She could nag me horribly sometimes."

Alan stared at her. "Well, I've been called a few things in my time, but somebody's mother is a new one!"

Delia, who was sitting on the floor, completely relaxed, suddenly came to full attention.

"Oh Alan, I'm sorry. I didn't mean to be rude. Please forgive me."

"There's nothing to forgive. You're young and talented and you're very good with your needle . . ."

"You mean I stick it in quite neatly?"

"No, I didn't mean that at all. Can't we talk peacefully? I often imagine sitting at ease with someone and just enjoying the murmur of voices."

At that moment there was a sound from upstairs. It was like a loud laugh, a good-natured shout from someone who was being teased or tickled. It was quite distinct.

Delia looked at Alan. "Was that them?"

He looked slightly uncomfortable. "Yes. I'm sorry. The couple in the blue room are showing off."

"It's better than living alone. I suppose."

He shrugged, looking suddenly young and foolish and love-able. "I haven't a clue who they were. This was way back. When I bought the place the estate agent passed it off as some sort of joke, but it scared me witless the first few times I heard them. I know little more about it than that. Honestly, darling, I don't step out of my room and they quite definitely stay in theirs. I did find out one thing. The lady of the house kept a diary at the time. And it referred to a Mr C begging a night's shelter because he was catching a train the next day. There was no mention of his lady love."

Delia slipped a comforting hand into his and they both felt the impact. "And they're not harmful?" she said to cover the sudden silence.

"Not in the least," Alan answered, and gave her the kiss he had been contemplating all the evening.

It was as powerful a thing as either of them had ever experienced. The only thought going through Delia's mind was why had she waited so long for this exquisite embrace to happen. Alan's was far more down to earth. He hated being on his own and had been looking around for some company when Delia had first caught his eye. He had thought her too magic a little creature to make love to anyone — but that had been as terrible a mistake as a man could make. She was born for passion. And Alan, quiet ordinary little Alan, blazed with it.

They drew apart and stared at one another, not saying a word. In any case, there was not a word that could have summed up that moment. They kissed as if they had always known they would — and they looked at each other in a warm and loving glow.

"Oh Delia, I wish I had done this weeks ago."

"No," she answered wisely, shaking her knot of red hair, "it would have been wrong. Believe me, this is the right time for us."

"You fairy creature. Despite the ghostly couple who dwell in the haunted bedroom, may I take you upstairs?"

"You most certainly can."

And they made their unhurried way upwards.

CHAPTER NINETEEN

Jenny — Past

Chopin could not remember when he had felt so angry. Normally he was a quiet being, although he enjoyed conversing and meeting people. At his highest point he enjoyed being the centre of attention, at his lowest he let others do the talking. But at the moment he thought that he would scream aloud and hit the woman who was chattering away in that ridiculous voice, a cross between a highly educated Highland accent and mincingly spoken French. He had to wheel around and stare out of the window at the fog-laden atmosphere before him in order to control himself. Trees dripped miserably, birds shivered in their nests, even the blades of grass had drops of clinging mist attached.

". . . so what do you think of that idea, eh, sir? You will adore Lord Wegulinchaps, I promise you. He's all abuzz to meet you. Of course, he has never . . ." — Miss Stirling took a breath and cast her well-bred features into a smile — "actually heard you play. No, the poor dear has been housebound these twelve years past but loves to hear chitter-chatter, you know the way it is with the older folk."

Chopin dropped his raised hands and clasped them before him. "No. I don't actually. I have had little experience of the senior set."

"Well, they are very dependent on us visitors to keep them lively. They love conversing about the old days and the old ways and, of course, their many and dead relations. Once they get started there is no stopping them, the poor sweet things."

Chopin cleared his throat, rather noisily, but made no further comment. He wondered, briefly, if he was going to drop dead and finally be free of that pair of women who haunted him and yet on whom he leaned so heavily. *For what other way out is there?* he thought grimly. If he married Jenny — and, oh how he would love that — he would have to live in a style he couldn't afford, because her earnings were enormous in comparison to his poor pittance. Life was so bloody unfair at times.

". . . and poor Lord Torphichen is down with a terrible cold — which the poor darling does definitely not deserve. What do you think, Mr Chopin? You're very quiet today."

But hope was pouring into the musician's bones as he caught sight of a rider plodding miserably through the fog. It had to be — and indeed it was — the post boy aboard an unseemly looking hack. And — may the Lord be thanked and praised — the animal was stopping wearily outside the front door. The boy slithered to the ground and presented a pile of letters to the servant who answered. The musician let out an audible sigh of hope as they were taken inside. He turned to Miss Jane.

"Please excuse me, Madam. I see that the post has arrived and I am expecting a letter. I do hope you don't find me rude."

And that said, he bolted down the vast flight of stairs and approached the highly polished servant. The man thumbed through the letters and picked one out, which he handed to the composer who stood silently, giving him such an earnest stare.

"Most kind. Thank you," Chopin said, his few words of English coming out with pride. Then he turned and raced upstairs to the quietness of his room where he flung himself on the bed and opened it.

It was from Jenny, of course it was, and it was written in French so that the composer had no trouble in reading the message. Which he did, a dozen or so times, before finally dropping off into a delightful and deliciously deep sleep.

* * *

They met in Edinburgh, where Miss Lind had hired a suite of rooms in a charming hotel. Chopin had — not without a great deal of difficulty — extricated himself from the two Scots women, who were tight-lipped in their annoyance that anyone should want to take their leave of the beauties of Torphichen — after all, was not my lord the brother-in-law of Miss Jane? — and go off to that den of iniquity in the lowlands. Patiently, Chopin had pointed out that he had to raise some money and been greeted by a snort — yes, an actual snort — of derision. Finally, his transport had arrived and he and Daniel made their way into its cheerful confines.

"Thank God I am still of sound mind," said Chopin, as soon as the wheels started to turn. "Those two ladies have to be the most boring females on God's Earth bar none."

"They are not exactly lightweight," answered Daniel.

"And that is putting it mildly." Fryderyck sighed and shook his head from side to side. "It was ever thus," he added — and smiled a trifle wearily.

But Jenny was so excited and eager to be in Chopin's company that she hardly knew how to control herself at Edinburgh station, where she and the redoubtable Mrs Grote were awaiting his arrival. Fortunately, there was virtually nothing one could do or say that would shock the married lady, she who wore scarlet tights and glinting jackets, and Fryderyck had no hesitation in grasping her firmly to his bosom.

"Say yes," she murmured into his ear before breaking away from him. Chopin stared at her, wondering what she meant. But no further words were spoken and shortly afterwards the woman took her leave, leaving the pianist in a state of doubt.

"Now," said Jenny, "are you prepared for the worst?"

Chopin went suddenly immensely pale. "You want to put an end to our affair?"

"No, my darling idiotic man. On the contrary. I want to strengthen it."

"But how can we do that?"

The great singer for once looked coy, an unbecoming flush rising in her cheeks.

"Well, how do you think?"

Chopin stared blankly. "I don't follow what you are getting at."

She stamped her foot in temper. "Oh, really! How can you act so stupidly?"

"Oh, darling. How can you be so angry? I don't know what I'm doing wrong. Tell me now and I shall stop it immediately."

"I want to marry you, you horrible and cruel wretch. I have never loved anyone in the way I love you. I loved Mendelssohn with all my heart but even his memory is dimmed by thoughts of you. Oh, Fryderyck, make me the happiest woman in the world and marry me."

He stared at her in blank horror. If she had been an ordinary mortal — a singer trying to make her way in the competitive world of singing — he would have proposed himself, long ago, but instead this hugely formidable creature, tiny but packed with enough talent for a dozen of them, had arrived to tease and delight him.

"No, darling, it would never work."

He could not have said anything worse. Jenny's usually sweet face glared into his with an expression he had never seen before.

"Why do you say that? What would stop it?"

"The fact that you are earning three — no, four — times as much as I am."

Convinced he was speaking the truth, Chopin clutched Jenny in a grip far tighter than he had intended, almost squeezing the breath out of her. Visions of the past rushed up to overpower him. The lingering smell of hashish which had always wafted around the presence of George Sand, who was rarely without a cigar. Those large eyes had followed him everywhere, *lovingly* he had first thought; *greedily* had come second. And to think he was comparing that lump of demanding womanhood with the naughty kicking little creature in his arms.

"Oh, my God!" he exclaimed and burst into a sudden fit of weeping, clutching Jenny to his heart as if she would always stay there. "I love you so much."

Secretly, she smiled. She knew she had won the day but she must never let him think so. After all, what did money matter? It was just something you earned and should never be taken seriously. It should not be too long before the announcement could be made to the entire world. *Miss Jenny Lind, the renowned Swedish soprano, will shortly be marrying the distinguished Polish composer, Mr Fryderyck Franciszek Chopin.* Would she wear bridal white? Yes, why not? Her triumph was complete.

She wriggled a little in his arms and her dress rode up a fraction, revealing that her rather frosty steel-coloured garment was hiding a vivid pink slip. She felt, rather than saw, his glance and when this was followed by a rapid intake of breath, she smiled.

He was speaking. "This reminds me of something that happened when I was a boy of about eight or nine. My father had taken me to play before an elderly titled lady, I am fairly certain it was an older Countess Radziwill. She was in her country residence which turned out to be a large strange cottage, rush-roofed, you could smell the lovely harmonious odour wherever you went. Anyway, she asked me to play some gentle music and I did so. It was the most extraordinary experience. I felt that crystal was falling from my fingers and the whole thing was turning into one of the most wonderful sounds I had ever produced. I started to cry and the old lady joined in and we sat sobbing like a couple of old fools."

"It must have been brilliant, like a great happening, the sort of thing one remembers with pleasure always."

"It was," answered Chopin, shifting her dress up a little more so that the vivid pink shone before his eyes. "Believe me, it was."

Later that day there followed one of the most beautiful acts of lovemaking possible. Brave little Jenny allowing herself to be stripped slowly and beautifully, each new place being revealed greeted with Chopin's wonderful kisses, starting slowly and working up to a frenzy of salutation. As for him, inch by inch, his clothes were removed, till he stood above her, naked and bare, except for a certain part which was fully erect.

"Oh, my darling," he said, "nobody will ever love you more, nobody in the whole world. Do you understand me?"

She nodded. "Yes, my darling, I understand perfectly. You are my favourite lover and my future husband."

Chopin hesitated a moment before consummation. "You are certain of that?"

"As certain as one can be about anything."

And then a sexual fantasy embraced the couple and for a while they were lost to this world.

"I love you," Jenny breathed. And Chopin answered her with a mighty shout as he climaxed deeply, then lay perfectly still, quite incapable of making another move.

CHAPTER TWENTY

Jenny — Past

"Of course," that voice was saying in a high-pitched French monologue, "we're all going to have the merriest time with old Lady Barchinski. One may wonder — of course, one would wonder — on hearing her name to think of her in her magnificent dwelling, living alone and existing mainly on onion soup, but believe me she is the merriest soul for many a mile around. Ha ha ha!"

Chopin thought that he should rather leave the room than strike Miss Jane Stirling who — yet again — was taking him out to meet her family, the upper class of Scottish high society, none of whom spoke French except for in laboured sentences followed by a great deal of huffing and puffing and *Mon Dieu*-ing. He considered it the most horrible torment he could endure but from somewhere he had to conjure a smile and a look of interest, this being harder and harder to do.

Today they were taking several coaches to ferry several people, all willing to make the slog to Lady Falsewig's establishment — as Daniel had wickedly described her and her dwelling. On this occasion Chopin was allowed to have his manservant as his travelling companion, so that they could gossip together to their hearts' content. After considering the matter for a while Miss Stirling

— who sat in deep judgement on this fine point of etiquette —
had nodded and agreed to the unusual arrangement, then taken
off surrounded by her widowed sister and various other females
all speaking in laboured French punctuated with Scottish cries of
enthusiasm.

Chopin turned to Daniel, ready for a good chat.

"Does this nation do nothing but have sex? For example,
their conversation is mainly on who begat whom, and then he
begat, and he begat and he begat, and so on for two pages till you
come to Jesus. How do they find the time for normal living?"

His servant laughed uproariously. "Perhaps they don't.
Perhaps they just lie on couches, rapidly twitching their kilts to
one side and begetting like mad."

"Small wonder that there are so many of them about."

Chopin sighed. His beloved had gone off on tour; he had
seen nothing of her for several weeks and now had grown positively to hate the position he was in. He had got to the point of
feeling himself kidnapped by the two formidable Scots women.
That the younger of the two was in love with him was glaringly
obvious to the entire universe, though she would deny it with
a smile that suggested, *I would like to tell you all but I can't.*
Nothing could have been less to his liking. Yet because of his
terrible financial position he was forced to accept their charita-
ble kindness. And he hated it. Furthermore, he had grown very
anxious about the thought of whether he should marry Jenny. It
was not that he didn't love her — he did, with all his heart. Yet he
had been brought up to believe that the man of the relationship
should be earning the money. To accept it from a woman would
show poor spirit indeed. Yet, what other choice had he? He knew
that the love of his life with her tight, sweet figure, her glorious
voice, her kindness and goodness of heart, had set her mind
on him and that nothing — short of a blunt refusal — would

change her from her purpose. He gave a deep and heartfelt sigh and turned his attention back to Daniel.

They chattered amiably, telling each other the latest gossip and laughing at some of the ruder parts when, with a horrible lurch, their coach pitched forward, their horse let out a loud scream of fear, and the poor driver vanished into the mists of the afternoon.

"Good God," said Chopin, torn between weeping and screeching with laughter. "I think we've tipped up."

Daniel looked at him. "Probably it's time for begating."

"Of course," Chopin shouted as they hurtled to the bottom of a small embankment. "First things must come first."

After a rapid rescue, which was conducted by Miss Jane Stirling in person, white of cheek and trembling with emotion, Chopin, who was by then near to tears with suppressed laughter, was hauled out grinning madly. Jane started to speak.

"Oh now, dear Mr Chopin. Are you injured or hurt in any way?"

"I don't believe so," he answered, patting himself. "I'll let you know if I develop any symptoms."

Beside him, Daniel bellowed a laugh, which was totally inappropriate in the company of an elderly virgin. Miss Stirling went an even more vivid shade of white but neither Chopin nor Daniel noticed, being too busy roaring with jollity.

The rest of the afternoon followed in its established ritual. Jammed into another coach with a bevy of ancient ladies, all of whom were trying to speak French, Chopin felt desperately in need of some stimulant and practically snatched a bevy from the hand of a glass-eyed man who had joined the company and was smiling at everyone with slipping teeth.

The end came after Chopin had seized the glass with much relief and downed the contents, only to bend double and shout something untranslatable in Polish. The piping voice of Miss Stirling informed him that it was a glass of medicine which the old boy carried around with him "just in case". After the initial shock, Chopin rapidly ordered another one and proceeded to get amusingly drunk, reciting Polish poetry to anyone who cared to listen. Which turned out to be practically everyone present, who tittered and lost their teeth and steamed up their eagle-eyed monocles and generally had a damn good time with such an entertaining little fellow as Chopin giggling and dancing before them all.

Jane Stirling made the best of it and pretended to join the fun but deep within she wondered what God would have thought of the spectacle of the great Mr Chopin, drunk as a skunk, parodying her beloved deep-rooted Calvinism.

Chopin woke the next morning with a head like a log of wood. Having avoided Miss Stirling as much as possible, he sat down to pen a long letter which he wrote with all his heart.

I am cross and depressed, and people bore me with their excessive attentions. I can't breathe; I can't work; I feel alone, alone, alone, although I am surrounded. Here it's nothing but cousins of great families and great names that no one on the Continent has ever heard of. Conversation is always entirely genealogical, like the Gospels . . .

He laid down his pen and crossed to the window. He was getting out of this place, for the sake of his sanity, for the sake of not throttling one — or both — of those grim sisters with their piping accents, in which they spoke French purely because he did. He must escape — and quickly. He must see his Jenny again, must look at her sweet smiling face, her lovely figure, must kiss her as she deserved. Oh God, even thinking about her was having its usual effect on him.

He must travel to Edinburgh where normal people lived, not whey-faced women with studied French in ridiculous accents, who were madly in love yet striving to be offhand like the former mistress of Nohant. It was more than he could stand.

A quiet word with Daniel sorted things out. Through one of the serving man's contacts a horse and cart — more could not be afforded, Daniel said — would await them on the morrow of the day after next. This would take them back to Edinburgh. Miss Stirling went white when Chopin mentioned it casually at dinner. He could not help smiling. He was very far from sadistic but the sight of her usually tight lips quavering struck a small inner chord and tickled a grin.

"Now, now, Miss Stirling. I have visited all your friends and relations and been as pleasant as possible in view of the paucity of my language. It is time I concentrated on my career, which is in sad need of an overhaul."

The first thing he did once he was free of the place was rush to buy a seat in the stalls for 25 September, on which date his beloved was singing the lead in *La Sonnambula*. Oh God, it was just so wonderful to be able to see her on his own, to gaze with rapture into her glorious crystal eyes. Though that would have to wait until after curtain call. He hoped that this message came through to her, after all he was wearing a coat lined with deep-pink silk. A colour they both loved to put on when together.

* * *

Her dressing room was packed with people, all artificial and neigh-ing into champagne glasses, but there among the usual throng of theatregoers were the good Polish faces of Princess Marcelina and her glittering husband. Even looking at them, Chopin felt his spir-its lift. He bowed formally to the prince and kissed the princess's capable hand.

"Looking at you like this makes me feel Polish again."

"Oh Fryderyck, don't tell me you're turning into a Scotsman?"

"I would, if a certain person had her way."

The princess, who had at one time been Fryderyck's pupil, looked askance. "You don't mean . . . Surely you can't . . ."

He nodded silently.

"Then more fool you for having let yourself get in such a position."

Chopin pulled a face. "It was thrust upon me. But no more of that dull talk. Here comes our great soprano."

And he simultaneously bowed and kissed the outstretched hand.

What gave the Polish princess the clue, heaven alone could tell. Yet she knew as certainly as if it had been printed in a book that the greatest singer in the world and one of the greatest composers of living memory were madly in love with one another. And she was pleased, delighted for them both, and because she was a kind princess and liked people to be happy, she exclaimed aloud "Oh good!"

But neither Jenny nor Fryderyck suspected anything, so deep in that initial embrace that they could have been on the moon for all they knew. And afterwards when all the fans had gone and every invited guest had left — with the exception of one — the way that the Swedish girl slowly and enticingly slipped out of her clothes, and poor Fryderyck — rather ashamed of his extreme thinness — after a few minutes of uncertainty entered the place in which he was the most capable in the world and moved himself rhythmically.

This was the start of a magnificent few days. In the experienced hands of Muir Wood — the Broadwood manager — the very elite of Edinburgh's and Glasgow's West End, to mention nothing of the queens of beauty and fashion, attended the matinée on Wednesday, 27 September at the Merchants' Hall. Curtain up was delayed by thirty minutes to accommodate the arriving carriages. Finally, Chopin made his appearance, looking fragile in a pale grey suit, including a frock coat of identical tint. Then he sat down at the Broadwood piano and the whole room transformed under his spell.

Listening to him that afternoon, Princess Marcelina could hear a whole different timbre in his playing, including episodes of both strength and grandeur. It was as if Chopin was whispering to the audience of strings of pearls and beauty and perfumed zephyrs. *The man is in love*, she thought, and smiled, determined to find out as much as she could.

The exuberant dinner at Johnstone Castle, which followed, was given in honour of the prince and princess. Chopin whispered in answer to a question as to why the Scots women had not joined him, "Alas, Katherine is for ever bereaved. Jane for ever a spinster. Black-clad sufferers, they live a life where the enjoyment of the moment is to be borne but not indulged."

The royal looked knowingly, nodding her head in sympathy.

"They are both very religious women. Mrs Katherine comes after me regularly with the Psalms. It seems that the other world is better than this one."

"And what about the sister? The one who makes wide eyes at you whenever she has the chance."

"You may well ask. Thomas Carlyle — please do not quote me — calls her a 'hoarse-voiced old bore.'"

"Really?" asked the wide-eyed princess, nudging her husband who was deep in conversation with another guest but looked up and said, "What is so funny?"

"Nothing really. Just that Fryderyck has a new admirer."

"Ah, you mean the mysterious figure, heavily swathed in wrappers, who left the minute the concert was done."

"So she *was* here," breathed Fryderyck, looking ecstatic.

"Indeed she was," answered the laughing princess.

After that, with Jenny disappearing rapidly, obviously off to some other engagement, Fryderyck was left with no choice but to head for Keir House near Dunblane, owned by yet another of Jane Stirling's relations. This was pitiful, as every living creature observed the Sabbath day and Fryderyck found himself included. He wrote: *Perth Shire. Sunday. No post, no railway, no carriage (even for a walk); not a boat, nor even a dog to whistle to.*

He had another worry, too. His lungs were getting so congested that he could now no longer climb stairs. So when he went to stay with yet another of the interminable relatives of Miss Stirling he had to have Daniel carry him upstairs and undress him and put him to bed as if he were a suckathumb child. But not when he was alone and in raptures with his darling nightingale, she would help him undress — in fact it gave her enormous pleasure to do so. Oh, what a woman she was — and thinking of her made him give an involuntary shudder of delighted memory.

And yet he worried unceasingly about marriage. She was determined to wed him and — very importantly — later give birth to his children. "Can you not see them, darling heart? I can, as clearly as if they were standing beside me. Oh, don't look so sad, sweetheart. If you marry me all your troubles will be over because I will earn enough to support us and whatever children we care to produce. And that's a promise."

But it did not comfort him. In fact — if anything — it made him feel worse. The congestion of his lungs was making its presence felt in front of the other guests. They were as kindly as they knew how to be, eating and drinking both heartily and noisily while he ate a mouthful of meat and sipped a very small glass of wine. After a couple of hours of this torture Chopin had to make his way to the drawing room, where he uttered the occasional witty remark. The ladies all listened to him, perched around the room, heads cocked like a nest of robins, little exclamations of wonderment, cooing noises as they murdered the French language and jumped on its dying form. But through it all his secret love affair continued to prosper and his incomparable Jenny remained madly in love with him, particularly while helping him remove his close-fitting garments and giving a cry of pleasure at what she saw.

CHAPTER TWENTY-ONE

Jenny — Past

Chopin had finally decided what was best. He could see the entire situation, there was only one sensible way out. That was by doing the honourable thing and removing himself to London, to escape the fever-bright gaze of the overwhelmingly spinsterish Stirling and that cold fish religious maniac sister of hers, while pleading with the great and beautiful nightingale that he had — as yet — no offer of marriage to give her. Future touring of the great houses of Scotland where he was greeted by the same woman — or this was how he jokingly thought of it — disguised as a deaf old fool, a loud-mouthed poseur or a brilliant half-wit — could not continue. The time had come to make a gracious exit. But he was going out with a roar that they would all remember. A night that would linger unforgotten in anyone's memory.

> *Monsieur Chopin has the honour to announce that he will give a SOIREE MUSICALE in Edinburgh on the evening of Wednesday, 4 October.*

The notices were going up and the bright rich things had arrived in the city for the Caledonian Rout; a week of drunkenness,

over-loud laughter, balls and hidden sexual intercourse whenever possible. Chopin travelled to the capital to stay at his poste
restante in Warriston Crescent with Adam Lyszczynski, a Polish
homeopathic doctor who had remained in Scotland and enjoyed
the life there.

The weather was warm, the sun was out and Chopin breathed
more deeply than he had for an age. He spoke Polish to his host
and retired to bed early, for tomorrow was to be set aside for saying
a brief— so he hoped — farewell to Miss Lind. He knew that she
was going to try with all her might to persuade him to marry her.
And when Jenny tried hard, it was very difficult to resist her. And
the one thing he really disliked was resisting Jenny.

Chopin's health, however, concerned him bitterly. In the
mornings he would cough until he thought his guts would leave
him, then, having calmed down a little during the day, at night
he became so congested that he had to be carried like a baby,
because climbing the stairs was beyond him. Dare he take on the
warmth and consuming love that Jenny was begging him to have?
God, how he wanted to — but it would be so unfair, saddling
that wondrous and packed-with-talent person with the burden
of caring for an invalid. He could not do it to her, Lord give him
strength to resist.

They met at noon, he — dressed head to foot in dove grey
— going to her apartment in a nearby hotel. She took one look at
him, her eyes widening, and said, "I never realised how handsome
you actually are. Did Daniel dress you?"

"Good God, no. I dressed myself, Miss Lind. And what of
you, Swedish Nightingale? Surely your maid helped you?"

But Jenny did not answer. Smiling mischievously, she lovingly peeled the clothes off him till at last he stood in nothing
but his under drawers, which, thankfully, were new and smart
in cut and made of tartan material — a fashion introduced by

Prince Albert. She looked at him closely and he almost blushed. She nodded.

"A good choice, Mr Chopin. Your underwear supports your body and also deliciously maintains certain aspects."

He thanked the heavens silently that even when he was coughing his guts up, nothing had damaged his most privy part.

"And what of yourself, Miss Jenny Lind? Are you corseted in to achieve so fine a figure? Or is it more your pleasure to study a gentleman's under garments?"

"I warned you that I was a theatre child and that we were all of us rude. It was the atmosphere — but I thoroughly enjoyed it."

"Are you challenging me?" he asked.

"Yes, indeed I am, sir."

When she was alluringly and beautifully naked some while later, he stood in his drawers and gazed at her.

"Are you truly mine, sweetheart?"

"For now and always," she answered. "Whatever happens in the future, I will belong to you."

"Then take me, my wonderful girl," he said; and allowing her to slowly and lovingly remove his very new tartan under drawers, he with much love became one with her body.

Much as they hated it, she was catching the evening train to Glasgow, then going on to Dublin.

"So it will be in England when next we meet? Nothing can persuade you to remain in Scotland?" Jenny asked.

"Nothing, my dearest girl. The place has actually nearly killed me. Round and round all those beastly grand houses and castles, with my two ladies watching me like hawks. They are so boring, poor things, that I truly pity them. They wallow in their Calvinism. The old one is always shoving leaflets into my hands on how to improve myself in this world, preparing me for the hereafter. The other one is a martyr to spinsterhood and relishes being so in love with me that one day her corsets are going to burst into bits and her naked fol-de-rols will wobble all over the place."

"Not a pretty sight," responded Miss Lind, sighing.

"As she takes a flying leap at me," Chopin continued, "and I fall coughing to the floor my new drawers will be rent asunder and I shall die of shock and you will pause in the middle of one of your arias and say 'Poor old Chopin's gone, I hear.'"

They both screamed with laughter, so much so that they had to rush to the station and find the train already puffing at the platform.

"Don't forget me when you arrive in Ireland and fall into the clutches of those mighty Irishmen."

She looked at him very straightly. "You will be always in my thoughts."

"How dull for you. Go there and sing, Miss Lind, my own beautiful girl. Go there and sing." And having said that, he kissed her swiftly on the cheek and left.

CHAPTER TWENTY-TWO

Jenny — Past

It was the evening of 4 October and already the Hopetoun Rooms were packed to overflowing. The crowd of excited and noisy people had begun to arrive an hour before the time of the concert's commencement. They were down for the Caledonian Rout, of course, and were having a good time regardless of the fact that nothing had started.

Chopin, showing a great deal of courage, had taken on the responsibility of the programme himself and had hired no supporting artist or singer. It was the last that Scotland would hear of him, and he would give them something to remember for the rest of their lives. He hovered out of sight until the light over the piano came on and the audience burst into prolonged applause.

He looked rather small when he entered, wearing his dove-grey clothes, his hair freshly washed, and feeling quite confident in his new tartan under drawers, which were also washed and clean for the occasion. Already he felt the good humour of the audience, their willing him to do well, and he stood bowing, one hand resting on the piano, and smiling darkly as he thought of Jenny being greeted with shouting, with stamping feet, with cries of "Encore". And then he sat down.

Nobody, including himself, could quite explain what happened after that. There must have been magic in the air, because the audience listened, hardly daring to breathe, lest they should lose a second of his playing. And he transformed from the red-headed little man into a great maestro, someone plucked from the magic ages so that ordinary mortals could hear him. And when, after two whole hours had passed, the entire audience was in tears of joy and laughter as all present were swept back to the days of gold. And big grown men wept unashamedly as the wonderful — no, *brilliant* is the word — music softly died away. Chopin sat at the piano in a moment so intense that he didn't dare breathe. And then he finally looked up, it was to realise that the whole room had risen to its feet and all were applauding without reserve. At last he stood, a neat figure in his dove-grey clothes, his red hair gleaming under the lights, and all he could think of was Jenny Lind, his lover, his woman, his glorious Swedish Nightingale.

After that, it was a brief round of the dreaded castles and stately homes to say farewell. Every old girl he met insisted on playing something or singing at him, one old creature whistling to a squeaking guitar accompaniment. Every performance by everybody always ended with the words 'leik water!' It meant that each representation flowed like water — or so Chopin discovered later.

There had been a frantic scene with Jane Stirling shrieking that there were castles to be visited and people who were longing to meet him. And he really mustn't go back to that filthy London or she would die of shock. Chopin answered, "Well, you can always visit me," then wished that he had kept his mouth shut as a gleam appeared in one of her frantic eyes and she silently mouthed the word 'Yes'.

So that was it. Now he was back in London, and he had an engagement to play at the Guildhall. In a moment of feeling recovered, he sat down and wrote to Jenny Lind and wished to see her as soon as was possibly convenient.

CHAPTER TWENTY-THREE

Delia — Present Day

It was Sunday morning in Hastings. The sun was out — not hot but taking the edge off the greyness; all the Sunday sellers were there in force; the book shops had arranged small stalls outside and the general atmosphere was one of old-fashioned fun. Strolling magnificently through the crowd, his shoulder-length hair gleaming in the sun, catching the eye of absolutely everyone he passed, was a gorgeous young man. He was walking arm in arm with a somewhat older woman, who went by the name of Tinker. She was, in contrast to him, terribly tiny and fragile-looking and obviously adored her companion. Several members of the crowd thought they recognised the man and nudged one another as he strolled past. Then one daring girl stepped out from the rest and said, "Can I have your autograph please, Mr Krasinski?" The crowd round him grew quiet. He stopped walking and gave the girl a very warm glance.

"Of course, my dear. I didn't think anyone would recognise me."

"Go on," a local lad jeered, "after last Saturday I thought you would have been mobbed."

Deryn Lake

And it was true. Justyn Krasinski and the group with whom he who had won the Eurovision Song Contest, had been on Saturday night TV playing their hit song.

"This is my grandmother," Justyn went on, "so you see, I am partially English."

There was a delighted murmur from the crowd and several folded magazines and pieces of paper were thrust forward from autograph-seeking hands.

"I've got a better idea," he announced grandly. "Let's all go to the Jenny Lind and I'll buy the lot of you a drink. That is, if Tinker agrees."

A loud cheer went up and, like children following the Pied Piper, a sizeable crowd followed the young man towards the hostelry, his grandmother nodding meanwhile. It was one of the most memorable moments the Jenny Lind had witnessed in its time. Word was soon out that a famous singer had walked in and the staff were brimming with curiosity. More and more people came from outside, curious and friendly, and all ended up in interested silence when Justyn treated them to a solo number.

Meanwhile, Tinker downed a large gin and listened to all the small talk. Her intelligent eyes were never still, flashing from one person to the next, sharp but smiling, never for a second dull or disinterested by anything or anybody. One aged woman, entering the pub for a light ale, drew back when she saw her and hissed through a mouth with rotting teeth, "I'll not drink with thee," and limped out again. Smilingly, Tinker made a rapid movement with her hand and then asked Justyn to get her another gin whenever he had a spare second.

It was an enjoyable break and afterwards Justyn and his elderly relative disappeared into a taxi to escape the mob and got out near the pier to have an enjoyable lunch.

"Let me tell you about Hastings, dear boy. I think it is quite a captivating town," the grandmother said.

"I don't really know a great deal. But then you probably have found everything out."

Justyn smiled at her. Having been born in Poland he was not particularly interested in British history, but there was something about this grandmother that particularly appealed to him. His other grandma had grown old quickly and now resembled a pickled walnut in the final stages of decay. He had always been slightly embarrassed when she came to the opera, bringing with her an odour like a drain in urgent need of washing out. But this other one — trailing some indefinable and bewitching perfume — was almost magical. He grinned broadly.

"I want you to come and visit me overseas. Which will be quite a change for you."

She looked at him in some surprise. "But you have a place in London. You're not leaving the show, are you?"

She knew immediately, his very silence giving her the answer.

Justyn smiled at her. "There's no need to pull that face, darling. I have had a wonderful offer from Italy and I intend to accept it."

"Oh, but you must," his grandmother responded, rather to his surprise. "It is such a beautiful country. I think you may well fall in love with an Italian woman. But don't listen to her. Always keep your thoughts to yourself."

His eyebrows shot up. "Well, well. I never knew you were psychic. What else do you have to tell me?"

She smiled enigmatically. "Wait and see, dear boy. All in good time, all in good time."

* * *

Delia was reading in bed, a pleasurable pastime, while Alan was wrestling with a really tricky part of his new work, a chorus for young adults set in a mining town in bygone Wales. She could hear him downstairs, fighting with the piano and swearing a bit, while upstairs all was well and the book was rather lovely — and, most importantly, the ghosts of her dreams had gone quiet, seemingly for good.

Earlier that day, Delia had caught the last train from Charing Cross and, as arranged, Alan met her at the station and had driven to his beautiful house, which always seemed to her to have a kind and welcoming atmosphere. But tonight the composer was definitely under a strain and smiled very thinly, looking anxious and unhappy.

"What's the matter?" Delia asked as Alan popped his head around the bedroom door.

"Nothing. That is, not really. It's just that there is some sort of trouble coming from the haunted bedroom. Sorry."

"What kind of trouble? Have you seen anything?"

"No. There's nothing to see. I popped my head around the door — you know what I'm like. What passes for a man is actually a terrified mouse. Anyway, all appeared to be calm within but then I heard this peculiar noise, very quiet but very persistent. It was a woman sobbing — not splashily or noisily — but in genuine and constant misery. I'm afraid I banged the door shut and went downstairs and started the Young Miners' Chorus and hid behind it."

"Oh, darling. Do you want me to have a look?"

"As long as you're not scared, yes please."

Delia put down her book and got out of bed. Having reached the haunted room, she boldly opened the door. Its incredible beauty struck her once again. There was something so fine about its elegant lines and the furnishings, which Alan had left exactly as he had found them. Nothing moved within, there was nothing in there. But then, just as she was going out, she heard it, listening carefully she recognised it as coming from the woman whom she had previously heard shout with love and laugh with pleasure. Presumably the love affair was over, given this terrible sadness.

"I hope you feel better soon," Delia said lamely, feeling as if she was quoting dialogue from a badly written soap opera.

Unbelievably, the weeping stopped; it was as if the woman had paused to listen. And it was then, in the semi-darkness, that Delia saw her. She lay on the bed and for a full minute, she materialised. She was of slim build, hair swept up, small hands and feet, and she had a face that Delia recognised but could not name. Delia stared at her for the whole minute and then the vision started to fade and there was nothing there except the bed covering. It *could* have been an optical illusion — yet Delia knew exactly what she had seen. But who was the woman? And why had that tear-swollen face looked at her so earnestly?

She made her way back to Alan, who was by now downstairs again. As soon as he saw her, Alan stood up and caught her in his arms.

"Darling, are you all right? Did you see anything?"

She nodded. "Yes, very briefly, I saw a woman."

"But who was she?"

"That's just it, Alan. Her face was so familiar. I knew it and yet I couldn't put a name to it. Those lovers must have stayed here."

"What period are you talking about?"

"Let me ponder — and meanwhile, can I have a drink? I need to recover my nerves. Are you all right? You look worried."

He laughed. "No, I'm just thinking how gorgeous you are and how you have mended a huge hole in my life and how much I love you and that you are everything I have ever needed."

"Oh, is that all?" Delia answered and winked over the brim of the wine glass handed to her.

They did not bother with supper but instead climbed up to the haunted bedroom so that Alan could listen from outside.

Before they were even halfway up the stairs, Delia had guessed that the woman had gone for good. Gone to whatever era she had been in when her lover died. Yet the question of who she had once been bothered Delia enormously — because it was a famous face and Delia had known it well, yet she could not name it.

She walked into the previously haunted bedroom, this time quite unafraid. The atmosphere had changed. It was more peaceful. The ghosts had gone. Yet try as she would, Delia still could not place who the woman had been. She beckoned to Alan who hovered in the doorway.

"They've gone. Truly. The atmosphere has completely changed."

He took an apologetic step or three into the room.

"Sorry to be so nervy. I've always been afraid of ghosts, ever since my father dragged me onto a ghost train on Brighton Pier. Scared the pants off me."

Delia turned to face him. "You are hopeless. Come on, I'll take you out for a drink, provided there's anywhere left open."

Actually, she thought he could do with a break. His face was showing all the signs of overwork. A delicate mauve around the eyes, occasional yawning, tired mouth. She realised in that second how very much she loved him and almost felt her inner self leap with joy. She was now quite certain that she wanted to marry him — as soon as he got around to proposing, of course.

* * *

Once again, Justyn bowed to his grandmother. "You are amazing, do you know that? Tell me your life story again."

"No. You've heard it so many times."

"Well, just the bit about the trousers. I love that."

"I have told you so often. I was eighteen years old and had just had a singing lesson. And then I went straight to the theatre where I had a very small part as a walker-on — or off, on this occasion — with the Carl Rosa Opera Company. Anyway there I was, in costume and wearing something resembling make-up on my face, when the tenor — a large man — came rushing onto the stage, late on cue as usual. Worse luck he bumped into me, sad-faced and plodding half-heartedly from the stage, and unfortunately his trouser button caught in my costume and I was dragged back onto the stage with him. It was not a pretty sight."

"Tell me how you looked."

"Suspiciously as if I had just been caught doing something that no young woman should know about, his trouser button lurking somewhere near my mouth."

"What did you do?"

"At that moment he let out a high note — I think it was meant to be a C but cannot be certain about that — and his trousers could not take the strain of a gawky child hanging on to him and putting extra weight behind mixed with singing a top note — and they fell off and clung around his ankles."

"And the audience?"

"Either fainted or screamed with laughter, especially when I crawled off stage, crying."

Justyn pulled a sympathetic face. "And what about the tenor?"

"Well, that was Grandpa Number One."

"I beg your pardon. How did that come about?"

"You never met him, of course. He died long before you were born. He was over thirty years older than I was. But he got me into singing, whereas I had only looked at it as a way of making money. I was quite good, you know. I might have kept it up as a profession but I got side tracked when I met Madame Teresa."

"Who taught you everything you know about witchcraft . . ."

Tinker looked up at him with eyes that flashed in the coming darkness. "Of course she did, my dear."

"So tell me, Madame Arcarti, am I going on to make a great success of my life?"

"Bless you, my handsome grandson, of course you will. Be steady with the drinking, light on the food, and don't let any woman steal your heart. That last rule is essential if you want to live a long and happy life."

"I'll do my best, Tinker. But I can't promise always to satisfy."

"I fully understand your predicament, my dear. Believe me, I do."

And she winked a brilliant eye at him as the pair enjoyed the rest of their evening meal.

CHAPTER TWENTY-FOUR

Jenny — Past

As the train pulled out of Edinburgh station, Fryderyck Chopin closed his eyes briefly and offered a small but dignified prayer to God, thanking Him for his lucky escape. Leaving the rooms where he had apparently performed a masterpiece, with the audience howling his name, many of them in tears, had been bad enough. But there was worse to come. A huge ensemble of people stood outside the door used by the artists performing, and although he bent double when leaving, so as not to attract attention, there was still an almighty cheer when they saw him. Chopin found himself swept off the ground as a group of hearty men lifted him and tossed him in the air. He closed his eyes and prayed that he would get through this ordeal without losing consciousness. But it was not over yet. There was a loud hallooing before he was thumped down on the ground again.

Chopin had a brief moment of worry about the state of his clothing, including his tartan underpants, but everything seemed to be all right. He managed a small smile. A drunken voice in the crowd began to sing "He's a Jolly Good Fellow," and the roaring and cheering was immense. Eventually he was lifted sky-high again and felt suddenly dwarf-like, surrounded by great braw Scotsmen.

Then somebody roared "Hush" and he realised that he was meant to speak. He was lowered to the ground.

"Thank you all. I deeply respect the applause you have given me." This was said in halting English. For answer, he was thrown into the air yet again, and the crowd began to move towards a nearby tavern that stood open and ready.

"We're buying you a drink, man," said a deep bass voice, and the people near him chorused, "Yes, we are."

But over the furore a woman's voice interrupted in high Scottish tones. "Oh no, you cannot. Put Mr Chopin down immediately. He is a private citizen."

Even as he was being thrown high in the air again, Fryderyck felt a rush of cold and bitter anger. "No," he bellowed in French. "Don't interfere. I am having a good . . ." — the last word was delayed as he hit a mass of bony arms waiting to catch him — "time."

"But . . ." wailed the woman loudly.

"But nothing, Miss Stirling. Goodnight to you."

And that having been said, he was carried triumphantly by a young audience that had wept with joy as he had played for them that night.

* * *

Now, sitting alone, Chopin put a hand to his aching head. He was suffering one of the worst hangovers he had ever experienced — and in his younger days he had suffered a few.

Daniel appeared with a beaker of water and a huge, malicious-looking tablet. Chopin raised a weary brow.

"Yes, sir, this is for you. And I am going to stand here until I see it gone. Now. The quicker you take it the faster you will recover."

Chopin raised his weary head. "Must I?"

"Sir, if I may make so bold, anyone who endured a night with the junior aristocracy of Scotland and is able to crawl on to a train bound for London the next day, deserves a medal. Now, no arguing. Down it goes."

Fryderyck gulped obligingly and, strangely enough, almost exactly one hour later he felt recovery set in. He leaned back in his seat and when he heard the call that luncheon was being served, decided he was hungry and stirred himself.

From all around him in the dining car came Scottish accents, but these were peppered with the sound of stout-hearted English people making their way back to smelly old London. Fryderyck cocked an ear.

"Tell me, my dear child, how you enjoyed the concert last night."

His companion, a young woman, replied, "Oh, Uncle Angus, it was wonderful. That little man played divinely. It is no exaggeration when I say that it was like listening to one of the gods."

Chopin ordered another glass of wine — *kill or cure* was his motto — and gulped it down. It was embarrassing, yet at the same time lovely, to hear such things. The young woman continued.

"He is terribly thin, of course."

"Ah, that would be caused by his constant days seated at the pianoforte."

"But he travels about in a coach with those two awful women who drag him around the palaces. I can't think what he is doing with that couple."

Angus looked knowing. "Perhaps they offer him free lodging."

"I hope that is all they offer."

"Really, my dear, you say quite the most shocking things for someone brought up as a lady."

"I am sorry, Uncle Angus, but I can't help what my friends tell me. Don't be cross."

"You, my little pet, I could never be cross with — only be careful in future to whom you say that sort of thing. You never know who might be listening."

The girl looked around the dining car, slightly ashamed, and then turned a bright pink and turned back to her uncle.

"Oh, you'll never believe this! He's sitting over there, on his own. He must have heard every word I said!"

Her uncle responded as only someone brought up in the old school could do. Standing up, he raised his wine glass high.

"Mr Chopin, I salute you. You have brought pleasure to all who have heard you, including the younger set, which I think is vitally important. Thank you from the bottom of my heart."

His booming voice had brought a silence to the rest of the dining compartment and now several people, hearing him, also stood up with their glasses raised.

"Mr Chopin," they chorused and Fryderyck, more than a little embarrassed, got to his feet and said, "Thank you very much," in his best English accent.

There was a round of very lively applause and one or two ladies — bolder than the rest — approached him and asked him to sign various pieces of paper, which he did. Feeling his hangover vanishing to a memory, Chopin accepted a bottle of excellent wine being given to him by a hearty-looking gentleman, who then stood by Chopin's side.

"I want to thank you most sincerely for your concert the other night. I personally could not attend but my boy was completely enthralled by your playing. He came home and wept to his mother when he told her about it. I have never seen him so moved."

Compliments started flying around the dining car with people standing up and clapping and shouting "Bravo". Though Fryderyck couldn't understand much of what was said he knew by their response that he was the hero of the hour and bowed repeatedly. A tray of drinks arrived from some enthusiast and Chopin decided that — once again — he was going to enjoy himself and hangovers be damned.

"Sank you zo much," he said in his best English and smiled with great enthusiasm. Fortunately, Daniel then arrived and whistled him back to his apartment so that he managed an hour's sleep before the train pulled in to the gloomy recesses of London. Chopin's manservant then arranged transport and they made off to the home of Henry Broadwood, with whom Chopin had arranged to stay while hunting for a new dwelling of his own.

That night he wrote to Jenny to tell her of his mad adventures and his somewhat drunken state. At least he would see her before too long — or so he hoped.

CHAPTER TWENTY-FIVE

Jenny — Past

Chopin was fast asleep, dreaming deep and silently. In his dream he could feel a light hand caressing him and with a merry groan of pleasure he tried to turn over to find out who it was — only to come up short. There was another body in the way, pressed up close against his.

"Jenny?" he whispered hoarsely.

"No, no. It is Fifi la Derriere, the one you left behind in Paris. Oh monsieur, how could you do that to me, your faithful mistress?"

Chopin woke up, mercifully with all his wits about him.

"I don't know," he growled. "She was not really my sort of woman. She had a most peculiar smell."

"A what?" shrieked Jenny at full voice.

"A loud stink that was quite unbearable. I prefer my women soft and gentle." He pinched Jenny's bottom, very slightly, exclaiming, "You are not her sort."

"You know perfectly well who I am when you are joking. You *are* joking — aren't you?"

"No, I am deadly serious," he answered, and gave her a kiss that would have rocked her off the floor, had she been standing.

"Oh, my darling," she answered, "I have missed you so terribly. You will never know how much. When are we going to get married?"

"I would like to now, immediately, at once — believe me. But I know that I am too sickly at the moment. I really mean this, Jenny, because I love you so damned much that I couldn't bear to be your ailing husband."

She lit a candle, blowing out the match carefully, and they looked at one another in the flickering light. Her eyes were the high point of her beauty, crystal bright and most becoming. Chopin was even more in love with her, full of emotion to the brim.

"Darling," he said, and kissed her again to hide the fact that he had started to weep; very quietly but with a great deal of feeling.

Jenny Lind, looking at him, also began to cry and so they lay together on his bed, weeping like a pair of infants.

"I love you so very much," he said, "and I always will. Until the day I die."

She swallowed briskly. "Don't talk about it — it is unlucky to do so. Think that you are getting better. Listen, sweetheart, have you thought about sea air? They say it is very good for the lungs and heart to breathe it in."

"Really? I didn't know that."

"Well, you do now. I have been invited to sing in Brighton soon and I wondered if you would care to join me. Perhaps we could have a small holiday afterwards. I have a few days free. Would you care to come?"

"I would love it. It might mean . . ."

"That we can be married after all. There, I've said it. Now hold your peace and don't spoil my dream."

They both fell asleep peacefully; Chopin for once not gasping but breathing deeply and with a very faint — but extremely tuneful — snore. Jenny, used to noises which could disturb even the heaviest sleeper, remained studiously unconscious, despite the sounds of Daniel clambering round the premises. Chopin — on the threshold of waking, opened one eye, thought it wasn't worth it and promptly dropped back into a relaxing slumber. They looked like a pair of angels, Daniel thought. Rather naughty ones, but still angelic.

Miss Lind smiled in her sleep then woke up, yawned, and said, "Good morning."

Daniel caught himself thinking that she must always remain like this. Not spoiled by too much success or great fame. She must stay fresh and young for ever and never fall into the hands of a miserable man who would make her do things that were foreign to her artistic nature. She should shine through the universe so that even death would not — and could not — erase her memory.

An hour later, they were sitting down to breakfast, both looking extremely scrubbed and clean. Daniel glanced at them, his face expressionless.

"And did madame enjoy her bathing arrangements?" he asked, his face a lesson in blandness.

"Very much. I particularly liked my back scrubber."

She could have been speaking, of course, about an old loofah, but the wink she gave Chopin indicated otherwise. He — looking particularly pleased with himself — said, "I'm glad to hear that."

Daniel had to turn aside, masking his laugh into a cough. His master was something of a mystery to him and with every day that passed in his company, Daniel felt he knew less, not more. He had gathered from people he gossiped with that that last night in Edinburgh had been magical.

"No, not quite," a young woman had commented. "You see, that night Chopin talked to God."

But now, sitting down to break his fast, wretchedly thin but for all that handsome, the composer was grinning like a well-groomed male feline. Jenny noticed it.

"You're looking very pleased with life, if I may make so bold."

"Partly because I have escaped from those wretched Scots women." Chopin paused, then added, "God forgive me. The trouble is that that family comprises the most boring people on Earth." He sipped his coffee. "They don't mean to be like that, but they just can't help it. The widow woman is the worst, full of Calvinist teaching and desperate to convert the most innocent bystander to her beliefs."

"But what of the younger?" Jenny asked innocently. "I hear that she is quite a good musician — in her own way, of course."

"It is true," Chopin admitted, a trifle tersely. "She can play well enough. It is just the rest of her that is so trying."

"What do you mean exactly?" Jenny asked, the very faintest of edges sounding in her voice.

Chopin was momentarily silent, chewing a piece of toast. "She has all the physical attraction of an elderly street post which, in fact, she resembles closely."

At this Jenny Lind exploded, roaring with laughter and spilling some of her cup onto the table.

"How can you be so cruel? The poor soul is not here to defend herself!"

"But for how long, I ask myself. Shortly, she and her Calvinist sister will appear in London. I am not psychic but believe me when I tell you this. For I know as sure as Fate that they will pursue me until my dying day."

The room had suddenly grown quiet as Chopin's words sank in.

"But why?" Jenny asked. "Won't they get bored with the whole thing?"

Chopin shook his head. "The younger one — Jane Stirling — would give her life's blood to live with me for ever. She is obsessed by me — to the point of lunacy."

"Oh dear," said Jenny, shaking her head and frowning deeply. "She sounds insane, from the way you describe her."

Chopin looked extremely solemn. "I think there might be some truth in what you say. But enough of the sisters and their peculiarities. Let's enjoy our breakfast and each other — and Daniel, of course."

They raised their cups in mock salute, but a certain silence had fallen over the pair of lovers, who ate the rest of their meal without speaking a word.

* * *

The trouble with Jane Stirling, born Joan Wilhelmina and feeling that name as quite the end of the road when aiming to be inter-esting, was precisely that — she *tried* with alarming heaviness. Her parents had been strict Calvinists, hence the fact that Mama was constantly pregnant and gave birth at such regular intervals that one could have almost set the clock by each baby. Fortunately — or perhaps not — Jane was made first fatherless, then motherless several years later, and was adopted by her sister, Mrs Katherine Erskine. Mrs Erskine was a widow who constantly wore black and whose one purpose in life was to bring the word of God to any who would listen — and to shout it at those who would not. She kept a very careful eye indeed on her young sister— at first allowing her to wear no drawers whatsoever but gradually relaxing to permit the open-legged variety. The one thing that raised the young girl above the rest of the squalling and quarrelling crew was her talent for playing the piano.

Jane had sat down one day at the stately instrument, which was hidden in the receiving room, and started to pick out a tune that she had heard a brass band play at the opening of a church hall. Mrs Erskine had been somewhat impressed, though she had said nothing except, "God is helping you." Because of this, Jane continued to practice patiently though she had a feeling that she might expand her style a little with a proper teacher — or any teacher at all, come to that. One day, she had sat down with Mrs Erskine for a serious chat.

"Oh dear sister, I am sure that I could become a stronger pianist if I had some tuition."

"Well, it would mean taking you into Edinburgh occasionally. Also, I wonder whether I could afford it on a regular basis."

"But surely our father left me some money?"

"Just a wee amount, yes he did."

So they had traipsed into Edinburgh once a fortnight taking a horse and buggy and an experienced driver. They had picked a teacher from a catalogue that listed various people as suitable for dealing with the younger folk and — having checked his references with a fierce determination — Katherine had settled on one Oliver Farquharson, hoping that he would be elderly. As it turned out, he was not. A good-looking youngish man with hair a vivid shade of ginger had politely risen from his piano stool when the doorman called out their names. Mrs Erskine had literally taken a step backward and issued a faint cry of disapproval, but twelve-year-old Jane ran towards him saying, "Please be my teacher, please."

He smiled politely and said to the girl, "Will you play for me then, Miss Stirling?"

"I can't play well. They are just tunes that I have picked out. I can't read music."

"Well, that will be enough." He bowed deeply to Katherine. "How do you do, madam. Will you be staying with us while your daughter plays?"

"She's not my daughter. Jane is my sister."

"Forgive me, madam. I beg your pardon. How stupid of me."

"Several people make the same mistake. Jane, play for Mr Farquharson. Do your best."

So Jane sat down and had played "Baa Baa Black Sheep" as well as she could. The young teacher turned to Mrs Erskine.

"She has talent, madam. Quite a considerable amount, I think. I would like to give her weekly lessons."

"That would be very difficult. We live quite far out and hiring a carriage especially could prove very costly."

Jane interrupted energetically. "But, dear sister, not if we join other members of the family and make it a regular outing. They could share the cost."

Mrs Erskine sighed deeply. "That is true, I suppose. Very well, I will give it my consideration. What day did you have in mind, Mr Farquharson?"

"The day that suits you best, madam. I can rearrange my other pupils accordingly."

Just then there was a polite knock on the door and the porter put his head round. "Lord Glen Gordon and Duncan are here, sir."

"Show them into the waiting room, if you would be so kind. Well, Mrs Erskine, have you reached a decision?"

"Yes, yes, I believe so. You are teaching Lord Glen Gordon's son I understand?"

"Young Duncan? Yes, he is a very amiable boy."

"Excellent. In that case, Jane will begin next Friday."

And with that, business done, Mrs Erskine and her sister swept out into the streets of Edinburgh on a raw and chilly day.

* * *

Over time, Jane did two things; one of which was exciting, the other a reality that had to be faced. She grew tall and gawky, which did not really become her as she had no idea how to carry herself, how to sit or stand beautifully, no concept at all of what one should do to attract people. However, the other thing was that she learnt to really play the piano — and play well. When she was eighteen, Jane appeared with other students of Mr Farquharson in a concert to raise money for the Poor Widows' Fund — and it was from this that the first thoughts of her going abroad were born. She mentioned this one day to her sister.

"Duncan, Lord Glen Gordon's boy, said that I had to live abroad if I wanted to be a proper pianist."

"Really? Has he invited you to attend the ball he is having on his eighteenth birthday?"

"No, Katherine. I believe that only the daughters of titles can go."

"Good heavens! Why, our family has been around since the beginning of time. Titles indeed!"

"But we don't have one, do we?"

At this Mrs Erskine had drawn herself up, her face fiery. "That would have been the choice of our ancestors. They were probably offered to our great forefathers, who scorned them, refusing money and rewards for winning a battle or two. We are of a proud heritage, Jane, I'll have you know."

Like a chastened child, the girl said nothing further, retreating to the music room and playing something that Duncan had mentioned. Obviously she had a secret crush on the handsome, stocky lad — but with no answering tenderness from him. And it was hardly surprising. So far she had copied her sister in everything: standing tall as a ramrod, long dark hair scraped into a bun, not a scrap of cosmetic to help her blossom. She was copying her much older relative and getting more and more like her in gesture and thought.

Finally, however, Jane once again broached the subject of going abroad to study, an idea that wouldn't let her go.

"I beg your pardon?"

"I simply said that Mr Farquharson and all the people at music school think I should travel in order to improve my playing."

"Improve? Improve! How dare they? You are a fine musician and I think you are at the height of your career."

"But who hears me? My fellow students and no one else. I really would like to go to Paris and find a pianist who could teach me more."

Mrs Erskine was momentarily bereft of breath as the most shocking image crept into her mind. Her youngest sister winking at a young gigolo who had just entered the bar where Jane sat dressed to kill, watching the young man, who was fully kitted out as a sailor and moving his hips seductively as he walked. She went pale.

"But why go *abroad*? Surely you have learnt enough in Edinburgh?"

"No, I haven't," Jane retorted, more irritated than she had ever felt in her entire life.

Her sister did the obvious thing and collapsed, weeping silently into a linen handkerchief. Jane watched in horror. She had never seen Katherine so upset. Yet it was obvious to everyone of any sense who had heard her play that she needed to find another teacher, Oliver Farquharson having given her his all. But Jane was on her knees instantly, putting a loving arm around her sister's shoulders.

"There, there, Katherine. Please don't cry. I won't go away, it was just a silly idea I had. I shall stay here and practise at home."

"No, my dear, I am being selfish. If everyone but me thinks you should go abroad then I shall accompany you and stay by your side through thick and thin."

Jane could hardly believe what she was hearing.

"Oh, Katherine, don't say that just for my sake. But if you think we should enjoy it — and you *really* mean it — I believe it would be a wonderful thing to do."

"Of course, I could accompany you everywhere you went."

"Everywhere. I promise. We could visit art galleries and places of that kind."

"I'm not sure about that, Jane. They display a great deal of nudity — and of the opposite sex, too — as you are aware."

"No, sister, I was not. Thank you for telling me."

* * *

And so they journeyed from the land of lochs and gleaming waters and finally arrived, exhausted, at a lodging house on the outskirts of Paris. Mrs Erskine was too drained to speak but Jane looked around her with interest and hoped, as always, for the best.

The change in surroundings did not, alas, improve Jane's looks at all. She was one of those plain people who carried about her an air of absolutely dogged determination to do well and it was not long after their arrival that she began to receive business cards from people who taught pianoforte. Then slowly but surely, eased by all the right words spoken softly, Mrs Erskine thawed out and a strange kind of patronising love for France and the amusing habits of its habitués gradually softened her approach.

Then one day, on their umpteenth visit to France, when Miss Jane was thirty-four years old and unfortunately not looking her best, she was sent to a new teacher by her present one, a rather lackadaisical young man who advised that she ought to audition for Mr Chopin.

"He's Polish, you know, but he converses in French so you'll be able to understand him."

"I've never heard of him."

"Well, I must say that is very remiss of you. He is the flavour of the month with the musical gang. But then I suppose you wouldn't hear of such things in Scotland. Too many stags to kill." At this he laughed uncontrollably.

The next day, Jane pulled her hair up into the tightest possible bun and then peered at herself in the looking glass. Her skin was waxen and her pale blue eyes did nothing to brighten her appearance, but nonetheless she stepped forward with hope that she might finally be meeting the person who would rocket her career upwards.

He called out "Enter" in response to her timid knock, and was sitting at the pianoforte when she went into the room. He did not turn his head until he had finished playing. Jane stood in the doorway, utterly mesmerised. Eventually, he stood up and made a small, polite bow.

"And you are?" he asked in French.

"Jane Stirling."

"Oh yes. One of my students wrote to me. He said you were rather good. Will you play for me please?"

"Yes, sir."

He moved from the piano and Jane sat down slowly, staring at the keys as if she had never seen anything like them. The whole of her body seemed to her to have lifted from the piano stool and be floating high over the rooftops of the city. For the first time in her life she felt that she could laugh hysterically or break down and weep copious tears. She was thirty-four years old and she had never experienced anything like it. For a glance from those dark-blue eyes had been enough. This stranger, this man called Chopin, of whom she had never heard a word in her rigid Highland life, had reduced her to a palpitating wreck.

"Please begin," he said — rather irritably, she thought.

She stared down at the piano keys dumbly, like a sickly animal.

"Is anything wrong?" he asked.

"No, sir. I apologise. I just felt a little unwell."

"Do you want to go outside?"

"N-n-no, thank you. I will play. I promise I will begin."

"Good. Then start."

She held her limp hands over the keys and, uttering a small silent request to the Almighty, she began to play.

Despite her awkward manner, despite her female-dominated upbringing, despite all that she had had to put up with, she could play — and play well. It was almost as if someone else took over when her fingers touched the keyboard.

Chopin, who had been leaning back in his chair, trying to sum her up, was astonished. He stared at her: gawky and drab though she was, the woman had a touch of genius. When she stopped playing, he clapped his hands together and she looked up, surprised.

"That was quite good!" he said. "I would certainly like to take you as a pupil."

She lost colour and then regained it rapidly, flushing scarlet in her obvious pleasure at being praised. Looking at her, Chopin did not know whether to laugh or cry. She was such a ragbag in her choice of dress. He guessed that some elderly relative was involved when Miss Jane went shopping — in Edinburgh, no doubt. And that relative's advice would be, "Brown is such a serviceable colour." He grinned as he thought this while poor blushing Miss Stirling stood cringing and uncomfortable.

"Play one of my things," Chopin said. "Here — try this." And he casually gave her a small lilting waltz that he had written on the previous day.

She stared at him. "Oh no, I couldn't."

"Why not? I don't have the plague. It's not infectious."

This was the last straw as far as Miss Stirling was concerned and she broke down in a fit of silent weeping. Chopin stood astounded, watching her, not at all sure how to handle the situation. He liked women, particularly those that he considered good-looking. But a weeping bundle of Scots humanity was more than he had ever been called upon to attend. So he did nothing until she eventually bolted from the room. Somewhat against his better judgement, Chopin followed her.

Her head was plunged into the lap of an older woman who looked something like the walking dead; at least that is what the composer thought. With large beady eyes and a non-existent bust and an extremely harsh expression the composer could think of nothing to do but give a small salute. The woman glared at him while the weeping Miss Stirling gave a minute moan. Chopin was completely and utterly baffled and bewildered.

"I will be willing for Miss Stirling to become a pupil, provided that she does not constantly collapse. The choice is entirely hers, of course. Good afternoon." And he turned and walked into his private apartments without a backward glance.

Miss Stirling sat up and wiped the smudges off her face. "What shall I do?"

"What do you mean, dear? The man meant it. He wants you for a pupil."

"But I behaved atrociously. I couldn't help myself."

"Well from now on you will act as people of our clan always do. With rigid good manners."

Jane nodded mutely, afraid to tell any living creature that she had fallen deeply in love with the handsome Polish composer and would in future cling on to him as long as there was life left in her body. Nothing and nobody could persuade her otherwise.

CHAPTER TWENTY-SIX

Jenny — Past

Slowly and insidiously, she tried to take over his life. But she might as well have tried to arrest the flow of a bubbling brook. She was very experienced with filing — or so she said — and she began to arrange his compositions into a form of order. Solange — the daughter of his early lover George Sand — would visit Chopin and was somewhat perturbed when she saw two tall, severe women walking silently around his property. Chopin laughed at her expressions of surprise and merely informed her that they helped him with his filing.

But there was an edge to them, something indescribable that Solange could not analyse. One night she awoke from a bad dream and cried out as she saw the younger of the two seize Chopin to molest him. Solange had not trusted Jane Stirling from the outset and she became increasingly suspicious. But the ladies noticed nothing — or if they did, hid the fact superbly — and talked incessantly of the beauties of Scotland's landscape and the marvellous palaces in which they and their relations all dwelt. Thankfully, one of the ladies was taken ill and they had to depart, Chopin wondered whether he should kiss them goodbye and decided against it.

It was at this stage of his life that Fryderyck ended his relationship with George Sand: a woman who considered herself an admirable writer, a wit, a great lover, a stunning beauty and who was, undoubtedly, a smelly smoker of hashish. Such affectations and delusions could all be forgiven, had they not come from a woman who demanded love and attention entirely for herself, had a streak of cruelty that extended to hating Solange, her daughter, whom she treated badly and, above all, disliking intensely any rival who crossed her path.

She had practically eaten Chopin alive in the early days, whisking him into her "maiden room", stripping off her trousers and high boots, lifting her breasts high as they would go, slowly oiling her private part, but never giving up her stinking cigars. Not everyone was impressed with her. She was described as a *man-eating nymphomaniac*, and *gutter tongued as a lighterman*. Poor Fryderyck didn't know what had hit him and thought that — perhaps — this was love.

They lived together during the summer, for she had a country residence, Nohant, and after some initial hesitation Fryderyck had gone to stay. George put on her very best face, oozing gentle love and sweet, adorable caresses. He played the piano for her, she lay down on a sofa and listened. It was heavenly; George acting out the part of a giving, gentle, sweet woman who gave her body freely and whenever required to her handsome and highly talented lover. Chopin was in a kind of trance of composing and sexual satisfaction.

Then came the winter and the inevitable move back to Paris. They found different apartments so nobody — other than members of the arty set — guessed what was happening. According to Sand, *she was happy to nurture, comfort and inspire*. Blah upon blah. *I remain in the intoxication in which you saw me last*, and *nothing gives such languor in the bones as the delicious lassitude that flows from happy love.* Meanwhile her children were given something to eat and sent off to bed. Unfortunately, they were growing up and taking in more and more of their unusual surroundings. The boy, Maurice, did not like Chopin at all; the girl, Solange, did.

It had started during a disastrous holiday in Mallorca, where Fryderyck's chest played up, George was consumed with sexual — but controlled — fire, young Maurice was eaten alive with wicked jealousy and poor Solange had to go for long walks on her own. Maurice had never forgiven the skinny interloper who coughed up blood, Solange had felt sorry for him and wished he felt better. And now, having endured a summer where their mother walked around as if she would strip her clothes off if anybody so much as asked her, they were moving back to Paris.

The affair continued, Chopin pouring out music that delighted audiences and earned him substantial amounts, George writing works for the theatre that failed dismally, Maurice deciding that he had an interest in art, Solange feeling lonely and excluded. Meanwhile, George's penchant for her strange cigars persisted and no one was gladder than she when spring arrived and plans were made to go once more to Nohant. Chopin by now had become part of the furnishings and she still played out the role of adoring love. But all was not well beneath the surface.

Solange had a part-time governess, one Marie de Rozières, who passed on as much information as she could gather about Chopin's background and upbringing. She was a born gossip and Fryderyck could not bear her. She considered him a pain and he did not trust her. Naturally, she reported everything back to the lady of the house, the one and only George, who kept up the pretence of loving Chopin madly. But slowly and inexorably the rot had started. The person upon whom the punishment was bound to fall was Solange. Her mother wrote her a letter.

Your brother and I love you but we have no illusions about certain faults which you must correct and which you will surely try to eradicate: self-love, a craving to dominate others, and your mad, stupid jealousy.

Chopin truly liked the little girl and continued to play with and support her. More importantly, George Sand seemed happy to live with him in both Nohant and Paris. The summers were excellent as both of them played a part; he enjoyed amateur drama, she took on the role of great hostess, tossing back her black curls, making traditional jam and writing — and listening to the colourful medley of her guests' conversation.

Most of Chopin's friends visited during those precious summer months; but despite the sparkle they brought with them, he did not really like the countryside and Sand's feelings were slowly but surely changing. Fryderyck was doing his best to be nice to her but she was feeling more depressed and listless, while he was beginning to loathe the relentlessly rural environment.

Meanwhile, the children had been growing up and Maurice had turned into a sniggering twenty-one-year-old, full of himself and loathing Chopin; a loathing he made plain with obvious displays of bad manners and insulting behaviour. Solange had more and more time to spare and would often sit in Chopin's room. With the return of the son — well loved by the mother — the end of Fryderyck was finally in sight.

The season at Nohant took place with its usual cheerful company of visitors and friends coming to stay. But no one had accounted for the difference that Maurice would make. He had developed such a hatred for Chopin, resenting bitterly the hold that he had over George Sand, though admittedly that was now waning. Continuing to run the poor chap down, finding public fault with him, swearing and always slightly over the edge with alcohol, Maurice did his best to vilify the wretched man.

They managed to stay together through the winter months — out of habit, as much as anything else — and then came the Nohant get-together. Matthew Arnold, arriving from Oxford, was struck by Chopin's wonderful eyes, but found the lady of the house boring. Then came George's moment of triumph: the serialisation in a popular newspaper of her serial *Lucrezia Floriani* which she insisted on reading aloud after supper, to all of the guests seated round the fireside. The obvious similarities between the serial and the relationship between Sand and Chopin struck the assembled company forcibly, the only person apparently not affected — or was he just hiding his pain? — was Chopin. Some of those present wondered if perhaps he just didn't understand it. However, while Chopin wrote miserably to his family, telling them how disappointed he was with his own compositions, nothing further was mentioned.

The next distraction was caused by Solange, now eighteen and looking splendid. She was going to marry Fernand de Prelaux, an aristocrat but as dim as they come. Shortly after this another attraction appeared on the horizon, Auguste Clesinger, who was bearded and disorderly. He was "all fire and flame" according to one observer. Solange, swept off her feet, jilted Prelaux at the last minute and Clesinger followed her to Nohant declaring himself to be violently in love. They were married swiftly — George fearing the worst — and informed Chopin by letter. He was distressed because he had always found Solange sweet and kind but his hands were tied. He felt too ill to bother himself any further. He wrote a lovely letter to her and left it at that.

Of course, the marriage broke down and George complained long and loudly about her terrible child. Her most stinging remark was left to the end: *She has fouled the nest in which she* [Solange] *was reared by thinking — and saying — that it has been the scene of the most disgraceful conduct.*

But there was worse to come. Clesinger, infuriated beyond measure by George's nasty son, took a hammer to him — only to find himself staring down the muzzle of a loaded gun. George went wild and punched Clesinger, only to be punched back violently in the chest. She screamed in response and fell to the floor. Happy families indeed. Later, George wept copiously and wrote hateful letters to her friends.

Meanwhile, poor Chopin had no idea of the theatricals going on in George's household and when a letter came from Solange, asking for the loan of his carriage to take her back to Paris, he gladly agreed to let her have it, little knowing that George and her beloved son Maurice had already refused. This caused great dramas. George puffed on her hashish cigars and wrote endless letters.

Chopin who was to come and suddenly does not . . . has become completely different in his attitude towards me, he no longer dies from mortal love, which I could not requite, as his friends accused me, and he declares to me that I am a bad mother . . .

Another furious cry was: *He has openly sided with Solange against me . . .* while she told others . . . *the poor sickly creature, without wishing to, and perhaps he could not help it, behaved as though he were my lover, my husband, and the master of my every thought and action . . .*

It was over. Chopin was free of her insufferable embrace. He could breathe again. Standing alone in his apartment he gave a long, deep sigh of relief.

Miss Stirling and Mrs Erskine had been in Scotland throughout most of this turbulent period, which pleased Chopin. The last thing he wanted was for them to offer their well-bred advice and unnecessary comments. Solange continued to call and it was from her that he learned of the birth of her daughter, followed almost immediately by the tragic death of the week-old child.

Meanwhile, George Sand raised another hand-rolled cigar to her brown-stained lips and told the world in general that Chopin had once behaved as if he were her lover, her husband and the master of her every thought and action. While she — of course — had stayed totally in control.

He set eyes on her only once after their parting and this almost a year later. He informed her of the death of Solange's baby, then bowed and escaped quickly downstairs. George followed him and grabbed his hand. Chopin gave a horrified look and promptly rushed out into the street. The end of the affair indeed — from that moment on, she never saw him again. The only memory George Sand had of the love affair to end them all was a pair of feet running as fast as possible in the opposite direction.

The advent of the two sisters, fresh from their cross-sea travel, was punctuated with little moues and various other noises which Chopin was unable to interpret. He decided that they could not possibly have heard even a rumour of his relationship with the cigar smoker so he simply thanked them for coming to see him, gave Jane something almost impossible to play, and dinner. However, this turned into a weekly occurrence and Fryderyck felt once more that he was becoming a creature of habit.

Then something on the lines of civil war broke out in Paris, the people versus the monarchy. There were casualties lying everywhere, frightened children running to find their parents, grandfathers picking up ancient muskets and swearing to fight to the death the evil forces that threatened them. In the middle of one particularly noisy battle, Jane Stirling came in from a back room, within which she had been busily filing, and said, "I am sorry Mr Chopin but I find myself unable to continue."

A particularly noisy shell whizzed overhead at that moment and they both jumped. Fryderyck looked upwards.

"You remember that invitation you once gave me?"

She shook her head, bewildered.

"To go to England and visit you — and your dear sister, of course."

Jane nodded mutely. "Well, I think it would be a wonderful idea. But we live in Scotland, of course."

"Then Scotland it is. I could do with a change of scene. What do you think?"

But Jane's answer was drowned out by a loud bang and a puff of smoke. Chopin shivered as he helped her back up to her feet and poured out a cup of tea, which she stoically drank.

CHAPTER TWENTY-SEVEN

Jenny — Past

Afterwards, he wondered whether he should have faced the dangers of Paris — but that was too ghastly a thing to consider for more than a moment. The two women had sensibly gone ahead to England, Jane panicking sedately that Chopin would not be travelling with them. But they had worked hard in his absence, finding him rooms in Bentinck Street, the younger sister doing everything that a wife would do, including choosing his favourite drinking chocolate and even contemplating that thing that only married couples engage in . . .

They went to meet him at London Bridge station, standing together, draped in plain no-nonsense clothes, faces drawn until they caught sight of him, when a very brief small smile radiated across Jane's visage, fleeting and flitting as wicked thoughts ran briefly through her mind. Chopin, for no reason that he could afterwards describe, stood stock still, not moving a muscle towards them.

He was seized by the most peculiar sensation. He knew with absolute certainty that he had come to England for some divine purpose — an odd word to use, for he did not really believe such things. That Fate had lined him up for some peculiar event; that he was about to meet his destiny. He — there in the bright daylight, surveyed by two rather dull females — was on the threshold of some magnificent event.

"Oh dear, Mr Chopin," said one of them, "thank the Good Lord Above that you got here safely."

He did not even hear her, because he was already walking towards the fields of pain and pleasure that lay awaiting him. He came back to Earth rather angry that a high piping Scottish voice had spoken French at him.

"I'm sorry. What did you say?"

"I said welcome to England, monsieur."

"I think", he replied, "that I am going to be made very welcome indeed."

And so it began. Within a matter of days he had gone to the Haymarket Theatre to see a Swedish coloratura sing the lead in *La Sonnambula*. He thought her a *typical Swede, not in an ordinary light but in some Polar dawn*. A few days later he was invited out to dine and the only other guest was Jenny. He was immensely attracted. A true love was unfolding between them — and both of them knew it.

* * *

By the autumn they were heavily involved. Jenny was pressing for marriage because she loved Chopin and wanted to have children. Chopin felt that to saddle a so young a woman with a husband in his precarious state of health would be grossly unfair. Yet he couldn't keep away from her.

His summer had been a total disaster. With money short and pupils dropping off he had done the rounds of high society, had played superbly, had met Jenny on several wondrous occasions, but by the start of July the wealthy folk had all taken off for Scotland — Europe being in a state of utter turmoil — so there was not much living to be had for a musician.

Chopin had started his disastrous visit to Scotland to see two women who quite frankly bored him beyond measure. Of course, Jenny had met him several times and they were in love more than somewhat . . . but that wasn't enough. He tried his best to play in public but most of his time was occupied by the cooing French of the inevitable Jane, complete with her omni-present sister. He could have wept with despair that he was not fitter, younger or richer so that he could make a polite exit. But he was deeply in love with a great singer and nothing would ever take that away.

Somehow or other he managed to see quite a lot of Miss Lind, often at railway stations when she was setting off on yet another tour. But at other times he was almost physically shoved into a horse-drawn carriage by Miss Jane, saying in her high wee voice that they were "off to visit My Lady Swishpipe," who was "a brilliant musician and most amusing", only to find that the old dame yelled a song in terrible French to the strains of a clapped-out guitar and looked at Chopin in what she considered a beguiling way as if she expected tumultuous applause for her screeching rendition.

At other times, Chopin paced alone the corridors of Calder House, the home of Lord Torphichen, Jane's elderly brother-in-law. He thought constantly of Jenny and wondered just a tiny bit if perhaps he should marry her and let her look after him. Yet the role of the kept husband filled him with dread. Since childhood he had always believed that it was a fundamental duty of the man of the house to maintain the wife and children. To Jenny — who had heard him preach this gospel until she could scream — that was rubbish. She was the big earner but money was not of huge importance to her. The concerts she gave for various charities, quite aware that she would give all the money she earned to whatever cause had sponsored the event . . . she could have been a millionaire if she had kept it. But she didn't want it or need it — so she gave it away.

Fryderyck was thrust into an agony of indecision, a lifetime's belief being treated with blank comprehension by the woman that he loved above all others. But now, perhaps, he would have a chance to talk her around. Jenny had a tour of England booked and Chopin was bored with Scotland. His final concert, when he had performed for the young and happy crowd of people who had come to the capital for the pleasure of taking part in the jolly activities, had been splendid. He never knew what it was that made him play like an angel, because his memory of that wonderful occasion had become blurred by time. All he could recall was that the crowd of youngsters had adored him and had carried him aloft through the streets of Edinburgh, shouting his name aloud. And the next day there had been a rapturous reception in the train's dining car where, once again, he was feted. Fortunately, the ladies had gone on ahead to London to arrange things for him. Slowly, but very surely, they were robbing Chopin of what he had always so enjoyed — his freedom. Someone had to stop them and give him space to breathe. The words *killing with kindness* ran through his mind almost continually.

The first clue that something exciting was about to happen came when Jenny wrote to him as soon as she returned to England. Mysteriously, she left no address at which she could be contacted, driving Chopin madder than he felt already. And then a ticket arrived through the post, containing information about her forthcoming performance in Brighton. With it came a little note:

Please, my dearest, come to Brighton and then go on a short — but very sweet — surprise with me. I would so love to see you and I hope you will accept.

214

It was what he needed desperately. To sleep with her beside him, to — hopefully — have sexual relations with her, just to be in her brilliant company would be enough. He sent for Daniel, to have a frank discussion.

"Tell me, good friend, do you think I am all right for this?"

"Of course you are, sir. I know you have problems with your chest but I honestly believe that those ladies string you up like wire. It seems to me — I trust you will forgive my honesty — that Miss Jane's attentions would be enough to drive a fit man mad, let alone one who, in any case, needs a doctor."

"I do know that you are speaking honestly — and so will I. They are stifling the life out of me. Frankly, I rue the day when I agreed to take her on as a pupil. I think some unkind creature thought it a joke for me to get so embroiled as I am."

"Miss Stirling is passionately in love with you, sir, and you know it."

"She is like some creature out of a nightmare, Daniel. If only I could get rid of her."

"You have your chance with Miss Lind, sir. If I were in your shoes I would marry her forthwith."

"I can't saddle her with an invalid. I absolutely refuse to do so."

"Then in that case you must live with the pair of hags and bear it as best you can."

Even though he knew it was the truth, Chopin shook his head. "They are very kind to me."

"In one way, perhaps. In another, not so."

"We are wasting valuable time discussing them any further. Daniel, I want you to help me."

"How, sir?"

"Miss Lind is performing in Brighton and has invited me to go away with her for a few days."

The servant actually cheered out loud. "Thank God for that! How can I help?"

"I must go to Brighton on the night of the performance. Will that be difficult?"

"Not in the least, sir. Trains run regularly from London to Brighton. Take a cab to the station and you can get aboard."

"There will be horse-drawn vehicles at the other end?"

"Of course there will. You are going to Brighton, sir, not the Outer Hebrides."

Chopin grinned, then actually burst out laughing. "You'll not tell anyone where I have gone?"

"Your secret will be protected until the day I die."

"And what happens then?"

"I shall whisper it to an angel and to nobody else, sir. You have my word on it."

So ended their conversation and Chopin fell to wondering what he should wear to this marvellous assignation. He had lost weight — again — and was therefore poring over the clothes he had purchased most recently. Eventually he chose a velvet suit for the evenings and lighter, brighter, day wear. And in due course, escorted by Daniel in a horse-drawn cab, he made his way to the London station. After that he put himself into a kind of trance, remembering that excited and excitable crowd of cheering young who had carried him through the streets of Edinburgh. Such memories were like stepping into another world, a place of such exhilaration that he hadn't cared if he did indeed die of joy. He had known then in a moment of pure thought that dying would not be too bad a thing to do after all.

The Opera House in Brighton, Sussex, was built on traditional lines and therefore had boxes immediately above the stalls. Chopin had been dreading the prospect of having to call for help to mount the stairs, but in fact there was a gentle slope upwards which he had managed quite neatly. Then he was inside a lovely velvety box, completely alone as he would have requested, had he been able to ask in advance. He glanced at the programme and saw that *The Daughter of the Regiment* was going to be performed. For the first time that day, a great smile spread over his features. He leaned back in his chair and grinned as his true love gave a terrific trill off stage and then rushed on, smiling and sparkling. She had never looked more beautiful or quite so entrancing. Chopin decided that, somehow or other, he was going to put aside all doubts and ask her to become his wife.

He didn't go around to see her in the interval but instead sent a little note, scribbled on the back of his ticket. It said, *I had forgotten how beautiful you are* and was signed with a capital C and a sign for a kiss.

As always, the entire opera house went mad at the end, even the very elderly struggling to their feet, applauding wildly. Chopin, too, stood up and clapped with great enthusiasm. He was still shouting "Bravo" when the box door opened and a male attendant asked, "Are you all right, sir? I heard you shouting."

"Mere enthusiasm," Chopin answered in very laboured English. Then, in French: "Now can you deliver me backstage please?"

"Certainly, sir. Are you a friend of someone in the cast?" This was said in English, but Chopin got the drift.

"Yes, I am," he gasped.

The man nodded and offered a steadying arm, which Fryderyck gladly took. Then they made their way through a series of darkened corridors and doors which, when opened, joined the theatre with the cavernous world of backstage. Laughter and the clink of glasses could be heard, coming from several of the dressing rooms. The attendant knocked politely on the door of one and on hearing 'Come', pushed it.

Chopin grinned so widely that he felt his face might light up, for there stood Jenny, wearing a wrapper wound round her lovely body and very little else. She looked at him from enormous eyes.

"You're here," she gasped.

"Well, you did invite me."

"But you didn't answer."

"I wanted to surprise you."

"You have. Completely."

"Why are you not surrounded by a million fans?"

"I sent them all away."

"For what reason?"

"In case you came."

"Well, I have. So what are you going to do about it?"

"This," she said, and then flung herself into his arms.

Fortunately, he felt strong enough to cope and gave her a gorgeous kiss in return. She was absolutely delightful and feeling her body pressed so close to his awakened all his old thoughts and longings. Momentarily, a vision of George Sand fluttered before him and he had to try very hard to overcome a wave of nausea. He must have been so young to fall into that old spider's web, full of cigar smoke and her "giving" herself whenever she felt like it, though all the time looking into his eyes and murmuring ridiculous poetry at him. Now he looked at Jenny and knew that he was hers for life.

"Where are we staying?" he asked.

"You haven't booked anywhere?" He shook his head. "That's as well, because I have."

Chopin smiled. He could think of nothing to say to her except that he loved her completely and utterly and knew that he would continue to do so for the rest of his life.

"Tell me of it. No, on second thoughts, don't. Let me be surprised."

"But, dear man, you must hear the best part. I have three days of holiday, starting now. I next appear at Southampton on the eighth."

He was not strong, but the urge to sweep her off her feet was overpowering. Fortunately Jenny was not one of the enormous sopranos but built lithely and so Chopin — straining every muscle — lifted her up and danced with her a little way.

She laughed with sheer enjoyment, placing her hands lightly on his shoulders. "I am so glad you've made yourself free to join me, darling friend."

"You can show me how much later."

* * *

A pre-arranged cab was waiting outside as Miss Lind and Mr Chopin set off into the night. It was hardly believable but a handful of ardent fans had braved the darkness and the cold to see her and they rushed around in an excited knot, clutching their programmes and memory cards. She turned to look at her lover.

"Shall I sign?"

"Yes, of course you must. They love you — as do I," he added in an undertone.

And he took a courteous step back so that the way was clear for Jenny to sign and chatter with those that wanted to — and that was most of them. One of them — a pretty miss who rather fancied herself — cast her eyes in Chopin's direction.

"May I ask who is accompanying you, Miss Lind?"

Jenny smiled, and for a moment resembled a well-fed cat. "My partner, Mr Chopin. He always comes to the theatre when he has a free evening."

The girl looked him up and down and Fryderyck gave a small, polite bow.

"Did you say Mr Chopin, Miss Lind?"

"Of course I did. You obviously don't know the chatter."

"I'm afraid I do not, Miss Lind. Did you mean *the* Mr Chopin?"

"Fryderyck," Jenny called over her shoulder. "Are you *the* Mr Chopin?"

"I think so," he called back.

A very minor frenzy broke out as the fans all rushed to get his autograph as well, and the famous singer laughed with joy that she should have such a lover.

Afterwards, in the confines of the cab, they sat close to one another, not saying much, happy to be alone. Very quietly, under his breath, Chopin hummed some of her tunes from a variety of operas. She, in loving competition, sang some of his most famous melodies. Strangely enough, the combined effect was beautiful and melodious and so they sat, in perfect harmony, until at last the driver pulled in before an imposing residence, lulled by the soft waves of the stretch of sea which beat so very close to its heart.

"How glorious," said Fryderyck, running his eye over the house's elegant lines.

"As are you," answered Miss Lind as she opened the carriage door.

CHAPTER TWENTY-EIGHT

Delia — Present Day

It was a bitterly cold day in Hastings and the young man strid-
ing briskly over the cobblestones drew his thick coat and layers
of brightly coloured scarf tightly round him. Why on Earth his
grandmother had chosen to live in this Godforsaken place both
puzzled and irritated Justyn, but he knew better than to argue
with her. Once he had suggested an older person's retreat as an
alternative home: she had not objected, she had just screamed
with laughter and told him not to be so foolish.

But today he had more serious news to tell her.

He had finally dropped out of *Summer Roses* and accepted a
marvellous part in Sydney, Australia, where he was going to sing
the lead in *The Daughter of the Regiment*. It had been a ghastly
audition with every eligible tenor on Earth — or so it had seemed
to Justyn — trying for the role.

What defeated them was that famous series of very high notes,
which they had to reach in their big aria. Justyn had presumed
himself beaten from the start but, strangely, his voice had rocketed
through audition after audition. He did not understand how, or
what had helped him: perhaps it was the ghost of Pavarotti, quietly
chuckling, or possibly it was because he had recently worked with

a new teacher, from whom he had learned some new tricks. But whatever it was, it — plus the fact that Justyn was good-looking and popular — had won him the day. So this would be his last call on Tinker in Hastings for the foreseeable future.

He went down the steps to her little garden flat and pulled the chime, which she had had put in to replace a plastic bell that played "I Do Like to be Beside the Seaside". She answered the door almost at once.

"Oh, my darling!" she exclaimed, "how lovely to see you. You look so well and you've lost weight."

"I've joined a gym. I was getting far too rotund. I don't want to grow sloppy."

"That you could never be, dear heart. I was talking to a man the other day, who asked me to tell you that keeping slim was vital for a singer."

"Who was he?"

"I didn't really catch his name. It sounded something like *Garseah*, but it wasn't that."

Justyn shook his head. "I don't think I know him."

"But he knows you."

"Probably a fan."

"I expect so."

They walked into her living room and despite his protests about watching his weight, Justyn accepted a generously sized glass of gin.

"Tell me about Australia," said Tinker, and sat down opposite him.

Justyn began to speak about the country and his opinion of the people who dwelt there and talked to her about the secrets of the opera house — but he was finding it difficult to remain conscious. As he spoke he could hear his voice growing distant and a moment later his chin headed towards his chest and he was fast asleep.

Tinker smiled. "It is all right, Señor García. He sleeps, but he will remember what you say."

In her mind she could see the distinguished man, who smiled and nodded. Having got up and checked that Justyn was comfortable, Tinker slowly left the room and made her way into the kitchen. There, what seemed to be a bundle of garments gave a loud snort and opened one eye.

"Where you been?" said the woman who was, in fact, inhabiting the garments.

"With my grandson, in the other room. I told you he was coming to see me."

"Yerse, so you did. Now what about another drop of brandy to help keep me warm?"

"You old soak." But despite her words, Tinker poured out a small amount.

The other woman gulped it down her throat immediately and held the glass out again. Tinker looked surprised.

"Really! You have had quite enough. So unless you drink a different beverage, I believe you should call it a day."

"How about a cup of tea then?"

"I haven't time to make tea now."

"I'll put a curse on thee."

"Honestly, Em, be careful what you say. For if I were to use one of my ancient Russian curses, you would feel the pain for the rest of your life."

"You wouldn't though, would you?"

"I am very sorely tempted."

And then a rather surprising thing happened. There was a rustle of unwashed clothing and Em stood up. Then she bowed her head.

"I don't want that. I'm just a harmless old drunk who wanders the streets of Hastings and don't do no harm to nobody. That was a nasty threat you just made, Tinker. It frightened me."

Tinker smiled. "Many a true word spoken in anger, my dear. But it would take a lot more than your burbling to bring about that curse. Now sit down and I will give you a tiny nip more."

But sounds from the next room had Tinker saying, "He is waking up. Drink quickly and then away with you."

Em obediently did as she was told and was out of the back door a minute later. Meanwhile Tinker, assuming her usual kindly grandmother expression, walked back into the other room to see her grandson yawning and waking up.

"I'm sorry," she said, "there was something that needed my attention in the kitchen."

"Don't apologise, Granny. I had a marvellous dream."

"What about?"

"Not much really. I was having a singing lesson from some old guy who was telling me how to achieve the high notes in *Régiment*. Actually, what he said was quite helpful."

Tinker smiled and rolled her eyes upward. "Thank goodness for that," she said.

She was quite certain that Justyn — as long as he could lay off the women and the wine — was going to be an international star. The sort of whom future generations of opera lovers would nod and say, "Of course, I heard him when I was a youngster."

Now she said, "Some of the wisest things that people do have been suggested to them in their dreams."

"Really?" said Justyn, and then he laughed out loud.

* * *

In a house not that far away — as the crow flew — Delia was busy tidying up. She didn't really enjoy it but she felt that the shaky side of her life was now firmly under control, mostly because of Alan's influence, though at the moment even that was under pressure as he wrestled with creating a new musical about the Welsh miners and their various strange legends. Arianrhod, who gave birth to many sons, fascinated him and, thanks to what he had told Delia of her history, Delia herself was becoming enraptured by the mysterious creature who had such a hold on Welsh mythology.

Cleaning the groaning bookcase as she was, Delia let her eye wander over the various titles and was fishing out a battered copy of *Forever Amber*, wondering whether Alan had bothered to read it, when she saw another, more ancient, book wedged behind. Pulling with both hands she managed to dislodge it to discover that it was genuinely old, probably nineteenth century. It was a diary of sorts, obviously kept by a man of few — but amusing — words. Sitting down in the window seat, Delia started to read.

Last eventide there came a knock upon my door and who should be standing there but the prima donna Lind, in the company of a thin redhead, who grinned, which did much to lighten his visage.

So that was probably the laughing couple of lovers in the bedroom, laughing and weeping because that was how Delia had last glimpsed her, in floods of tears. And the man? Who was that with her? Delia thought back to what she knew of Jenny Lind. This was certainly before the Barnum barnstorm days and the pictures she had seen of the man Jenny eventually married — Otto Goldschmidt — suggested that he was hardly given to uproarious laughter, or any laughter at all come to that.

Feeling somewhat defeated, Delia walked over to Alan's portraits of the Great Masters. There was Beethoven glowering furiously, Schubert looking so sweet and innocent with his round glasses — strange to think he had died of a venereal disease — and Liszt, the glamour boy, who changed women as other men changed their socks. And there, with the rest of that bunch of geniuses, was Chopin — handsome, red-headed and pale as a ghost.

"Got you," said Delia, collapsing into a chair. "You cunning devil. So you came here, did you? And for a travelling companion you chose the prima donna herself. My God, what a pair."

* * *

Jenny — Past

The cab rattled along, consuming the miles between Brighton and Hastings at a regular pace, while Chopin sat with his arm round Jenny, realising as her breathing got heavy that she had fallen asleep. He looked at her with adoration, seeing that her hat had slipped sideways and that her mouth — that wonderful mouth out of which poured the most spectacular sound in the world — was open.

He thought about life at that moment, thought deeply about his various loves and mistakes and realised, with a sudden feeling of calm dread, that his own life was slipping quietly away. His episodes of spitting blood, his breathlessness, his coughing to choking pitch, had all got worse. Days when he was not fit to meet a fellow human being and only poor Daniel — that ever-kind, ever-good-natured man — was in control. That was why he could not marry Jenny. He would be saddling her with an invalid and that — to put it bluntly — was the sum total of his future. But meanwhile, if he could grasp a little love, a little taste of joyful life, he would not hesitate to continue.

Jenny woke up and cuddled him. Chopin knew then, at that precise moment, that life could still be amusing and promised himself silently that he would enjoy the next few days as if what was left of his life had to be lived to the full.

"Forgive me, this last tour has quite worn me out. Are we there yet?"

"No, darling, just a little further."

He held her closely until eventually the lovely cobbled streets and ancient buildings of the old town came into view.

"Where are we staying?"

"At a house called St. Just. It belongs to some friends of mine. I think you'll like it. It's fairly new in style."

"When was it built?"

"About 1820, I believe."

But no more was said as the pair were unloaded outside a beautiful building and made their way up the few steps to the front door. Fryderyck was speechless, overawed by the delicate style of the house, and the generosity of Jenny's friends to lend them such a magnificent place in which to stay.

Even though he was exhausted, he slept little, waking with such breathlessness that he was afraid his wheezing was going to disturb her. But she was too tired, having had to sing that very night, and just slept peacefully on. However, at dawn's first glow she woke up and said, "Good morning, my angel."

He looked at her and drew as deep a breath as he could manage. "Good day to you, my sweet girl," then he burst into a positive paroxysm of breathlessness that had Jenny leaping out of bed and shouting for some help. A startled manservant appeared.

"My husband is rather poorly, as you will see. I think he will need some attendance."

And even though she hated herself for doing so, with that she left the room. But once outside she burst into a fit of weeping that shook her physically, so badly that she had to feel for a chair into which she collapsed, crying bitterly. She suddenly knew why Chopin had refused to marry her — because to cope with a man as sickly as he was and lead the hectic life of a truly great singer was impossible.

She crouched, a drawn and haggard wretch, with all her desires and wishes in the dust. Finally, she pulled herself together and went to him. He was lying, paler than she had ever remembered seeing him, his eyes closed and a napkin laid beside him into which he could spit blood. She knew then that for his precious sake she must ensure that the great love affair was over. But meanwhile she must do nothing to hurt or spoil their relationship which — she hoped — would last for ever.

"Oh, my sweetheart," she said, sitting on a chair beside the bed. "How are you feeling now?"

He opened his eyes and tried his best to smile. "My sweet girl, I am so sorry. I am afraid that I am having a bad start to the day."

"Don't get up unless you feel like it. I will dress and come back as quickly as I can. Then we can discuss what we are going to do."

When she returned, gorgeous in an exquisite shade of emerald satin, Chopin slept peacefully, mouth open, hands loose. This was a good sign because when he was under any kind of stress he tended to clench his fists into balls of anxiety. Looking at him, Jenny knew that even though her love had changed direction she would never stop caring about him. She had not lived a life of discretion; there had been too many children in the Theatre School in which she had been trained, too many girls and boys all interested in experimentation, for them to grow up blameless. But she had always tried her best to be kind and generous, not only with herself, but also with her money. At that moment an idea came to her, and Jenny smiled.

Fryderyck opened his eyes and smiled back. "I'm sorry that you should have seen me like this. It is only that sometimes I feel so short of breath. And I hate it, my sweet girl. I hate being so weak that I have to rest. Do you forgive me?"

"There is nothing to forgive, sweetheart. Do you feel up to putting on some clothes and going for a short walk by the sea? I think the air will do you good.'"

"Yes, if your friend's valet could come and help me dress. I find it is a bit of a struggle getting in and out of things sometimes."

Her heart bled for him; she could have wept at the thought of such a curse being bestowed on anyone so talented. But she merely smiled and said, "Then we will see about luncheon later," before leaving the room.

The wind was up and the waves rose briskly to its call, as did Chopin who was walking with determination. Several people were about and parading along the small protective wall that had been built where the sand ended. Jenny could feel the breeze tearing at her hat, which she was in danger of losing at any moment. Chopin smiled to himself as she clutched it firmly onto her head. Behind them they could hear two people conversing in loud whispers.

"I don't think you're right, my dear. I mean what would a woman of her social standing be doing going out for a walk in humble Hastings?"

"Well, the Pontefracts went to the theatre in Brighton last night and said Miss Lind was absolutely on top form. They even thought they saw Mr Chopin himself in the gentlemen's drawing room. I suppose, if Lind and Chopin know one another, they might choose to visit Hastings."

"Oh, how ridiculous. He lives in London, doesn't he? What would he be doing, visiting down here?"

Jenny and Fryderyck looked at one another and he winked. "Slow down," he whispered.

They loitered a little and the talkative couple caught up with them and passed ahead.

"Good God," the woman was whispering. "I do believe that was Miss Lind after all. She's quite pretty."

"Then who's the chap?" murmured her partner.

"I think it's him — Mr Chopin. But it can't be!"

The man turned round and gave a long and mighty look to which Fryderyck responded by giving a short bow and an elegant smile.

"Pardon me for staring, sir, I thought momentarily that you might be Frederick Chopin."

"Honoured," Fryderyk answered and held out his hand and shook the other's as if he were greeting an old friend.

"Well, I never," said the startled stranger, and bowed low to the couple. "You never know who you are going to meet, do you? Miss Lind and Mr Chopin. Who would have thought it?"

Hastily, before they could engage them in any further conversation, Jenny glanced at her watch. "Oh, do forgive us if we hurry on. My poor aunt gets so nervous if we are late."

"I didn't know you had relatives in this country, Miss Lind. Please forgive us."

"Of course. It's been so lovely to talk to you. Hasn't it, Fryderyck?"

"Lovely," he said, and gave a beatific smile.

They escaped for luncheon to a small but elegant restaurant where Jenny attacked her food well but poor Chopin picked his way round the edges. He looked at her and gave a hopeful smile.

"Darling girl, I will be better tomorrow, I promise."

"But what about tonight, my darling? And I am not talking about bed but about a special church service that is being conducted to help the sick, or so the servants said. It is in St. Clement's church, one of the oldest in Hastings, apparently. I thought that after you had rested we could stroll to the entrance and maybe go inside."

But Chopin replied, in French: "I am not religious, my dear."

"It won't be for religion. It will be to hear the bells — and smell the smells."

"Do you believe in anything, Miss Lind?"

"Of course I believe. My mother was most suspicious of actors, thinking them all after women — or boys — or both. But despite all that she let actors persuade her to send me to the Swedish Opera School. I know that God helped me."

"But I have heard it said that Die Freischutz nearly killed you and that you took yourself off to Paris, and there Manuel García saved your voice and restored your life."

For a moment, Jenny was silent. "It is true enough. I did not sing for two years while he reconstructed what I had left — a pitiable sound. I was very low at that time."

"But look what arose out of the shell," said Chopin, and leaning across the table gave her a resounding kiss on the lips.

"Yes, I shall be grateful to him for the rest of my life."

"As will the rest of us."

After their brief pause they walked a little further and found the church, built on a slight embankment. Jenny had a strange feeling. It was not fear that Chopin would reject it when she told him that she had decided marriage was out of the question, or that he would sigh with relief. What she feared was that he just would not care, one way or another. But in that she was wrong. As they climbed, very slowly because of the amount of breath it took, she looked up at him, standing slightly taller than she was.

"What are you thinking, my dearest friend?"

"How very much I love you, Miss Jenny Lind. And I always will. In this life and beyond."

They had panted their way to the top — Chopin literally gasping for breath as Jenny pushed the great door open — and they found themselves in an expanse of quietness. It was almost physical. The need to look around, to take in all the magnificence, was irresistible. Silently making his way to a pew, Fryderyck sat down and buried his head in a pamphlet, which turned out to be the history of the place. Jenny, meanwhile, moved like a shadow around the church, studying its interior with those great eyes. Apart from an elderly man slotting in new numbers on the hymn board, they were completely alone.

There was a strange, exotic smell everywhere. Jenny loved its deep and almost magical perfume. In her mind she saw dancing girls, very scantily clad, gyrating their slender hips, a sultan bright-eyed, watching their every move, only the tremor of his lower lip revealing that he was sexually aroused. And she recalled how the handsome and slim Chopin — whose breathing had almost stopped when he had reached the top of the church steps, then gasped his way slowly inwards — had aroused her. She would always love him — she knew it — even when she had married someone else who would probably bore her rigid. Without really meaning to, she sighed and looked at Fryderyck, who was gazing around him, as overawed as she was.

One or two people had begun to come in, very quietly Chopin thought. It was as though the magnificent church had a unique spell that was cast as people came through the door. It was too magnificent for people to talk and laugh loudly, everyone who entered lowered their tone out of respect for the ancient building. The custom of centuries lingered on.

As always, the gentry sat in the front pews. To their educated eyes Chopin, who was later joined by Jenny who had looked care-fully at all the wonderments, was decidedly puzzling. The cut of his coat was obviously first class, his body a little too thin for one of the upper set. But his face — ah, his face — was of foreign stamp and was closely regarded through quizzers and one or two magnifiers. The woman, on the other hand, had such a familiar look — though nobody could recall where they had seen her.

Then the organ rumbled out its magnificent opening voluntary and the congregation stood. The hymn was well known: "At the Name of Jesus Every Knee shall Bow", and the congregation let rip. But there was one glorious voice that rang out above all the others, as thrilling and as exciting to listen to as any great opera singer. Heads turned, women whispered, men were visibly shaken. Chopin fell in love with her all over again, glancing at her glorious face as out of it poured a sound fit for only angels to hear.

The vicar, who had started his usual uninspiring rumble stopped in his tracks and listened, meanwhile staring rudely at the singer from whom all the splendour was coming.

"Good God," he muttered very quietly, "I think it's Jenny Lind." He put his spectacles back on his nose and frankly stared. And wasn't that . . . But it couldn't be . . . But it was! Fryderyck Chopin was standing next to her and giving the hymn as much voice as he could.

Without thinking further, the vicar sent up a prayer. "Thank you, God. Thank you so much for letting Chopin and Jenny Lind come to my church. Amen."

But it was not only the vicar who had been impressed. Slowly the sound of the rest of the congregation's singing died away as one spectacular voice rose above all the others. And she, unaware of the growing silence around her, continued to sing from the heart, totally innocent of the sensation she was causing. In the end there was only her voice and also that of an ancient beldam, who was churning out an endless caterwaul for accompaniment. Eventually the mighty organ ceased to play and Jenny, totally unaware, sat down. There was a spontaneous round of applause as most of the congregation remained standing, all staring at the pew in which Jenny had retaken her place.

"What's happening?" she whispered to Fryderyck.

"They are clapping you, my sweet girl."

"Why?"

She glanced around her carefully.

"Because you were wonderful, my darling — as always."

After the final hymn — during which a great many of the congregation remained seated and gazed fixedly at Jenny Lind — there had been a big round of applause. The vicar, anxious to come to the end of the service, hurried through the rest of it. The organist, very ancient and very loveable, peered down from his perch and wondered at the speed at which the reverend was concluding the business. He had just played the opening notes of the dismissal when he saw in his mirror that the vicar had held up his hand for silence.

"Christ be with you."

"And also with you," murmured the congregation.

"Before I give you the blessing I want you all to know that tonight you have indeed been blessed — for sitting amongst you is that world-famous singer, Miss Jenny Lind. Accompanied on this occasion by the well-known composer, Mr Fryderyck Chopin."

A small uproar broke out. People, normally reserved and mouselike, headed purposefully towards the pew. A young woman, sitting only a few feet away from them, fainted spectacularly, landing on Chopin's lap. There were shouts of "Bravo" and other things which Fryderyck could not understand but Jenny could. These came from the rougher, fishing gang. Rude though they might have sounded, they were all said with joviality and much cheering. Carefully replacing the young woman in her original seat, Chopin stood up.

"Where are you going?" Jenny asked.

"To speak to the vicar."

"In French?"

"No, in broken English." And pushing his way through the crowd, Fryderyck found himself at the reverend's side. "Sank you zo much," he gasped, putting out his hand.

"My dear chap, thank *you*. What a tumultuous evening this has been. And may I say, Mr Chopin, that my wife is a great admirer of your work. She sits at the pianoforte for many a long hour trying to play what you have written down."

"Sank you again."

Chopin bowed and turned as there was a loud cheer from the fishing fraternity and he saw that Jenny had been hoisted shoulder high and was being carried towards the door. She was looking somewhat flustered, wondering where he had got to.

"Bad, no?" he asked the vicar.

"No, my very dear sir, the fishermen are paying her respect, on a magic night like this has proved to be I think God is smiling."

Considering this to be a wonderful way of thought, Fryderyck hurried after Jenny's retreating form. As best he could he followed in the darkness that had fallen while he had been inside the church.

On leaving the portal, the mob turned left and proceeded down the street a little way before sharply turning left again and carrying Jenny, who by now had a weary look of resignation about her, down a little hill. Then they turned left once more and entered a strange cabin — big enough to hold a few families at most — and lowered her to the ground. Then they burst into song — obviously one of congratulation — and thrust a drink into her hand, changing the tune to a hearty fisherman's chant of greeting. Vividly reminded of his experience in Edinburgh, Chopin joined in in Polish.

Jenny cast her beautiful eyes at them and — he couldn't help himself — Chopin burst out laughing. Shouts from an audience were all very well but to be carried aloft by a group of well-meaning men — at least she hoped they were well meaning — was for her something of a different experience. Students had tried in the past, had pulled her coach for her, but being lifted on high was rather unusual to say the least. Still, with Fryderyck laughing like a mad thing and the rest of the mob giving her big grins with many, many missing teeth, Jenny was lowered to the floor and a drink was thrust into her hand.

"There you are, ma'am. This will put a smile on your face."

Jenny stared at the gleaming liquid then took a chance and drank the whole mugful down in one. She felt a very strange sensation and reeled very slightly toward Chopin who made the very best of the situation and clutched her to his side. The fisher people cheered as one and an old lady piped up, "Do you good, dearie."

Someone nearer the wall shouted out, "What's your name, love?"

Chopin shouted back, "Jenny Lind."

"Eh?"

He repeated it, letter by letter, and then saw that slowly the man was writing it high on the wall, climbing up a small step ladder in order to do so.

"What's happening?" she asked, her speech slightly slurred.

"Naming this meeting place after you, Missus. Unless you have any objection that is?"

"No." She giggled rather wildly. "No objection."

"What is going on?" asked Chopin, reverting to French.

"They are calling this fishing place the Jenny Lind, would you believe?"

"Bravo, my darling," he answered, clutching her to him tightly.

* * *

Delia — Present Day

As soon as Alan had entered the house, Delia called out and rushed to him, perilously carrying a tray with two glasses of sherry on it and an old book. Fortunately, he looked in a far more cheerful frame of mind than when he had left and eagerly consumed a drink, afterwards giving her a special smile.

"I went for a walk on the high cliffs at Hastings and got quite inspired. There was a strange old woman up there, dressed like a bag of rags, smelling most peculiar and not a tooth in her head."

"Did you talk to her?"

"More the other way around. She grabbed my hand and said that I was going to be world famous amongst my fellows — whatever that might mean."

"What it says, of course. You are going to become a legend inside your own lunch hour."

"Well, that's comforting. At least we can afford to keep the cat."

"Yes, we must not let the servants starve. Regardless of that, I've got something fascinating to show you."

And she thrust the book at him while she went off to refill the glasses. When she got back Alan was sitting on the sofa, reading spectacles on, studying the book.

"It says that they spent one night here. Apparently, the owner's daughter had been a pupil of Chopin's while he was living in London."

"Around the corner from those two Scottish creeps."

"Oh yes," answered Alan, putting the book down. "Why do things like that always happen to somebody else? No elderly lady ever invited me to have tea. And no old buffer asked me to his flat to see his father's collection of risqué snapshots. I got invited out by several of the male dancers but had to tell them my grand jeté wasn't up to scratch. Honest to God, it was a hard old life."

Delia wondered whether she should get a remark in about his former in-laws but decided it would be tasteless and changed the subject.

"Did you realise that Jenny Lind was a bit of a goer?"

Alan shook his head. "No. Biographies of her got that so wrong. Then there was that ghastly film showing her falling for

Barnum, who in fact was about sixty-something when they met and had ugly warts on his face."

"Why did she marry that pianist who was considerably younger than she was?"

He shrugged. "I suppose because she liked him and he was kind. God knows. She who had been loved by the most handsome and talented men in the world ended up with our Otto."

"I hope he was sweet to her."

"He probably did his best. And he gave her the thing she wanted most — children."

Delia's mind ran about. What a state Jenny must have been in. Loving Mendelssohn so madly, then falling for poor dying Chopin and ending up with a somewhat younger man who could only declare his passion for her by playing the piano.

"Do you think she loved him?"

"I think she needed him desperately. Otto was a good musician and obviously adored her — while she was losing the bloom and glitter she had first held for men and audiences alike. Add to this her longing to have children — and Bob's your uncle."

"Poor Jenny."

"I don't think that word can be used in relation to her. She was fabulously wealthy and splashed money around as if it was going out of fashion."

"But only in gifts. Remember she would raise mountains of cash by means of giving a concert — which would always be packed out — and then give the takings to some poor organisation or other. Recall that dodgy business with Chopin when a large sum of money appeared anonymously and he was most perturbed."

"That was given by the sisters, wasn't it?"

"Those windbags always appear, don't they? I'm sick to the teeth of them and I reckon the wretched chap must have been as well. They only had £300 a year each to live on, so where they got all the money from remains a dark mystery. What did they do with it?"

"Paid for his funeral, of course."

"Had they caught up with him when he returned to France?"

"You just bet your life they did. That high-pitched pair of ghouls were relentless in their pursuit. No sooner had they found out his address than plans were being laid to *visit dear Mr Chopin and feed him his porridge oats.*"

"They sound horrendous."

"They were. One day I'll tell you the whole wretched story."

Delia nodded. "I wish you would."

* * *

Jenny — Past

The night being so cold and the warmth of their stomachs so strangely welcoming, Jenny and Fryderyck made their way home as quickly as possible. He felt, in a way that he could not explain, that on this night and in some mysterious manner he had reached a kind of zenith. That his strength had come back to him. That he was no longer a shivering little wretch lying in a corner, feeling past it and wishing that he could slip quietly out of life. Instead, he felt full of youthful joy, ready to go into society and flirt and drink and eat too much. And above all and in particular make glorious love to the incomparable Lind.

She, saying nothing, had begun to undress slowly, tantalisingly slow as she took off each small garment and smoothed it neatly before laying it on the bed. He watched her, for once feeling totally confident in himself, remembering how, years ago, he had been stupid enough to get a nasty disorder and as a result had not been allowed to go near anything of a sexual nature for some months. But that had all cleared up and was a thing of the past. And tonight he felt ready for any challenge.

He took her gently at first, cradling her in his arms and singing softly an old Polish lullaby. And she was so enchanted that she lay, passive and totally under his spell, while he sang his cradle song in such a beautiful and melodious voice that she could have remained like that for the rest of her life. At that enchanted moment the two of them loved with all their hearts and if Fate had dealt them a different deck of cards might have gone on to lead a happily married life. But neither of them was aware of that and eventually they let go of one another as they fell into a deep and satisfied sleep. Neither of them knew this was the last time they would ever make love to one another.

In that wicked light that comes just before the first colours of dawn, they both woke but, like children, did not move, not wishing to give the game away, not admitting that their minds were both working savagely. Jenny was aware that she must renounce singing if he were to be properly looked after and therefore knew with absolute certainty that she must bring their relationship to a close, because to spend the rest of her life in silence was more than she even dared to think about. He, Chopin, knew quite certainly that he was dying and that there was nothing that could save him. He had consulted enough doctors, seen the look on their faces, had even heard one eminent surgeon murmur, "If only he had a wife." *What for?* he had thought. *To mop up those persistent pools of blood?* But he was too proud a man to wish for one and to subject his sweet Jenny to such a terrible ordeal was beyond human thought. So he smiled in the first rays of sunshine and said, "Good morning to the sweetest woman in the world."

And she answered, "How lovely to wake in your arms, my very dearest man."

CHAPTER TWENTY-NINE

Jenny — Past

They parted company the next day, rather sadly. Chopin almost immediately left London and disappeared back to France, prepared to face battles, resignations, murders and suicide threats just to get away from the presence of the two overbearing Scots sisters. Stricken by uprisings France might be, but at least there was peace of mind and no polluted fog to contend with.

Jenny, on the other hand, completely out on a limb and not sure where her life was going, selected that some dreary nobody — an army officer called Claudius Harris whose mother came from "good stock", was deeply religious and believed that all people connected with the theatre were polluted, both mentally and physically — and insisted that they were betrothed.

All hell broke out. Harriet Grote thought her friend had taken leave of her senses, Gunther went about talking of suicide, Jenny felt she was breaking down, Chopin wept bitterly and cursed the fact that he was too ill to intervene. The final straw was reached when Jenny's legal adviser, Nassau William Senior, arrived at Clairville Cottage at 9.30 in the morning to be greeted by a woman who appeared on the edge of a nervous breakdown, looking at him silently with wide staring eyes. Eventually she poured out, "You see me in the deepest affliction. All my career, public and private, is at an end. I have nothing before me but darkness and misery."

"Why is this?" Mr Senior enquired politely

There was a fit of very loud weeping and finally the words, said chokingly, "I believe that the man I am going to marry is the mere puppet of his mother — and her *eminence grise*, Captain Marsh."

Mr Senior's well-trained nose rose in the air. "I see. Can you tell me a little more about these people?"

The words came pouring out. Jenny was expected to give up the theatre entirely and live in Bath amongst the religious crowd and their pure-at-heart wives. She was never to refer to the fact that she was once an opera star and brought pleasure to multitudes. If she refused to do this, poor Claudius would die of a broken heart, of which she would be the cause.

Mr Senior indulged in a silent snort. "I have never yet heard of a fit young man dying of a broken heart. It is complete rubbish. And if the Harrises claim damages, then a month's performance would easily take care of that expense."

Jenny still pulled an unhappy face and Mr Senior was more than delighted to hear a cab come to a halt at the end of the garden.

"Let us hope that it is not the young man himself making one more effort to wring your withers."

Jenny did not answer but turned a pair of sad eyes in his direction and Mr Senior was positively thrilled when, after the briefest of knocks on the door, a maid threw it open to reveal Mrs Grote, clad from top to toe in shimmering purple, her skirt cut rather briefly to reveal a pair of puce pink stockings.

Jenny shot her a mournful look to which Harriet responded with, "You seem in need of a drink, my girl."

Bang on cue Jenny burst into loud weeping, hiding her face in a pair of quivering hands. Producing a brandy from a hidden alcove, Mrs Grote shoved one under the sobbing singer's nose.

"Get this down you. You'll feel better within minutes."

Jenny obediently gulped and Mr Senior rose to his feet.

"I have said all that I have to say, my dear Mrs Grote. I shall leave you two ladies to talk on. I shall shortly partake of a light luncheon and afterwards you will find me taking my ease in the garden."

He bowed formally and left the room.

"Now what is all this about?" asked Harriet forthrightly.

"Poor young Claudius. He will kill himself if I do not marry him immediately."

"What utter rubbish. I'll bet his evil old mother is behind the whole thing. How dare these people call themselves Christian? She is a wicked old beast and so I shall tell her if ever I have the mischance to meet her."

Jenny did not know whether to laugh or weep at this, so sat with a face like a chamber pot. Harriet narrowed her eyes.

"Tell me about Chopin. Do you no longer love him?"

The singer remained silent but watching her closely, her visitor saw Jenny lose all colour and suddenly fall sideways onto the sofa in a storm of cruel and bitter weeping. This told Harriet Grote all she needed to know. The fuss and bother about the snivelling little Claudius man was not the real cause of the anguish at all. Jenny had loved Chopin and he, no doubt, had returned those feelings in full — but something had held back their passion. The word *doomed* rang in Harriet's brain like a death knell.

Jenny whimpered on about the cruelty of life but Harriet merely responded with an "Oh, really" and a "Gracious, I didn't know men behaved like that. Real men, that is." Eventually Jenny herself was bored by the constant reiteration and timidly asked if Harriet thought she might have a drink to calm her nerves.

"Certainly, my dear. And I shall have one as well." Crossing over to the alcohol cabinet, Mrs Grote poured out some heavy measures, weakened by just the merest drop of some freshly made lemonade.

"Now," said Harriet, "tell me everything."

"He couldn't stay in London a moment longer. The polluted fogs and the lack of fresh air put his stricken lungs under the greatest strain. Although he knew that France was constantly on a war footing, he had no choice other than to leave England. But I expect those two harpies will sniff him out and soon come whimpering round, offering him cups of tea and oat cakes."

"Quiet!" ordered Harriet sternly. "The very thought makes me feel nauseous."

"I am sorry. They are so well meaning that they have choked the life right out of him." A spark of Jenny's usual fire suddenly flared. "And all they want is for dear Miss Jane to marry him."

"Surely that will not now be possible?"

"I think," Jenny answered bitterly, "that she would go through the ceremony with a Calvinistic priest standing at the dying man's bedside as long as she became his wife."

"Then shame on her. They have followed him from pillar to post and by doing so they have systematically killed him."

Mrs Grote refilled her glass, hunched her shoulders and sat in a vast and magnificent silence. Jenny, whose spirits, which had been rising ever since her friend's arrival, looked at her hopefully.

"Have you a plan, dear Harriet?"

"Yes, I think I have. Is it true my dear that you raise thousands for charities by giving a single concert?"

"True enough."

"And what happens to this money? Do you keep it?"

"Certainly not. I raised 220,000 francs at the last count. And, before you ask, with that I donated to five hospitals, paid the orchestra's fees, and gave to an artistic memorial fund."

Harriet took a deep sip of whatever concoction she had poured out. "And what would you do if you heard that poor Chopin was in trouble once more?"

"What do you think I would do? I would help him, of course."

"Then . . ." Mrs Grote's voice trailed away.

"Oh, my God. He is dying, isn't he?"

"To put it bluntly, yes."

Fresh tears came, in fact Jenny Lind broke down and buried her head in Harriet Grote's lap and cried so deeply that her friend could do nothing but sit and wait for her to weep herself out. Eventually she raised her poor swollen face.

"I will do it. I shall give him the money — and in a way that he shall never know it came from me."

The puce stockings flashed as Harriet stood up. "Give me time to think about that. Meanwhile, my dear, I think you should make plans to return to France. I hear that the hags from the heather are making full arrangements."

"Oh, the beastly creatures. Can't they leave him in peace?"

"Clearly not, my sweet."

* * *

It was May before she set foot on French soil. Jenny was glad in many ways to be leaving England behind her and along with it the loathsome Claudius who had taken the liberty of entering her house, defacing her Bible with sour remarks and generally behaving like a total twit.

Indeed, the excitement of entering the French capital once more thrilled her with delight. Her English friends had all moaned about how unhappy she had been during the years spent retraining her voice with the delightful García. On the contrary, she had treasured the hours with him, listening and copying the reshaping of her vocal presentation until it had returned, clear as a bell and twice as lovely. And now, thanks to him and all that had followed after, here she was back in France and climbing the staircase that led to Chopin's rooms in the Square d'Orleans.

She had never visited him there but once Solange — the unloved daughter of George Sand — had described it to her in full detail, particularly that a bunch of sweet violets was always put out to scent his living room. Jenny felt a tear form as she remembered how she had bought a bunch of the same flowers to remind her of him and she prayed that the sisters of doom — as Jenny had christened them — were not in residence.

* * *

Her wish was not to be granted. A high grating voice was saying in bad French, "You ought to take a wee bit more of your tea, dear Fryderyck . You know you will feel better when you do force a drop down."

A sharp ring on the doorbell cut her short and the woman — the older of the two judging by her general dilapidation — stood glaring. Grandeur oozed as Jenny swept past her and said, "Fryderyck, my darling, I'm here at last."

Looking up and seeing immediately the grim faces of the two Scots sisters, Chopin decided to jump in the game and hang the consequences.

"Jenny, my angel, my own sweet love, what has kept you in London?"

She fluttered her lashes, every inch the stage prima donna. "Things, people, you know what it is like, don't you, darling? My, when I think of the number of times you have waited for me — so sweetly and quietly — I could kiss you for it."

"Please do," he answered with a catch in his voice which reverberated around the room.

Mrs Katherine Erskine, ever the strict Calvinist and now guarding her younger sister like a hawk — which was a pathetic joke as the sister in question was older than Chopin and constantly wore a dour expression — grimaced, and Jenny smiled adorably as the Scots regarded her.

"Don't let my arrival put you off in any way. I know" — and she gave Chopin a confiding smile — "what a chatterbox he can be."

"Come along, Jane, I can see we are outstaying our welcome," Mrs Erskine said icily.

Jane pulled a face. "Yes, I suppose we are."

Chopin watched them, expressionless, his lips moving only slightly as he whispered a farewell. Jane dropped the tiniest of tiny curtsies. They stood in silence until they heard the street door close with a mighty thump. Then they looked each other in the eyes and burst into a fit of giggles.

"You wicked woman!" Chopin whispered. "How wonderful it is to see you again. I am sorry about my rapid exit from London but I felt that any longer in the place would have killed me."

"You could have sent me a note explaining."

"I was too ill. I'm very sorry. I just had to get out."

"I'd rather not talk about illness anymore. Can I sit on your lap, please?"

"I have grown so thin that I would much rather sit on yours."

They both laughed with extreme pleasure as they slowly changed places and cuddled together in his comfortable old chair, exchanging kisses as if they were going out of style.

* * *

Four days passed, during which they had no time to see one another. Then Chopin's doorbell rang and he answered it personally, Daniel being out shopping and the ladies deep in files. A man stood at the door, holding a package out to Chopin.

"So sorry this is late, monsieur. It has been languishing with Madame Etienne, your landlady, for four days."

"What is it?"

"I don't know. I tried to have it delivered to you — care of Madame Etienne — four days ago, as I have already said. Before that, it was delivered to my house with a brief message asking me to pass it on to your good self."

"And you are?"

"Alexis Didier, though I appear on stage as Alexis Somnambul."

Chopin paused, clutching at an idea that suddenly flashed into his mind.

"Aren't you a magician? Don't you give demonstrations of magnetism — or something of that nature?"

"That is correct, sir."

"Then why were you picked to run this errand?"

"I have no idea, monsieur. The first I knew about it being uncollected was when Mrs Erskine came to my house and asked who sent it."

"Well, who did?"

Somnambul spread his arms and shook his head. "I have no idea, sir. Nor do I know why I — a humble clairvoyant — should have been picked to deliver it."

Chopin stood silently, his head whirling with ideas. Why did the man have a stage name almost exactly like that chilling opera in which Jenny was so superlative? Was this a mere coincidence? None of it was making any sense.

"Where is the parcel now?"

"Here," said Somnambul, and produced a package from his back pocket and handed it to Fryderyck.

It was warm to the touch, as if something glowed within. Chopin stared at it suspiciously.

"If you could please tell me how you knew the parcel had been dropped."

"I don't know why I was picked to deliver it," added Alexis pathetically. "I don't deliver parcels. I was told it was quite important. Anyway, there were two women standing in the room I was called to and the taller one took it away immediately."

"So how did it all end up?" Chopin asked irritably.

"I have no idea. I don't know what to believe. There is somebody practicing hocus and pocus and trying to hide the truth."

And that was the limit of any information he was given. Had he been in better shape physically he would have gone and sorted it out, face to face with Jane Stirling, whose clumsy hand he recognised as trying to pull invisible strings. But one thing was certain. They could lie till they turned purple — Chopin had a brief moment of seeing this come true and grinned broadly — but he believed with all his heart that the huge sum of money within the package — £25,000 — that Jane Stirling and Katherine Erskine were pretending came from them, had not come from them at all. Each woman had an allowance of £300 a year to live on — and that was the end of that story. They could lie and pretend for all they were worth — but Chopin knew that wonderful amount of money had an entirely different source — and he would believe that until his dying day.

Nonetheless, it was a puzzle. Alexis Didier was asked to deliver the parcel to Fryderyk Chopin but instead handed it to a tall, thin Scotswoman who disappeared with it. It then turned up at the home of Madame Etienne, Chopin's landlady.

When Miss Stirling — her voice a fraction squeakier than usual — arrived in a storm of weeping and confessed that she was his benefactress, Chopin did not believe her. *Where and how could she raise a sum like that? She is merely showing off.* The fact remained that Didier's stage name was Somnambul — a fact which proved the case completely to Chopin. Jenny Lind, who could raise this sort of sum at a charity event — something she organised regularly — was the person responsible.

Chopin, determined to give Jenny one final treat before saying a final goodbye, hired a very handsome horse and a handsome driver, to say nothing of the coach which was decked out with the very latest things. He, meanwhile, climbed into the most stunning clothes that still fitted him; a supple leather jacket and soft stylish trousers and a top hat that shone like a dark sun in splendour. Fortunately, it was one of his better days and the happier he felt the more his face transformed, turning him into an attractive man as he once had been.

He had come prepared, bearing a smart, stylish hamper that contained a couple of crystal glasses, a bottle of quinquina wine and a further bottle of glowing red liquid. The quinquina was to boost the taste of the other, he explained as Jenny watched him delicately pouring it. That is as delicately as was possible with a young and energetic horse in the traces. She gave him a glowing smile.

"You seem very happy, if I may comment."

"Look at my beautiful companion and you will understand why."

She did indeed look stunning, dressed from head to foot in stiff satin of a colour that matched her eyes. Chopin gazed at her deeply.

"You have crystal eyes. Do you know that?"

"You are so sweet to me. You say the kindest things."

"Only because I truly love you."

"Fryderyck, we are not going to marry, are we?"

"No, my darling. It is too late for us this time."

She nodded. "I understand. But know that I will always love you, deep in my heart."

He raised one of her small, gloved hands to his lips. "As I will you, my very own Swedish Nightingale."

It had been a pleasurable ride, the carriage clean, the horse sprightly. But the parting was painful. He looked so sad and though immaculate in appearance, he could barely raise a smile of farewell. Jenny knew better than to linger, and as best she could she allowed Chopin to help her get out. He kissed her on the cheek, quite formally, then bent in a deep bow while she turned and made to leave. They smiled at one another, a long deep smile, still very much in love. Then she turned and hurried away into the brightness of the afternoon.

CHAPTER THIRTY

Delia — Present Day

As soon as she left the theatre, Delia felt the change in atmosphere. The soft autumnal weather had been drawing to a graceful close but tonight it had been given marching orders by a savage drop in temperature. A cruel little wind had sprung up from nowhere but, despite this, icy angry stars threw a blistering comment. Wishing that she was wearing a proper coat, rather than a quickly snatched cardigan, she headed for Charing Cross station.

Over the last month it had become her habit to pay weekly visits to Alan at his beautiful house in Sussex. She was incredibly in love with him and would gladly have moved in on a permanent basis but something — what? Deep and depressing respectability? A memory? — would not allow it. So she had continued to live in London, a place of rootless enjoyment and toughening-up.

But Delia wasn't really the type for that. She longed to organise a stately house, to see it run efficiently, to be open for visitors and people wandering and exclaiming and pointing. But she would have lived with Alan if he had had nothing but a shack. So even her thinking was muddled.

It was a dark train, the clocks having gone back, so people either stared at their mobiles expressionlessly or telephoned their friends in loud voices. Delia stared out of the window and was glad when that height of respectability, Tunbridge Wells station, arrived. Out got the usual crowd of men dressed in high-street-purchased suits, bristling like bulldogs as they ascended the staircase at a frightening pace. Delia grinned despite being worried about Alan and giggled when a man lost his shoe which went hurtling downwards to the bottom of the flight.

He was there, waiting for her at Wadhurst, smiling at her as she got off the train. She had to stop herself scampering childishly towards him and focused on walking with a sophisticated stride.

"What's the matter?" he said.

"Nothing? What do you mean?"

"You're walking oddly."

"My feet hurt. Too much London."

"Well, you're in the country now. Time to relax." He cleared his throat meaningfully. "I'm afraid you're going to be rather on your own doing that this time, sweetheart."

"Don't tell me, let me guess — you're composing."

"It's more than that. It's that bloody musical. It's turning into an opera. I can hear it in my head and I know damn well that that is what's happening. It's even got a blasted chorus who have crept in from somewhere to annoy me."

Delia nodded and put on her wisest face. "Then why don't you let it become one?"

"What do you mean?"

"What I say. Okay, you wrote a musical — but what is to stop you progressing? Andrew Lloyd Webber did so; why can't you? I can picture it quite clearly. The chorus alive and well and singing their hearts out in the Albert Hall."

He looked at her, thinking about his reply. "Are there children in it?"

"Of course," she answered seriously. "They have been hand-picked from school choirs. They are all there, with little shining, earnest expressions. They are singing the great Gloria that will come at the end."

He stared at her, looking down into her face. "You really mean it, don't you?"

"Every word."

"Promise me?"

"I solemnly do."

"Then it shall be written and dedicated to you."

"It will be my treasure."

"As you are mine," he answered. "For always."

* * *

Delia, who had recently bought a cookbook, managed to make a rather handsome gathering of cold salmon and cucumber, which was devoured later on. Alan ate silently, his mind full of music which he occasionally hummed aloud. She, not wishing to interrupt, thought about the house and how it could be restored to its former glory and the possibility of one day having visitors who would come and make exclamations of delight.

Later, at about ten o'clock, she wandered outside just to breathe in the frost-filled air and look about her. However she was amazed to see, despite the lateness of the hour, a small car slowly making its way up the drive. It stopped, and a familiar figure got out. It was Justyn, who slowly made his way around and helped out another person, much smaller — in fact, quite tiny. Then they stood, in silence, gazing at the great pale house, neither speaking.

"Hello," Delia called loudly. "Is it you?"

Justyn jumped into the air — quite a sight, given that he was already six feet four. "Oh, dear girl, you gave me a fright. This is my grandmother, Tinker."

The old lady bowed graciously. After a second, Delia bowed in return.

Justyn continued: "I am on my way to London now, catching an early flight to Australia. We haven't come to call on you exactly. It was just that Tinker wanted to see the exterior of your beautiful house."

"I just needed to make sure that everything is fine for the future. That may sound fanciful but I am a medium, you see. I do hope you don't mind."

"Mind? I don't in the least. I've always been terribly interested in the supernatural," said Delia.

There was a mighty thunder of chords as Alan burst forth a great majestic sound and the small group were reduced to silence, listening to the music's stirring compulsion.

Justyn said, "Alan is a great composer. He is writing now for a full chorus."

"Do you believe there will be one?" Delia asked him.

"Beyond doubt. They will play at the Albert Hall. But the full work will be performed at all the leading opera houses of the world. I shall audition."

It was said with such utter conviction that Delia gave a laugh of pure pleasure.

Tinker spoke up. "Your house has a long and intriguing history, as you well know, my dear. And it is true that Jenny and Fryderyck spent a night here during a terrible storm."

"But it is true that she wept here, too. I saw her."

"She wept because the whole of her life was changing. She had been taken up by an American showman called Barnum. He introduced her to the concert halls of the United States. She was not the same from that day forward."

"And what about her marriage?"

Tinker gave a small, sad smile. "What about it? She, the Swedish Nightingale, became Mrs Ordinary. She who had had men like Mendelssohn and Chopin throwing themselves at her feet exchanged all that for an existence of Victorian pleasantry." She sighed. "Such is Fate I suppose."

Delia found that her eyes were moist. "I do hope that nothing like that happens to me."

Tinker gave her a hug. "You, my very dear girl, will inspire the man playing now to great things. You will become the power behind the throne."

Delia laughed, partly through joy, partly through wonderment. Tinker turned to go.

"One minute more, Justyn, I want to leave my Russian prayer of good fortune."

He nodded his head. "As you wish, madame."

Tinker spread her small arms outward and at that moment the moon — magnificent and majestic — emerged from behind a cloud. Delia lowered her gaze, feeling it too much to watch while this magic old lady wove her spell. When she looked up again, they had gone. The ancient car was just going through the gates, so quietly that she wondered whether she had dreamt the whole thing.

She turned to go indoors but glanced once more at the magic moon. It stared back expressionlessly. Unable to help herself Delia curtsied to it, low and deep as her mother had taught her. Then she laughed at herself and ran on swift feet back into the house.

THE END

AUTHOR'S NOTE

An unusual story, this one. Most people have heard of the two great composers, Mendelsohn and Chopin. Mendelsohn was more than attractive, women found him ravishing, he was married — of course — to a sweet little thing who scampered along beside him but mostly stayed at home looking after the children. Then there was Fryderyck Chopin, red-headed, slim, and a genius, who attracted women like the mighty 'thinking bosom' George Sand. From hashish cigars to trousers and stove-hat, she liked her men young and ready for action. And the third person in this mighty triangle was a small nobody whose voice had been trained so badly that it gave out and she took herself off to Paris and Manuel García — the only teacher left who could restore the terrible sound.

The love lives of these three were complicated. Mendelsohn blazed, became a great conductor, and left women swooning. Chopin had to free himself from his cigar-breathed mannish lover — and poor Jenny Lind was just emerging from two years training which at long last had produced a glorious voice.

That there was any connection between them came as an extraordinary surprise to me. I was reading Ates Orga's — the celebrated musician — book on the life of Chopin when I saw that he had drawn attention to a special note. It was written by Cecilia and Jens Jorgensen and claimed that Chopin and Jenny Lind were very much in love and were having an affair. It was published by Icons of Europe and quite honestly it took my breath away. The couple met in London — Jenny in recovery following the death of Mendelsohn — at a dinner party. Afterwards they went to the piano and stayed there till one o'clock in the morning. Quite honestly, it took me and shook me as I read the words 'It was a "coup de foudre"'. Love at first sight.

After that I bought the book and read it from cover to cover. Then I began my historical research and found the facts leaping out at me. Once you knew what you were looking for they were all there. The fact that they loved each other is clear. That Jenny was committed to a tour and could not spend enough time with Chopin is obvious. The two Scottish ladies are so typical of women on the hunt for a husband that it is almost — but not quite — amusing. It is a fact that Jane Stirling wore black for the rest of her life and announced to the world that she was Chopin's widow! As for Jenny, a Hollywood version had her singing to a handsome hero — Barnum — who was, in fact, of mature years of age and had warts.

This is just a resume of the treasure trove I found. I was helped enormously by Ates Orga — a mine of information — and by members of my family including my gallant son Brett, who strode about with a modern computer that made mine look as if it had travelled the Arctic, which it probably has. Kate Lyall Grant, senior director at Joffe Books, was kindness itself. Thank you to everyone.

THE LUME & JOFFE BOOKS STORY

Lume Books was founded by Matthew Lynn, one of the true pioneers of independent publishing. In 2023 Lume Books was acquired by Joffe Books and now its story continues as part of the Joffe Books family of companies.

Joffe Books began in 2014 when Jasper agreed to publish his mum's much-rejected romance novel and it became a bestseller.

Since then we've grown into the largest independent publisher in the UK. We're extremely proud to publish some of the very best writers in the world, including Joy Ellis, Faith Martin, Caro Ramsay, Helen Forrester, Simon Brett and Robert Goddard. Everyone at Joffe Books loves reading and we never forget that it all begins with the magic of an author telling a story.

We are proud to publish talented first-time authors, as well as established writers whose books we love introducing to a new generation of readers.

We won Trade Publisher of the Year at the Independent Publishing Awards in 2023 and Best Publisher Award in 2024 at the People's Book Prize. We have been shortlisted for Independent Publisher of the Year at the British Book Awards for the last five years, and were shortlisted for the Diversity and Inclusivity Award at the 2022 Independent Publishing Awards. In 2023 we were shortlisted for Publisher of the Year at the RNA Industry Awards, and in 2024 we were shortlisted at the CWA Daggers for the Best Crime and Mystery Publisher.

We built this company with your help, and we love to hear from you, so please email us about absolutely anything bookish at feedback@joffebooks.com.

If you want to receive free books every Friday and hear about all our new releases, join our mailing list here: www.joffebooks.com/freebooks.

And when you tell your friends about us, just remember: it's pronounced Joffe as in coffee or toffee!